YOUNG
NICK'S
HEAD

K A R E N   H E S S E

YOUNG NICK'S HEAD

Simon & Schuster, London

First published in Great Britain by Simon & Schuster UK Ltd, 2001
A Viacom Company

1 3 5 7 9 10 8 6 4 2

Simon and Schuster UK Ltd
Africa House
64-78 Kingsway
London WC2B 6AH

Simon & Schuster
Australia Sydney

A CIP catalogue record for this book is available from the British Library

ISBN 0 689 83508 6

Printed by WS Bookwell Ltd, Finland

This book was first published in the USA by Simon & Schuster under the title
Stowaway.

My heartfelt thanks to David Bisno and Mel and Norma Shakun; the staffs at Brooks Memorial Library and Dartmouth Library; Randy, Kate and Rachel Hesse, Mami Ikezaki, Eileen Christelow, Liza Ketchum, Bob and Tink MacLean, Wendy Watson and Heather Ahrenholz.

And to Brenda Bowen, who waits at the dock through each long journey, hand outstretched, ever ready to catch the rope and pull me in.

To Rachel,
whose future I cannot endeavour to imagine

I, Nicholas Young, swear on the grave of my dead mother, Elizabeth Sullivan Young, that this is the full and true account of the remarkable occurrences on board His Majesty's Bark Endeavour *between the years of our Lord 1768 and 1771. Any person wishing to dispute what I record here shall find me at the Kew Estate on the bank of the River Thames. I'm the one with red hair.*

PART I

Stowaway

AUGUST 1768

SUNDAY 7th TO FRIDAY 19th *[Plymouth]* With the help of Seamen Francis Haite, John Ramsay and Samuel Evans, I have managed to keep my presence aboard *Endeavour* secret. She's a small Bark, and her Company over eighty in number. It's a wonder I've not been discovered, with all the coming and going of the men aboard, but I have not. The three seamen I paid to get me on bring biscuit and water. They make certain I exercise each night during middle watch, when there are fewer hands on deck. But there is little to relieve my situation till *Endeavour* sails.

It's a good hiding place I've got, in the aft of what Samuel Evans calls the Pinnace, a small boat *Endeavour* carries aboard her. I can look over the edge and see the deck without being noticed. But it is difficult, lying still, day and night. Sometimes the urge to cry out nearly gets the better of me. I haven't yet. It would go hard on the men who have helped me if I did. And I would be returned to the Butcher, who would take it out of my hide, if Father didn't kill me first.

Endeavour creaks without rest as she sits at anchor. The breeze chatters her ropes against the masts. The ship's bell clangs on the hour and half-hour, and the bosun's whistle ever pierces the air with its piped orders. With all the din of London, I thought it could never be so noisy on a ship. But it is.

I've chickens for neighbours, and pigs and a goat. They snort and cluck and bleat day and night, in pens on deck. I'm glad of their company and wish I might go near them more often. I've had milk out of the goat, straight from her teat. John Ramsay says she's aboard for the Gentlemen and Officers, so they might have fresh cream when they please.

Today, the 19th, Captain Cook gathered the Ship's Company on deck and read the Articles of War aloud. Captain is a clean-shaven man, strict and stern, with cold eyes. The Articles he read stated there would be no swearing of oaths on board, no drunkenness, nor uncleanness. Good thing Captain hasn't had a whiff of me. The Articles declare cowardice, mutiny and desertion to be punishable acts. They say naught of stowaways, but Francis Haite, John Ramsay and Samuel Evans each glanced my way during Captain's reading.

SATURDAY 20th *[Plymouth]* Rain, rain, rain. Even with the cover pulled over me, I am thoroughly wet.

SUNDAY 21st *[Plymouth]* We toss at anchor. My stomach heaves and cramps and heaves again. And I'm bruised from head to toe.

I half wish Father would come aboard and take me home. I'm tired of being wet and hungry. Father knows by my letter that I've run out on the Butcher. But I did not write where I meant to go, nor what I meant to do, for when I sent the letter, I hardly knew my plans myself. Even if he knew, he would not come. I am a disappointment to Father. All my brothers are scholars. Only I could not settle to my studies. Father has no use for a son who will not learn his Latin.

MONDAY 22nd [*Plymouth*] A storm has made the sea sorely troubled beneath us, even as we sit at anchor. This noon a servant boy saw me heaving out of the Pinnace as he ran to be sick himself over the side. I pray he was too much in his own misery to take notice of me and mine.

TUESDAY 23rd [*Plymouth*] Last night the servant boy came right to my hiding place.

'Lad', he whispered, 'are you still alive in there?'

I held silent. After a moment he poked his head into the Pinnace and stared straight at me. I stared straight back. He looked to be fifteen or sixteen years of age. When he made out I was well, he smiled. Blisters, I have never seen such a beaming smile.

Samuel Evans called out from the forward of the ship, 'Hey, there. You, boy. Get away from the Pinnace.'

The servant boy was gone in an instant, but not before he'd dropped some hardtack and a piece of junk into my hand.

WEDNESDAY 24th TO THURSDAY 25th [*Plymouth*] More wind and rain, and the air thick and heavy on my chest. I stink worse than a London gutter. I wish I could just shut my eyes and sleep until everything was right again.

I told Francis Haite about the servant boy who found me.

'That would be John Charlton,' Francis Haite said. 'He's a good lad. He won't give you up.'

Francis Haite is an old man, older than the Captain, with crooked and missing teeth and a face well lined. He clasped my shoulder for a moment. 'Be patient, lad,' he said.

I shall be patient. Father thinks me worthless when it comes to sticking with a plan. He says I run from everything. Well, I did run from Reverend Smythe's school. And from the Butcher. But I had good cause on both counts. And unhappy as I am, cramped in the hard confines of the Pinnace, I am better off than I was with the Butcher. And so I shall remain, recording my trials in this journal. I shall prove to Father that I am not a quitter. That I am good for something. That I am more than a Butcher's boy.

Finally, the rain has stopped. Empty casks taken off. Fresh supplies of Beer and Water brought on. This afternoon, at last, we weighed anchor. Now there are new sounds to join with the others. The wind clapping the sails, the men singing out in the rigging, the water churned by *Endeavour*'s prow. Fine sounds. Sailing sounds.

FRIDAY 26th *[Off the Coast of England]* Samuel Evans, who has the largest hands I have ever seen, larger even than the Butcher's, found me at my journal, which has suffered from the damp despite its wrappings. He cannot read nor write and thinks it wondrous that a boy of eleven can do what a grown man cannot. 'I could teach you,' I told him. 'When I am out of hiding.'

He laughed and nodded his large head. 'Time does sit heavy

on a seaman some days. It'd be a blessing to read away the hours.'

SATURDAY 27th *[Off the Coast, North Atlantic]* Fair-haired John Ramsay, the youngest of the three men helping me, shipped out the first time when he was but eight.

There are several Gentlemen aboard. I often hear the name of Mr Banks called. He's a very educated man from the sound of him. His brown hair goes wild in the wind, and his dark eyes are lit with an eager curiosity. Mr Banks's Company watched porpoises off the side this afternoon. From my hiding place I could hear their remarks and see the pleasure the Gentlemen took in their sightings. I only wish I might have stood at the rail beside them and seen what they saw.

As I write, the sea is ever in my ears and in my bones. *Endeavour* creaks and groans and sighs as she goes. I creak and groan and sigh, as well, but I must do it all in silence.

SUNDAY 28th *[Off the Coast, North Atlantic]* Gale in the night. But today the rain gave way to haze and a light breeze, and I dried out a bit. Mr Banks and his Gentlemen dipped up some seawater and discussed the creatures found swimming in it. The Gentlemen were full of exclamation and wonder.

MONDAY 29th TO TUESDAY 30th *[Off the Coast, North Atlantic]* The weather has turned foul again, and the ship heaves and tosses. I am sick. The Gentlemen have been sick, too. Been at the side regularly. I can say now that Gentlemen heave the contents of their stomach same as eleven-year-old stowaways.

WEDNESDAY 31st TO THURSDAY 1st SEPTEMBER *[Lat. 44°56′ N, Long. 9°9′ W]* All day the sea rose, breaking over the deck. Captain had the men everywhere in the rigging, trying to save the ship from being torn to pieces by the wind.

Just before first watch the Bosun staggered to the side and shook his fist at the sea, cursing it for stealing his skiff. But ship's cook, Mr Thompson, was angrier still. A dozen of his hens drowned in the storm. Mr Thompson kept muttering how he was never to feed the entire Company if the sea kept killing his livestock. I'd never seen ship's cook so close before. He has but one hand!

The storm, at last, is blown out and *Endeavour* floats easy in the sea again. The servant boy, John Charlton, comes past when he can, leaving bits to eat. He also brings with him good cheer with that kind face of his and that beaming smile. I don't know much about him but that he is from London, has a friendly nature, and at fifteen years of age has spent his last three years at sea. He says my red hair reminds him of his mother. He knows his way about, John Charlton does, and he knows the men who brought me aboard. They can be trusted, he said. They're good men.

The men at night sing songs of Spain, and John Charlton says soon we are passing there. He brought me the latitude and longitude readings so I might enter them in my journal and has promised to do so whenever he can. I asked John what I should do about coming out.

'Stay hidden,' he said. 'If you are discovered now,' he said, 'Captain may yet put you off on land and see you returned to England.'

FRIDAY 2nd *[Between Cape Finisterre and Cape Ortegal]* Spain! I cannot see it from my hiding place, but I heard the cry. The Gentlemen brought their casting nets out and fetched in such creatures I can only imagine. Great were their exclamations of wonder. Their excitement makes my hiding so much more difficult to bear. That and the dampness of it all.

SATURDAY 3rd *[Off the Coast of Spain]* Saw little of the Gentlemen on deck today. At times they are careless and leave a morsel, spiced meat or cheese. Mr Parkinson, one of the artists Mr Banks brought aboard to draw the plants and animals we shall see on this voyage, is particularly forgetful with his food. He is a young man with a woman's hands. I am always interested to hear his observations. He speaks in a clear, light voice unlike any other on board. I have seen much in my imagination, listening to Mr Parkinson's reflections.

SUNDAY 4th *[Off the Coast of Spain]* As the sun was setting, the Gentlemen spied an endless field of little crabs feeding upon the surface of the sea. They cast their net and brought in a dripping lot of the little scuttlers. On deck the crabs glistened in the last rays of sunlight, clicking and slipping over one another. The Gentlemen exclaimed excitedly, and Mr Banks could not gather the creatures fast enough.

MONDAY 5th *[Off Cape Finisterre]* Mr Banks received a bird from one of the sailors this morning. It had been tangled in the rigging. The bird died in Mr Banks's hands. He had one of his servants rush it to Mr Parkinson to be drawn. I like all animals, but birds are my favourites. The year after Mother died, when I lived with

Grandmother, I would climb trees and watch the birds in their nests. I learned to imitate their calls, so that they would come almost to my hand.

Mr Banks has two greyhound dogs aboard. They sniff at my hiding place in the shelter of the Pinnace. Ordinarily the sight of them would gladden me, but I fear the bad turn they could do me now if they should give me away. But with the pens of live-stock around me, no one questions their excitement. Must be the pigs making them act so, Mr Banks says.

TUESDAY 6th *[Off the Coast of Spain]* Spain retreats and the Gentlemen gather species from the sea with a wonderful wor-ship. They exclaim at their finds, calling them sparkling jewels. Could these creatures possibly be as rich as my mind imagines? Mr Parkinson and Mr Buchan, the other artist aboard, must be very busy men, to draw all the creatures Mr Banks discovers. He says no sailor has ever troubled before to make such a record. Now his discoveries are forever recorded in Mr Parkinson's and Mr Buchan's pictures. I listen and imagine what everything looks like.

WEDNESDAY 7th *[Lat. 40°29′ N, Long. 10°11′ W]* Captain and crew sailed with a spirit of happy speed. Mr Banks looked out to sea a good part of the day. His posture suggested he was prepared to walk directly upon the water. I think he would ask Captain please to slow down so he might not miss a single fish swimming in his path. But John Charlton says Captain would not listen to such a request. *Endeavour* goes with the wind.

I asked Francis Haite as he coiled rigging nearby if I might come out soon. He swung his old head no.

I shall rot here. It smells as if I've already begun.

THURSDAY 8th [*Off the Coast of Spain*] John Ramsay says, 'We are pulling away from Cape Saint Vincent, lad, the last of Europe. And soon you shall come out.'

It's difficult deciding what to do first. A wash – what with the fleas and a coat of saltwater on my skin, I itch like mad – or dinner. I think it shall be dinner.

FRIDAY 9th [*Off the Coast, North Atlantic*] We are fairly flying over the sea.

SATURDAY 10th [*Off the Coast, North Atlantic*] In the night I dreamed of the Butcher and woke with a start. My back burned, remembering the bite of his whip. Silently, I slipped out of the Pinnace and crept over to Goat. She nodded, looked me over with a single golden eye and leaned her weight comfortingly against me.

SUNDAY 11th [*Lat. 34°1′ N, Long. 14°29′ W*] John Charlton says, 'Wait until we leave Madeira, Nick. Only that much longer.'

I don't wish a quick end to our voyage. In fact, I'd like to go on a very long time. The men assure me we shall, as they did that first day I approached them in Deptford Yard. But how much longer can I last in hiding?

MONDAY 12th TO TUESDAY 13th [*Isle of Madeira*] I've wondered how John Charlton knew so much about Captain. Well, it seems John is the Captain's own underservant and has sailed with him before.

The bits he brings me to eat come from the Captain's own table

John Charlton checked on me as he tended the livestock pens. 'We're heading from here to Brasil, Nick. Then round Cape Horn to King George's Land. We've orders from the Lord High Admiral himself. We're to observe the Planet Venus whilst we're there. It's very important, this observation, Nick. Captain says it will tell us how far the Earth is from the Sun and help all men who go to sea ever after.'

I only wanted a long voyage. I did not know I had stowed away on such an important one.

WEDNESDAY 14th *[Isle of Madeira]* A terrible accident today. Captain moved *Endeavour* to a new berth this morning. The anchor did not hold fast on the first attempt and required to be set again. It was brought up and hove out, but this time Mr Weir, the Quartermaster, found his leg entangled in the anchor rope. In a heartbeat Mr Weir was over the side along with the anchor. It was a desperate work to bring him back up. The men hove up the line with the greatest urgency. But despite their efforts they were too late. Mr Weir was drowned.

I want only to sleep, but when I close my eyes, I see the Butcher at work on Mr Weir.

PART II

Crossing the Line

SEPTEMBER 1768

THURSDAY 15th TO SATURDAY 17th *[Isle of Madeira]* John Charlton
stood by the Pinnace Thursday and called my name. I wished to
open my eyes and see his kind face, but I couldn't make myself
move. He and John Ramsay got me out of the Pinnace and carried me to Surgeon Monkhouse, who, along with his assistant,
Mr Perry, is looking after my health.

SUNDAY 18th *[Isle of Madeira]* I lived with my grandmother the year
I was seven. Grandmother's cook, Ganny Pajet, doctored the
people in the village, and I picked up a thing or two about doc-
toring from her. After Grandmother's death, when I found myself
under the roof of Reverend Smythe, the healing skills I learned

from Ganny Pajet came useful. The Reverend was a man who took pleasure in beating others. He would have flogged me and the other boarders, but he knew we would tell. Instead he beat his own children, staring at us all the while, forcing us to witness his cruelty. The healing skills I learned from Ganny Pajet came useful again yesterday. My friend John Ramsay, who helped smuggle me aboard and keep me well hid, and carried me here to Surgeon Monkhouse, was brought here himself with injuries from falling down the After Hold. I rose from my sickbed and gave what assistance was called for. Mr Perry said Surgeon Monkhouse was well pleased with me.

Captain is determined to keep his men healthy and well fed, the spotless Mr Perry says. Two men were given twelve lashes a piece for turning away their portion of beef, though I can't imagine why they should do so. All hands were called to witness the flogging. I also came on deck. The whipping put me in mind of Reverend Smythe and the Butcher, and now I am more frightened of Captain Cook than ever I was before. John Ramsay, who is still down with his injuries, said I shall be fine if I do as I'm told. Captain shall certainly not have to whip me for not eating.

I've been given a hammock and assigned a mess. I'm to be a servant and work into becoming an A.B., able-bodied seaman, by watching and helping where I'm told. Most of the men ignore me, except for the rough-mannered Mr Bootie. Captain reprimanded him, asking Mr Bootie how I had escaped detection for more than two weeks. Now Mr Bootie acts as if I kept hidden solely to injure his reputation, to make him appear the fool. He smacks hard at my head when he passes and calls me wicked and useless. Mr Bootie has recommended Captain put me off. But no order has been issued regarding my fate.

Surgeon Monkhouse has done his best to keep me out of harm's way. I had fever when I was brought to him. He saw me bathed and found the wounds left me by the Butcher. Surgeon Monkhouse is always in disorder, in marked contrast with the ever tidy Mr Perry. But Surgeon Monkhouse has been kind to me and seen to it I've come to no great trouble so far.

Now we are under way, with the hold filled with fresh Beef, a Live Bullock, Wine, Water, Fruit, Onions, sweetmeats. I know these things because I went down in the hold and, with the help of Mr Banks's servants, Thomas Richmond and George Dorlton, retrieved a spare casting net for Mr Banks from beneath the barrels and crates of supplies.

Slipped out during middle watch to visit my friend Goat, for the air is far more pleasant on deck than it is below. Goat was well pleased to see me. Her tail wagged and she bleated loud enough it's a wonder the entire Company wasn't alarmed. Goat was happy for my knuckles rubbing the top of her hard head between her horns. The pigs, too, greeted me and pressed their snouts to my hands, their hot, moist breath and their whiskers whispering over my skin.

We are under sail, into the heart of the Atlantic and I am still aboard.

MONDAY 19th [Lat. 31°43' N] Surgeon Monkhouse presented me, officially, to Captain today. I stood before him, quaking. He regarded me with those cold eyes of his and that stern lift to his chin. I am to be under Surgeon Monkhouse's supervision, Captain said, until I prove myself worthy. I am fortunate, Captain said, that the Surgeon has taken an interest in me. However, if I do not prove able, Captain said, I shall be put ashore in South

America and left to my own devices. He was most stern, Captain was. But then, after dismissing me, he called back over his shoulder. 'Nicholas Young,' he said.

'Aye, sir?'

'Be certain to eat your onions,' he said.

'Aye, aye, sir,' I answered.

A smile flickered over Surgeon Monkhouse's rumpled face. I was grateful for it.

TUESDAY 20th *[North Atlantic Crossing]* The Gentlemen are glad to get their hands on another casting net. Today they brought a fish aboard of the most wonderful colour. I'm so pleased to be out from the shadow of the Pinnace and see all there is about me.

No one but Surgeon Monkhouse and his brother, the midshipman, and Mr Perry and John Charlton and the two servants of Mr Banks speak to me. But still it is better than before, much better. And I've made friends with Mr Banks's two dogs, Lord and Lady Grey.

I'm watching over John Ramsay, who is still recovering from his fall. Captain has changed the length and number of watches so the men have more time to rest between duty.

WEDNESDAY 21st *[Atlantic Crossing]* Captain gave out hooks and line today that we might employ when we are not busy with the care of the ship. Ship's cook, Mr Thompson, is willing to prepare whatever we catch. The men received pipes and tobacco, as well. There was none of that for me. I don't need a pipe, not having the taste for tobacco Father and my brothers have. But I am very glad of my own hook and line.

THURSDAY 22nd TO TUESDAY 27th *[Lat. 21°26' N, Long. 20°14' W]* The air is clear, and fish leap from the water, shining silver, then knife back into the depths again. It's a grand thing to be under the sail, racing across the great Atlantic.

A flying fish came right through Mr Green's porthole. Mr Banks took it directly to Mr Parkinson to have it drawn, and I was called to clean up the puddle on the cabin floor. I had trouble keeping back the laughter, imagining fat Mr Green when the fish flew in through his window.

Midshipman Bootie came stumbling over me in the night as I sat with Goat. He cursed, then squinted down at me. 'It's the little demon', he said, and he lifted me by my ear and held me until I thought my ear would come off. Lieutenant Gore came past just as I could take no more. Mr Bootie dropped me to the deck and stumbled on.

I asked John Charlton what to make of Mr Bootie.

He said, 'Mr Bootie likes his drink. But he isn't a very likeable drinker.'

Mr Bootie does not resemble the Butcher in face or form, but his manner is just as cruel.

WEDNESDAY 28th *[Atlantic Crossing]* Whilst I scrubbed and polished and shovelled and fetched, I watched the Mates and Midshipmen at their drills. Not a member of this Company would trust me with Arms, not even the two kind Monkhouses, the rumpled doctor, William, and his handsome brother, Midshipman Jonathan Monkhouse. I'm but a stowaway. Nothing more.

THURSDAY 29th *[Lat. 17°32' N, Long. 21°11' W]* The Gentlemen brought a great shark in today. It was a sleek and fearsome thing, with its cold eyes and its mouth of teeth. Mr Thompson made dinner of it for the Company. The Gentlemen praised its excellent taste. Mr Bootie, overhearing that I was revolted by the idea of eating shark, carried a morsel of meat over and tried forcing it down my throat. I bit him. He smacked me hard so that I fell backward into the lap of my messmate. The men had a good laugh over that. Called me Sharky all evening. I don't care. I would have none of that shark meat. I'll eat anything else, thank you. But not shark. Sharks eat human flesh.

FRIDAY 30th *[Isle of Bonavista]* Dawn brought land into view. Bonavista the Mates called it. And close we were. Close enough *Endeavour* nearly caught her bottom on a Ledge of rocks. Very bumpy she was, this island of Bonavista. All mounded up with hills, except where she met the sea in beaches of sand. Mr Buchan made a picture of her, but Mr Parkinson didn't even come out for a look. He's hard at work in the Great Cabin, drawing the shark still.

The men had a joke on me yesterday, every one of them. I thought Mr Thompson had truly served the shark last night for dinner, but it was another sort of fish and they all knew. To think I passed up my dinner believing it to be shark when in fact it was a dish I might have savoured. And how long has it been since I swore I'd eat anything Captain offered? The men tease me when they can, those that bother with me at all. The coarse Mr Bootie is hateful. The fox-faced Master Molyneux, too. John Charlton said there are some who think stowaways are bad luck and never do warm up to a fellow who comes on that way.

This evening the Gentlemen were employed watching Mr Parkinson draw pictures of Ticks taken from the head of a bird. I understand how the Gentlemen might be inclined to study every living thing. But Ticks?

SATURDAY 1st OCTOBER *[Lat. 14°6' N, Long. 22°10' W]* How funny the Gentlemen are when they put their hands upon a new fish. They race to the Great Cabin, where they keep a library of books, and they tear through the pages trying to match what they hold in their hands to what they see in the book. They are ever looking for something new, something never seen before. Mr Parkinson barely notices when I bring refreshments to the Great Cabin. He's too busy painting and drawing.

SUNDAY 2nd TO TUESDAY 4th *[Atlantic Crossing]* Captain ordered we should all eat sour Kraut with our Portable soup. Kraut is vile. Hurts my jaws just to smell it. The Gentlemen and Officers eat it with exclamations of wondrous appreciation. I eat it only to avoid a whipping.

I'm up in the rigging every chance I get. It's not so different from climbing trees at Grandmother's. Some of the seamen are friendlier, now they see I can do my share of the work, even if I am a bit undersized.

WEDNESDAY 5th *[Atlantic Crossing]* A night of excitement with storms of flashing lightning and sheeting rain. There is no escaping such weather. Not on deck, nor below. I was wet through in moments, drinking the water down as it blew into my mouth and nose. Held on to Isaac Smith, seaman, when a wave hit him square and tried to take him over. I may be little, but my arms are strong enough. Isaac Smith said nothing after the incident, but he treats me like a mate now.

THURSDAY 6th *[Atlantic Crossing]* We are at the mercy of the storm, working the sails in the driving rains. Captain is always on deck. His eyes have a way of looking outward, as if he were questioning the ship and the sea and the wind. And he has a way of listening so that I think the ship, the wind, and the sea, they're answering him.

FRIDAY 7th *[Lat. 9°42' N, Long. 22°19' W]* After the fury of the last two days, it was a relief to scrub the deck this morning under a fresh sky. We are off course from the wind that carried us in the storm. And now we are becalmed. The sails hang slack, in want of a breath of wind. Mr Banks brought aboard what the crew call a Portuguese man-of-war. It is a beautiful creature, a bubble of light with ribbons of colour hanging down. It was hard getting close enough to see it when they brought it aboard, so many crowded round, and the men were ever careful of its sting. But I got a good, long look as Mr Parkinson painted its picture.

SATURDAY 8th *[Atlantic Crossing]* Employed at taking inventory of the stock. I counted the barrels and bags of Bread, Flour, Beer, Spirits, Beef, Suet, Raisins, Pease, Portable Soup, Oatmeal, Wheat, Oil, Sugar, Vinegar, Sour Kraut, Malt, Salt, Pork and Mustard Seed. Between the smells and the motion belowdecks, I have no appetite.

SUNDAY 9th *[Atlantic Crossing]* Great excitement this morning as the Gentlemen endeavoured to land a shark with their lines. The shark won and I suspect is now swimming as far from *Endeavour* as possible. Another shark appeared at evening. This one showed a harpoon wound. The Gentlemen thought they might make up for this morning's botch by bringing this one on before the day ended. That shark, too, had another idea.

Showed Samuel Evans some of the letters he needed to read simple words. He put his big hands up and rubbed his eyes. 'I can't even tell how to look at it,' he said.

MONDAY 10th TO TUESDAY 11th *[Atlantic Crossing]* Everyone is out of sorts. Mr Perry boxed my ears for moving too slowly with the mop. And then again later because he couldn't find me. I was tending Lord and Lady Grey. Lightning flashes around us and thunder rumbles down to the very hold. Rain, rain, rain. It slams on to the deck, runs down the hatches.

Mr Banks thought he could catch a dolphin in all this mess. I was happy to see it get away. Father said I must overcome my soft-heartedness. That's why he apprenticed me to the Butcher last Christmas after my second escape from Reverend Smythe's school. 'The Butcher'll make a man of you,' Father said. He made a thief of me instead. I stole money from him to run away.

WEDNESDAY 12th *[Lat. 7°21' N, Long. 22°39' W]* Captain keeps us hard at work, scraping and scrubbing and working at the ship, from the decks to the hold. Mr Pickersgill refused to work today, and Captain lashed him to the Mast. There are plenty who don't fancy Captain's busywork. As for me, I'm grateful not to be bruised and battered inside the Pinnace or flung over the side to Mr Banks's sharks.

THURSDAY 13th *[Atlantic Crossing]* Some little wind. Mostly becalmed. The Gentlemen keep up their netting of blubbers and sharks. Blubber's what the men call the clear jellied fish. Those

Blubbers have a nasty sting. Mr Banks thinks the little fish that hide within the Blubbers' tentacles are safe there from fish looking to eat them. What a dangerous game, to hide from one enemy within the poisoned cage of another.

FRIDAY 14th TO SUNDAY 16th *[Atlantic Crossing]* At last a gentle breeze. John Ramsay came on deck during my watch. I asked if he'd really sailed when he was eight.

'I did,' he said. 'And I was scared that first time. Didn't know anything. But I was better off than if I'd stayed on land.'

'Was it bad for you at home?' I asked.

'No,' he said, sweeping his fair hair back from his forehead. 'But I was running with bad boys. My mother thought it best to get me away.'

It was then Mr Bootie sprang on us. I hadn't even heard him coming.

He pushed me to the deck and put his boot on my chest and began to crush my ribs. John Ramsay ran for Lieutenant Hicks and brought him quickly back.

'What's going on here?' Lieutenant Hicks asked.

'The boy abandoned his watch,' Mr Bootie said.

Lieutenant Hicks helped me up. 'Is this true, boy?'

I caught Mr Bootie's sharp, ratty features in the moonlight. His green eyes looked like murder. 'Yes, sir,' I said.

'Mr Reading,' Lieutenant Hicks called.

The bosun's mate reported immediately.

'The boy needs starting,' Lieutenant Hicks said. 'He's forgotten how to stand watch.'

Mr Reading produced a rattan stick and struck me.

'Again,' Lieutenant Hicks said.

The stick bit my flesh.

'Once more', ordered the Lieutenant.

The last was the worst.

'I've let you off easy, boy', Lieutenant Hicks said. 'Don't let it happen again.'

Mr Bootie smiled menacingly at me as he followed Lieutenant Hicks away.

MONDAY 17th *[Atlantic Crossing]* John Charlton scrubbed the deck beside me this morning. 'I heard about last night', he whispered.

I was careful to keep a sharp eye out for Mr Bootie, but he was busy aft.

Mr Perry noticed the new bruises. I didn't tell him how they got there.

TUESDAY 18th *[Atlantic Crossing]* I watched on deck through squalls of rain. But the sails caught a breath and we are moving again.

Mr Banks struck his head this evening, exercising in his cabin. Mr Perry and Surgeon Monkhouse tended him and assured him all would be well, but he was worried he'd done himself some dreadful harm. I fed and watered and walked Lord and Lady Grey. When I returned with them, Mr Banks himself asked for water, which I got him.

WEDNESDAY 19th *[Lat. 3°44' N, Long. 25°23' W]* We're moving sure now across the sea at a good run. Mr Banks happily reported great improvement over the night. He is interested in me, Mr Banks is. His dark eyes study me when I enter the Great Cabin, carrying refreshments or clearing them away.

THURSDAY 20th *[Atlantic Crossing]* Mr Perry and Surgeon Monkhouse kept me hard at scrubbing today. Glanced inside the Great Cabin in passing. The Gentlemen were deeply concentrated on their dead things, their birds and fish and such. I do not wish to be drawn to their pursuits. Looks too much like schoolwork to me, with all the books they've got in there. Still, I can't help looking in when I pass.

FRIDAY 21st *[Atlantic Crossing]* Captain wishes to keep us from suffering the effects of scurvy, though we haven't seen a single case, Dr Monkhouse says. But now Captain bids us swallow vinegar. I told John Charlton that vinegar makes me gag. 'Next time I shall offer my share to Mr Bootie,' I said.

Smoke, the ship's grey-striped cat, has fallen into bad favour with me and Mr Banks. She ate one of Mr Banks's birds. A live one.

SATURDAY 22nd *[Lat. 1°45′ N, Long. 28°12′ W]* A grand day for weather and wind. We sailed well. And the whales sailed with us, blowing their spouts of mist. Mr Banks tried any number of ways to persuade our men to steer closer, but the men followed Captain's orders and the whales remained at a distance. All the better for them, given Mr Banks's liking of dead things.

SUNDAY 23rd TO MONDAY 24th *[Atlantic Crossing]* We had a white squall. It came on us without warning. A quick and rattling wind. The men were suddenly everywhere in the rigging. And then just as suddenly the squall had gone. Usually squalls come with some warning. But not this one. Still, it has passed and no damage done, but for Mr Parkinson, whose pots of paint tipped over. I was sent to clean the mess and found the Great Cabin empty. One of the drawings was blown into a corner by the storm. Here, captured on paper, was a bird I'd carried to Mr Banks from the rigging two days earlier. Mr Parkinson draws with a true hand, each feather softly rendered, the hardness of the beak told in line and shadow. Mr Banks came in as I stood over the drawing.

'What are you up to, Nick?' he asked.

'Just . . . picking up, sir,' I stammered. 'No harm done, sir, to the drawing, I mean.'

'No, Nick,' Mr Banks said kindly. 'No harm done.'

TUESDAY 25th *[Lat. 0°15' S, Long. 29°30' W]* Captain is certain of our location after several readings of his instruments. We have crossed an invisible Line dividing the Ocean north and south. The Equinoctial line, Mr Banks calls it. It's tradition that all first-time crossers be ducked in the very sea itself. That's what the men say.

After dinner a sort of chair was fashioned from pieces of wood and secured to the main yard on a pulley, and all the North Atlantic Men who would not pay their way out with brandy were lashed, one at a time, into the chair and lifted over the side, then dropped three times into the sea, to the tune of the bosun's whistle. Because I did not appear on the list of Crew, I thought I might escape, but someone had included my name amongst the twenty-two first timers. NICHOLAS YOUNG, THE LITTLE RED-HEADED DEMON, it said. I think it was Mr Bootie's hand.

Not even the dogs and cats were exempt. Mr Banks paid for his company to stay dry with a good quantity of Brandy, though it pleased him, I think, to see Smoke, the grey-striped cat, ducked. Goat did not have to be ducked. She'd been over the Line before, and she got to stand around with the others and watch.

I was terrified, waiting my turn. Some of the men went down, their faces white with fear, and came up half drowned after three times under. Some of the men yelled and grinned and shook like ducks, head to tail, coming up with an explosion of curses. When my time came, I held so tight to the chair my hands hurt. But I found the ride more frolic than fearsome. The trick was in catching a deep breath the moment before going under and holding it till I broke surface again. Blisters! The ducking felt grand! Cool and refreshing. My cheerful countenance at the last did not hurt my standing with many of the Company. Even Mr Bootie wore a grin on his ratty face when I came up laughing.

This was Captain's first time over the Line, too, but he did not take a turn in the chair. Likely he paid off in rum, just as Mr Banks. I'm glad the dogs weren't sent over the side. I don't think they'd have liked it. The cats yowled piteously. John Charlton, who had gone white with his ducking, sat with me late in the dark, with the first watch calling softly one to another. Everyone seemed cheered, even the ones like John who'd come up half drowned. It was a very good day to be amongst the men of *Endeavour*.

PART III

Rio

OCTOBER 1768

WEDNESDAY 26th *[South Atlantic Crossing]* The flying fish have found us again. They are everywhere in the sea, and many of them land on deck, flopping and slapping. I flung back every one I found until Mr Thompson, ship's cook, caught me at it. It seems flying fish make good eating. Mr Thompson said he'd serve me up for dinner if I threw back one more.

THURSDAY 27th *[Atlantic Crossing]* Mr Banks is quite eager to see a certain island and has encouraged me to keep a sharp eye peeled. John Charlton knows I'm worried Captain will leave me behind when we reach South America. Mr Bootie whispers ever at Master Molyneux's ear, and Master Molyneux is often in with

Captain. John listens at Captain's table. So far he has not heard Captain mention ridding himself of me, though I have hardly been a perfect seaman. It helps that Isaac Smith, who is cousin to the Captain's wife, has befriended me since the day I kept him from washing overboard. Captain is fond of Isaac, who at sixteen shows great promise to become a Captain himself someday. Isaac, who found me today at my journal, has offered ink and paper, if I should need more. If I am permitted to remain aboard *Endeavour*, I shall accept Isaac's offer.

FRIDAY 28th *[Lat. 3°41' S, Long. 32°29' W]* By tonight Captain was fair certain we had passed east of Mr Banks's island. I told Mr Banks I would not give up looking.

SATURDAY 29th *[Atlantic Crossing]* Helped fill the empty casks with saltwater to give ballast to the ship. Tonight as I gazed out, searching for Mr Banks's island, rays of white light sprang from the water's surface wherever I looked. I ran to fetch the Gentlemen, and they cast their nets and brought up all manner of sea creatures. The light, it seems, came from a sort of Blubber. Ginger Bigfoot, the ship's orange cat, came over and rubbed against my leg. I lifted her into my arms and we stared over the side, watching the show of lights from the great, dark ocean. Mr Banks took a moment to thank me for fetching him. 'You needn't watch for the island any longer, Nick. We've missed it.'

I said that I would look for South America instead.

SUNDAY 30th *[Atlantic Crossing]* We make remarkable good speed. Showed Samuel Evans the letters in his name. He continues to be a slow, though willing, student.

The air is so thick and moist I can hardly catch my breath. Mr Banks and the Gentlemen are out with their lamps, catching light-bearing crabs. These are animals never written of before. Mr Parkinson works late with his pencil and paints.

MONDAY 31st TO WEDNESDAY 2nd NOVEMBER *[Lat. 12°48' S, Long. 32°20' W]* The wind rushes us through the sea. Mr Banks grumbles at our speed, for he cannot catch any of the fish he sees off the stern.

THURSDAY 3rd *[Atlantic Crossing]* I think it's not as hot, nor has it been since we made our way out of the calms. Tonight, after my watch, I sat a bit with my friends Goat and Smoke, the grey-striped cat. In the sky the stars were like milk spills. 'What have you done?' I asked Goat. 'Have you sent your milk out to the heavens?' Goat did not bother answering. She simply turned her gold eyes to me and demanded a rub behind the ears.

FRIDAY 4th *[Atlantic Crossing]* I am of two minds. Desperate, after so long, to see land. Fearful that Captain will put me off when we reach it. I like life aboard *Endeavour.* I have friends here. This ship is more like home, this Company more like family than anything I've ever known. Captain must not put me off.

SATURDAY 5th TO SUNDAY 6th *[Lat. 19°3' S, Long. 35°50' W]* We sail on through perfect days of wind and sun. The colour of the water has changed some. The men say we are moving over a great shoal of coral and we must use care. 'To run upon coral is to run upon destruction,' Samuel Evans said. The men are ever singing out the soundings.

Isaac Smith says we have been close upon the coast of Brasil for more than a week and that we might have pulled into port in less than a day's sail in all that time. But Captain has his plans and will make land where he feels it most useful.

MONDAY 7th *[Off the Coast of Brasil]* The soundings show us in deeper water, though Isaac insists we are not far off the coast of Brasil.

Mr Banks was confounded by enormous stains of yellow on the sea. He and the other Gentlemen brought some of the yellow matter up to examine near noon and were still scratching their heads at nightfall. They could not determine even if their discovery was animal or vegetable. Mr Banks does not particularly like being confounded.

TUESDAY 8th *[Off the Coast of Brasil]* Brasil! I see it! It's the first body of land we have seen in what seems like a lifetime. What a place of towering mountains it is. We have come upon Espírito Santo. At least I think that's what the fishermen who pulled alongside were trying to tell us this land is called. Mr Banks and Dr. Solander boarded the fishermen's boat. The Gentlemen returned with many specimens for their studies and for our dinner.

We are so close to land, but Captain tacks off and on and we get no closer.

WEDNESDAY 9th *[Lat. 21°29' S]* Steady soundings, day and night, with the shore inching closer and closer. All is preparation for making land. My eyes fill with the sight of the shore and the hills lifting into the distance.

Captain is ever on deck taking readings. I am trying to be

helpful in every way without actually getting in the way. I still managed to displease Mr Bootie. Whilst coiling the rigging in the fore of the ship, I accidentally tripped him with a rope end. Mr Bootie grabbed the end and beat me about the feet and legs with it until Mr Monkhouse, Surgeon Monkhouse's brother, made him stop.

THURSDAY 10th *[Coast of Brasil]* The mountains of Brasil soar into the very clouds. The Gentlemen collect seaweed and worms. I am careful in the rigging today, though I go aloft as Mr Bootie orders. Still, I climb more with my arms than usual, having a pain in my foot since Mr Bootie beat me yesterday. Looking out from the topgallant mast, I long to feel land under me. I'll wager Goat wouldn't mind a bit of fresh grass herself.

FRIDAY 11th TO SUNDAY 13th *[Rio de Janeiro]* Our ship is in the company of many, many others, anchored in the harbour of Rio de Janeiro. Lieutenant Hicks and Mr Clerke took the Pinnace to shore to arrange for fresh Water and Provisions, and a Pilot to lead us closer in, but our men were not welcomed as guests. *Endeavour* was boarded by Portuguese soldiers who questioned Captain and the Gentlemen about our intentions in coming. Captain had not expected such treatment, and though he remained patient, all of us who knew him felt his displeasure.

MONDAY 14th *[Rio de Janeiro]* No one but Captain is permitted off *Endeavour.* I suppose I should be glad. Captain can't leave me in South America if the Portuguese won't let me off the ship.

Captain returned after the first dog watch. He was escorted by a Portuguese officer. Samuel Evans, who is coxswain of the

Pinnace, caught us up on the events of the day. It seems our Gentlemen are particularly not wanted ashore. The Portuguese think they are not scientists at all.

The weather this evening is all sweet breezes carrying the smell of land, but our confinement ruins the pleasure of it. It is not enough to see land. Never has *Endeavour* felt so much like a prison as it does now.

TUESDAY 15th *[Rio de Janeiro]* How unfair. There are many ships at anchor in the harbour, and they all have free passage to and from the city. Yet last evening, when the Gentlemen tried to launch a boat, they were stopped most certainly by the soldiers guarding *Endeavour* and had no choice but to return on board.

Captain, who is permitted, the only one permitted, went ashore and protested. But the Viceroy would not relax his restrictions. He says our Gentlemen are spies and harbour ill will to the Crown and Commerce of Portugal. He refuses to believe the Royal Navy would suffer scientists aboard when there is no profit to be gained from them.

Mr Perry said he expected King George's Land to be peopled by backward souls, but not Brasil.

Each morning and each evening we're in Port, Captain fires off our guns according to Navy custom. Perhaps the people of Brasil do not believe we are who we say we are, but Captain does not stray from his duty.

The weather holds fair, and supplies of fresh beef and greens come aboard.

The Gentlemen are as bristly as hedgehogs.

WEDNESDAY 16th *[Rio de Janeiro]* A breeze blows from the sea around noon each day and keeps blowing until the sun sets. Then the land breeze comes up, carrying out to us the smells and sounds of Rio de Janeiro. That's the hardest time for us all.

THURSDAY 17th *[Rio de Janeiro]* Mr Banks says the Portuguese insult the British with this behaviour, particularly putting a guard on Captain. But John Charlton said Captain will not raise a word in anger. He must provision *Endeavour*. If Captain surrenders to anger, we will have neither food nor drink for the next leg of our journey round Cape Horn to King George's Land.

FRIDAY 18th *[Rio de Janeiro]* Captain sent the Viceroy a letter listing his complaints. John Charlton says the Viceroy wrote back, saying if we do not like the rules of the Port, we should leave. I think we should. They don't even have good fruit here. Except for the watermelon, there is better to be had in England.

SATURDAY 19th *[Rio de Janeiro]* Captain takes his anger out on us by keeping us employed in hard labour through the long day. John Thurman received twelve lashes at Captain's order for refusing his work detail. I turned my head as the cat-o'-nine-tails lashed his back. But the sound filled my head with memories of Reverend Smythe and the Butcher, and I made myself watch John Thurman's whipping to chase away those memories from my past.

SUNDAY 20th *[Rio de Janeiro]* The Viceroy's main charge is that our ship is ugly. That such a vessel as *Endeavour* would never belong to the British fleet. Mr Banks, his wild hair flying, said something not very complimentary about the Viceroy this afternoon. I've heard worse. But never from a Gentleman.

MONDAY 21st *[Rio de Janeiro]* Mr Banks keeps close confidence in the Great Cabin. I believe he is scheming to go ashore. I only heard snatches through the open windows, but I'm nearly certain I'm right.

TUESDAY 22nd *[Rio de Janeiro]* Mr Banks sent his servants Thomas Richmond and George Dorlton ashore before dawn. They managed to return safely, carrying back with them all manner of plants and insects.

WEDNESDAY 23rd TO THURSDAY 24th *[Rio de Janeiro]* A Spanish ship sailed into the Harbour. We watched to see how she would be treated. No guard was placed. No restriction was made. The ship's men came off her and rowed to shore without a word of protest from the Portuguese soldiers!

FRIDAY 25th *[Rio de Janeiro]* I wish the British had been first to set foot upon this land. What great things we might have done with such a place. It is wasted on the Portuguese.

SATURDAY 26th *[Rio de Janeiro]* Around midnight last, I was on watch outside the Great Cabin when Mr Banks pulled himself out the window. As soon as I realized what he was about, I had to choose between calling out or letting him go. All his attention was on getting secretly to shore. He didn't notice me watching him until he had lowered himself into the waiting boat. He slipped away into the dark night without a word of alarm from me.

When he returned, bringing specimens for study, he also brought some green creepers, which he made certain I received. Goat was well pleased and her tail never stopped wagging for hours. Mr Banks said nothing to me about his adventure, and I kept still on my part.

SUNDAY 27th *[Rio de Janeiro]* Word is out of Mr Banks's visit to shore, though I never gave him away.

MONDAY 28th TO TUESDAY 29th *[Rio de Janeiro]* We are full up to our top decks with fresh water and supplies. And we prepare to set sail. Though Mr Bootie is suspicious of my involvement in Mr Banks's trip ashore, I have not been questioned. Mr Banks swears he made his escape in total silence and could not possibly have been observed, either by ship's Company or the Portuguese guards watching us. And so I am saved from a whipping.

WEDNESDAY 30th *[Rio de Janeiro]* It will be good to get away from this place and the unhappy restlessness it has infected us with. A Pilot came aboard at Captain's request, sent by the Viceroy. He will lead us out to open sea.

THURSDAY 1st TO SATURDAY 3rd DECEMBER *[Rio de Janeiro]* Seaman Flower has drowned after dropping from the shrouds into the sea. Surgeon Monkhouse gave me a drink of rum and told me to pull myself together. But how do you watch a man drown before your eyes and just go on?

John Ramsay said, 'Cheer up, Nick. Sailors never learn to swim. Should they fall in, better to let the sea take them quickly.'

PART IV

South to Cape Horn

DECEMBER 1768

SUNDAY 4th *[Rio de Janeiro]* No breeze for sailing, but thousands of butterflies. Mr Banks danced on deck. Lord and Lady Grey barked and leaped about him. Only Goat paid no mind to all the goings-on. Went over the letters of his name with Samuel Evans.

MONDAY 5th TO THURSDAY 8th *[South Atlantic]* How good to be under sail again. Mr Banks brought in a dolphin and a shark for his studies.

FRIDAY 9th *[South Atlantic]* Our weather is fair, but the ocean swells are towering high and *Endeavour* rides hard as she slams down into the troughs. Lieutenant Gore says we've missed a great storm. As it is, the ship broke her topgallant mast last night in the rough seas. I am glad we were not in the full force of such a blow. SATURDAY 10th *[Lat. 25°34′ S, Long. 41°12′ W]* The sea is littered with debris.

SUNDAY 11th *[South Atlantic]* Mr Banks took another shark. It behaved in a manner most foul. When caught, it ejected its stomach from its mouth, then took it back in again. It did so several times. I saw it with my own eyes. When Mr Banks and Dr. Solander opened it up, they found six baby sharks within. Five they placed alive into a tub, where they are swimming still. The sixth was dead. Slops for dinner.

MONDAY 12th *[South Atlantic]* A gentle breeze has returned and we move slowly through the clear sea air. Captain runs the gunners through their Monday drills. And we caulk and repair and tend to the never-ending needs of *Endeavour*.

TUESDAY 13th TO SATURDAY 17th *[Lat. 32°15' S, Long. 42°48' W]* Captain has put the Company on 'watch and watch.' We stand for four hours, then are below for four. It is hard to get sleep enough in four hours. Particularly with the sea tossing us about.

SUNDAY 18th *[South Atlantic]* There's a chill in the air. The Gentlemen have closed the windows in the Great Cabin. Now I shall not hear as much. Goat has grown accustomed to my keeping her up to date on the Gentlemen's doings. She will be greatly disappointed. At least we still have John Charlton posting us at the scuttlebutt.

MONDAY 19th *[South Atlantic]* The sail maker and his mates are busy preparing the ship for the hard seas round Cape Horn. The men who have rounded the Cape before say we are entering the worst part of our journey. Blisters! Can it get worse than we've already seen?

TUESDAY 20th *[South Atlantic]* Last night a sudden and quick storm smacked us so hard I have never felt such a thing since we've been at sea. But today the temperature rose to a gentle degree, the windows came open again, the wind whistled in our ears, and we flew over the water. Mr Banks requested my help in setting the Great Cabin right after last night's storm. Mr Bootie, being close by, offered his assistance in my place, saying I was incapable of doing a proper job. The wild-haired Mr Banks looked upon Mr Bootie as he would upon a pile of dog's leavings. 'Come, Nick,' he said, beckoning to me. Mr Bootie glared as I followed Mr Banks away.

WEDNESDAY 21st *[Lat. 37°8′ S, Long. 48°30′ W]* A kind of bird called a sheer water has caught up with *Endeavour* and follows us across the waves. The appearance of this bird signalled Captain that we must be closing in on the Cape. Mr Bootie grabbed my head under his arm as he came past this morning. 'Cape Horn has been the death of many a sailor,' he whispered. 'I'll be sure to have you aloft in the worst of it.'

Then he let go and walked off as if he'd never seen me.

THURSDAY 22nd *[South Atlantic]* We kept company for a time with Porpoises of such a large size that even Mr Banks did not attempt to take one. He contented himself with watching, and when the Porpoises pulled away, he and Dr. Solander took the boat out and shot birds for their studies. Mr Banks often takes me as one of his oarsmen. He heard me one day entertaining the men with my bird calls and found it a useful skill. I'm not certain I like that he employs me to call the birds down to their death. But until Mr Banks, I never saw so many birds so close. It is something to see them that way.

Mr Banks kept up his shooting for hours. There was no hurry, as we had little wind. Now the new sails are bent and ready for the Cape. Mr Ravenhill, the sail maker, who manages to stay drunk day and night, is more drunk than I have ever seen him.

FRIDAY 23rd *[South Atlantic]* A day of little wind but mighty events. Early this morning a cloud, small and white, appeared in the west, suddenly erupting in an explosion of fire. Moments later, a crack fractured the air, like close cannon shot it sounded. And then the cloud vanished. We suffered no damage, but that cloud, wherever it came from, came too close for my liking. It had my heart racing. Goat wasn't happy, either.

Mr Banks killed an albatross and a turtle for his studies. I asked him why he killed so many things. He said you can't know a thing unless you study it. Inside and out. He said it was a scientist's job to study things. To know things. To record them so others could study, too. 'It is for King and country,' he said. 'It is for the betterment of all.'

I suppose if a bird or a turtle must die, it is good to do so for the King.

SATURDAY 24th *[South Atlantic]* Captain was out taking his sightings by the moon. I sat quietly in the shadows and watched him, so sure of himself, so certain in his every movement. Captain may be stern. He may punish a man harshly from time to time. But I know a bad man from a good one, and Captain Cook is a good man.

SUNDAY 25th *[South Atlantic]* Under a clear sky and with a good wind in our sails we race towards the Cape. It is Christmas, and I think of Father and his new wife, and my brothers off at their studies and my sisters at home. I imagine right this moment they are sitting down to their Christmas feasts. The first time I ran away from school was at Christmas. I thought I might have dinner at home and a holiday from Reverend Smythe for one day. It took me hours to get home. I was tired, hungry, cold. Father's man dried me off before he brought me up to Father. When I was taken in to him, Father said nothing to me. Not a single word. He simply put me in his carriage and drove me back to school. The only words he spoke were to Reverend Smythe. He told the reverend that if I ran off again, I should be withdrawn. That night Reverend beat his youngest daughter, Josephine, eight years old, my age, with a particular ferocity. Only I was required to watch.

On *Endeavour* tonight the entire crew drank until they were stinking, falling-down drunk, even John Charlton, his beaming smile bigger and looser than I have ever seen it. I slipped in with Goat and stayed out of their way. Some of the men grew harsh, particularly Mr Bootie. He strutted around, making fun of Mr Banks and the Gentlemen in a rough and ugly way. He came looking for me but grew distracted by a loose hen that flew into his face. He killed it with his fists. And then he handed it to Mr Thompson and said, 'Here's a hen for Christmas.'

MONDAY 26th *[Lat. 40°19' S, Long. 54°30' W]* *Endeavour* strayed off course during Christmas celebrations. Captain has worked to right us, and now we're back in the sea road, heading towards the Cape.

Mr Banks hung over the side watching great beds of rock-weed drifting just beyond his reach. But he did not shoot anything today. I think the men, whose heads still suffer from their Christmas rum, might have thrown our Gentleman over-board to be with his rockweed if he'd fired off a shot.

TUESDAY 27th *[South Atlantic]* The wind is fresh and full of squalls. Some tricky sailing required, but the men swung into action as easy as lanterns on their poles. I am quick and sure in the rigging, and I grow stronger each day. But still I am no A.B., not yet. I do whatever I'm asked. As Surgeon's servant it's most often scrub-bing and washing and polishing, fetching and carrying, that sort. Mr Banks sometimes calls me to the Great Cabin to do similar work for the Gentlemen. And I never mind tending the livestock and Lord and Lady Grey. Mr Thompson, the cook, calls me to lend a hand at times. And I do my share of picking oakum and making rope.

At times today we caught a stink in the air, like rot, like death. At night the men talk. Cape Horn has caused the destruction of many a ship. Mr Bootie says there are monsters living there. And horrible beasts. I huddle in with Goat and bury my nose in her side when the stink comes upon the air to me. Goat does not smell very good, but she doesn't stink of death.

WEDNESDAY 28th *[South Atlantic]* It's an odd colour, this sea. I don't like it.

THURSDAY 29th *[Lat. 41°45' S, Long. 59°37' W]* Mr Green and Captain were out with their instruments taking sightings to fix our location. The soundings show the seabed is neither falling nor rising, but staying forty some fathoms below. The water is nearly white, a dreadful colour for a sea. Mr Banks and Dr. Solander pull up feathers and corpses of creatures floating dead to study in their cabin.

FRIDAY 30th *[South Atlantic]* What a day. The ship was festooned by insects. Butterflies, moths, crickets, and beetles. They were everywhere in the rigging and upon the deck. Whilst he dipped with his nets, Mr Banks had us gather everything we could from the rigging. Then he sorted what he wished to study and what he wished to discard, and the discarded insects went over the side while the Gentlemen worked with great energy on the ones they kept. We were given rum for our assistance. I shared mine with Samuel Evans, Francis Haite and John Ramsay. Francis Haite said butterflies and moths and beetles and such could not fly far out to sea. What with the shallow soundings and the white colour of the water and the butterflies, we must be very close to land, Francis said.

While we sat, thunder popped softly, like the sound of the sails snapping in the wind, and lightning feathered the sky in a wonderful show. Later some saw land to the west, but I was below deck and missed it.

SATURDAY 31st *[Lat. 43°14' S, Long. 60°26' W]* Mr Banks says there is perhaps a passage leading from the Atlantic Ocean to the Pacific. He says the passage is a great river and that is what brought the butterflies to us, but Captain Cook has his own ideas and stays his course for Cape Horn. Mr Bootie says that's a good place to put off a useless, red-headed demon. 'Leave him to the monsters of the Cape,' he says.

I hate Mr Bootie.

SUNDAY 1st JANUARY *[South Atlantic]* As the clouds deepened from day to night, a wondrous thing happened. I went to the side of the ship to empty buckets, and I saw the sea asparkle with a brilliant light, as jewels the King might wear in his crown. It is a sight I shall never forget, as long as I live.

A new year begins this day. Life at sea is not what I thought. I never imagined the endless work of it. Nor the discomfort of it all. But I also never dreamed of the beauty, and the peace, and the way it feels to have found my place with the men. I would not be back in London, cowering in the corner, taking blows from the Butcher . . . not for all the tea in the King's pantry. I don't know what I shall do when *Endeavour* returns to England, but I shall not put myself in the Butcher's reach. That is the one thing I know for certain.

Worked with Samuel Evans on his letters.

MONDAY 2nd *[South Atlantic]* Hail fell today in lumps the size of my fist. And the water turned red with great numbers of small creatures. Both whales and sea lions fed eagerly upon them. Mr Bootie called them red shrimps. Mr Banks scooped them up and brought them to the Cabin for study. They were not as big as the tip of my finger.

TUESDAY 3rd *[Lat. 47°17' S, Long. 61°29' W]* The men thought they saw land, and we turned the ship westward in pursuit. I kept my gaze fixed on the horizon until my eyes burned, but the horizon never changed, nor came any closer.

The men thought they'd found Pepys's Island, but all they

found was Cape Fly Away. That's what the men call sightings of imaginary land.

Mr Banks captured seaweed of giant size today. Lieutenant Gore says such a weed can grow twelve fathoms tall from sea floor to surface. I asked Goat if she would like that kind of weed to eat, and she lowered her head and butted me.

WEDNESDAY 4th *[South Atlantic]* Back on course and driving before the wind. It's quite cold here and I have no coat, no good hat, no proper boots and no socks at all.

THURSDAY 5th *[South Atlantic]* Gales morning and evening.

FRIDAY 6th *[Lat. 51°20' S, Long. 62°19' W]* It's perfectly bitter. There are birds in the sea called Penguins. I never dreamed of seeing such a thing as Penguins. They show black across their backs and dazzling white chests, and they fly through the sea as a swift might traverse the air. But they are built in such a manner that they could never get airborne. Captain issued Fearnaught Jackets and heavy Trousers to the company. Though they say it's bad luck to wear the gear of a dead man, Surgeon Monkhouse said I was to wear the clothes of the drowned Seamen Flowers. The Jacket and Trousers are large enough I look like I'm slipping my skin, even with the sail maker's assistant taking them in a bit for me. But the clothes are thick and warm.

Mr Banks has brought his own warm clothing. He stands on deck and keeps a lookout for the Falklands.

SATURDAY 7th *[Nearing Cape Horn]* The wind blew and the ship tossed during the night, so that everything shifted. All of the

Gentlemen's books spilled and slid and banged back and forth in the Cabin. And the hammocks creaked from their nails, and the rafters moaned as they shifted. I could not sleep. The Penguins shriek. It is a most unbirdlike sound.

Whilst I put the Great Cabin to rights, I stopped and looked inside one of Mr Banks's books. It was about birds. There were dozens and dozens of pictures. I would have not minded Reverend Smythe and his school so much if I had had such a book for my studies. Carefully, I replaced the volume on Mr Banks's shelves.

When I went to milk Goat for Mr Thompson, I managed to take only half of what I usually get. 'What's the matter, old girl?' I asked. Back in the galley I showed Mr Thompson the half-empty pail.

'She's not sick,' Mr Thompson said. 'Only put off by these seas, she is, Nick. Get on with you.'

SUNDAY 8th TO TUESDAY 10th *[Nearing Cape Horn]* Captain has the men tacking. A group of speckled porpoises tack with us, leaping from the water entirely, then quickly slipping back in again. If I could only swim like that. If I could but swim at all.

WEDNESDAY 11th *[Tierra del Fuego]* Land! Isaac Smith says this is Tierra del Fuego and we are just before the Cape. The Gentlemen, with their glasses, report seeing beaches and trees, but no monsters. Mr Banks is eager to go exploring ashore, and I should like to go with him just to touch land again. Monsters be damned.

PART V

From the Horn to King George's Land

JANUARY 1769

THURSDAY 12th *[Tierra del Fuego]* The wind changes from moment to moment. And yet Captain found a breeze he could use. Immediately he put our nose into a small cove, and we came within a mile of shore. Then the wind went wrong again and forced us out. Though Isaac Smith says it is summer in this hemisphere, early this evening a cloud came upon a rise and left a fall of snow across its top.

FRIDAY 13th *[Tierra del Fuego]* Today we had stinging hail and bitter rain and even our Fearnaughts brought little comfort. Three times we tried to make headway. Three times the tide and winds pitched us back. If this is their summer, I shouldn't want to know their winter at all.

SATURDAY 14th *[Tierra del Fuego]* It feels hopeless in this wild and raging sea. How shall we ever make it round the Cape? The tide turns, and roiling mountains of water rise up and smash against one another, barring our way.

We found a Cove east of Cape Saint Vincent in which to take shelter. From this anchor Mr Banks and Dr. Solander took a boat to shore and collected plants for hours. I was not chosen as one of the oarsmen and, disappointed, I remained aboard, where there was much work to be done. The Gentlemen returned at a level of excitement I have not seen from them yet – everything they carried was new to them and not in any of their books.

I asked Mr Banks if he saw any monsters whilst he was ashore. He said, 'No. Only two huts.'

I asked, 'Are they the sort of hut monsters might live in?'

He said he did not think so.

SUNDAY 15th *[Tierra del Fuego]* Mr Banks and Dr. Solander went ashore again today with Captain Cook. He was in search of fresh water to replenish our supplies. They brought back not plants, nor water, but three natives! The three were of a colour like rusted iron, with long dark hair, thick and unkept. They were very tall. But they were not monsters. Their bodies bore stripes of red and black paint; their clothes were woolly animal skin. The natives were offered bread and beef, which they accepted with obvious pleasure though we could understand nothing of their language. They did not like the taste of wine and gave that quickly back. They did not stay aboard more than half a watch. Mr Banks escorted them back to shore.

MONDAY 16th *[Tierra del Fuego]* Captain has found a good place for the men to gather fresh water and wood. He took Isaac Smith ashore with him, and Master Molyneux, to make charts. We can see the native women from the ship. They are like the men in colour and build, but they wear a piece of animal skin over their privy parts. The women gathered shellfish at low water, loosening them from the rocks with a stick, then placing their harvest in baskets.

Mr Banks took a large party, including Dr. Solander, Mr Green, Mr Monkhouse and Mr Buchan, to explore the hills that are patched with snow. George Dorlton and Thomas Richmond have gone along to carry the gathered plants. Lord Grey went, too. I hoped Mr Banks might choose me as he assembled his party, but he had his mind on other things, and Mr Bootie had his eye on me. Nor did Samuel Evans tap me to take a seat in the Pinnace. I have tried to teach him his letters on the Sundays when Captain Cook gives us the afternoon free, but he forgets what he has learned from one week to the next, and it seems we start all over again each time. I am beginning to understand Reverend Smythe's frustration with me. It is tiring teaching someone who won't learn.

It is late and Mr Banks and his party have not returned. I fear for them, ashore, exposed to this bitter night.

TUESDAY 17th *[Tierra del Fuego]* Mr Banks's party did not reach the ship until near noon today. When they finally came in sight, they were a sorry lot. Most, too weak to climb, had to be handed up to us. We got the whole story from Samuel Evans. Mr Buchan, Samuel said, suffered a fit as they explored the terrain yesterday. Because of that the party was caught too far in the hills when day ended. The weather turned from the warmth of an English May to the frost of winter. Dr. Solander, who is even heavier than Mr Green and not the fittest, lay down in the snow first and swore he could go no farther. Thomas and George lay down with him and refused to go on. Lord Grey remained with the three of them as snow began falling. A fire was built and Dr. Solander was brought down to it, but by the time the men returned for the others, it was too late.

They died. George Dorlton and Thomas Richmond died. They froze to death right there in the snow. Lord Grey would not leave their bodies this morning. He took much persuading, Mr Banks said.

We brought the dazed party aboard, or what remained of it, and warmed and fed them and put them into their beds, but for Mr Banks. Mr Banks wished only to return to shore and harvest more plants. I think sometimes the Gentleman has not one bit of sense in his head for all his learning.

Tonight I look up from the deck into the hills of Tierra del Fuego knowing there lay the bodies of my friends. Even galley work at Mr Thompson's stove could not warm me.

WEDNESDAY 18th TO MONDAY 23rd *[Attempting the Cape]* We work to get every inch we can out of the wind, but then a calm sets in and the wild tide carries us back with great speed.

Captain leaves much of the sailing to the men as he works tirelessly in his recording of the land we pass. He is much satisfied at including land not upon any chart in his possession nor any chart known to man.

TUESDAY 24th *[Attempting the Cape]* Captain keeps us tacking between the Mainland and the rocks dotting these ferocious waters. All about us both land and sea rise to sharp and craggy peaks. Mr Bootie orders me aloft as often as possible. John Charlton's ready smile turns sour at the midshipman's orders. 'Don't worry, John,' I tell him. But there are times when I have nearly fallen from the rigging as the wind howls and freezes my hands to the ropes whilst the ship pitches in the churning sea.

WEDNESDAY 25th *[Attempting the Cape]* A thick fog enveloped us midday and no observations could be made of land. We sounded constantly, inching slowly towards Cape Horn. The fog cleared for a quarter-hour and there, Captain said, was the Cape! We were rounding it!

THURSDAY 26th *[Rounding Cape Horn]* We've done it! Rounded Cape Horn! And now we feel the wind in our sails from fresh Pacific gales! Blisters! The Pacific!

FRIDAY 27th *[South of the Cape]* We fight for every mile.

SATURDAY 28th TO MONDAY 30th *[Lat. 60°4′ S, Long. 72°48′ W]* The sea remains a place of great turmoil. It swells and falls with alarming extreme. Sometimes I forget why we are here. I know only that daily we climb the rigging, repair *Endeavour*, fight to survive in this brutal sea. There is no more to know.

TUESDAY 31st TO FRIDAY 3rd FEBRUARY *[Across the South Pacific]* Every day we inch out of the grasp of the Cape. But the days are clouds and fog, rain and bitter cold. And Captain has turned us into colder sea yet in search of a better wind.

SATURDAY 4th *[Lat. 57°45′ S, Long. 82°16′ W]* Mr Banks is unwell and Mr Perry says it's the scurvy, the disease Captain most fears. I helped Surgeon Monkhouse prepare for Mr Banks a drink the doctor calls a rob, made from the juice of lemons and oranges.

SUNDAY 5th *[Across the South Pacific]* The cold has crept into our bones and I fear it shall never leave. My feet and face are the worst. The skin is cracked and bleeding.

Mr Banks is better. He ventured from his cabin this noon. The rob of lemon and orange must have helped.

I assisted Mr Thompson in the preparation of Mr Banks's dinner. Mr Thompson often requests my help in the kitchen though I can't always be spared. Mr Thompson doesn't know I was last apprenticed to a butcher. He just thinks I'm quick about such things. I've said little on board about myself, except to John Charlton and Surgeon Monkhouse. But there are those who notice. Enough of Reverend Smythe's attentions have worn off on me to mark me as a boy with education. I believe it's the thing Mr Bootie hates most about me.

Today Mr Bootie came to the Great Cabin whilst I was there. He asked if he might borrow one of Mr Banks's books. Mr Bootie is ever trying to have a pleasant talk with the Gentlemen, but the Gentlemen seem little interested in what the midshipman has to say. Mr Banks told Mr Bootie the books were not to be touched. Yet only last week Mr Bootie heard Mr Banks offer that I might come and read anytime I pleased. I shall pay for all this, no doubt. Mr Bootie shan't let it go easily.

MONDAY 6th TO WEDNESDAY 8th *[Across the South Pacific]* Slow progress North-west.

THURSDAY 9th *[Lat. 52°22' S, Long. 86°17' W]* We travelled like we have not done in months. Felt like flying. Peter Briscoe saw a beetle fly over us. We've been awhile without insects.

FRIDAY 10th TO SUNDAY 12th *[Across the South Pacific]* Surgeon Monkhouse is instructed to feed us Wort if we look even slightly like scurvy coming on. We are given Portable Soup, Malt, Saloop and Sour Kraut in the hope that at least one of these foods will battle the scurvy. When Captain first asked us to eat the Sour Kraut, we had no taste for it. But the officers' table had such high praise for it, we thought to give it another chance. Before long Captain had to set a limit, else we'd eat it all before we got more. It makes the mouth shudder, Kraut does, and some of the men make passing bad smells after, but we are healthy.

MONDAY 13th TO WEDNESDAY 15th *[Across the South Pacific]* Went as oarsman with Mr Banks in his boat as he brought down birds.

THURSDAY 16th TO FRIDAY 17th *[Across the South Pacific]* What a wind blows! It split the Main Topsail, right down the middle. A string of curses came from the Sail maker such as none I've ever heard. But we quickly had the torn sail down and another in its place. The Sail maker, even in his drunken state, repaired the split with the greatest skill. *Endeavour* flies too fast for Mr Banks to collect anything but a face full of wind.

SATURDAY 18th *[Lat. 44°50' S, Long. 99°7' W]* She blows fresh and steady and we run across the sea.

SUNDAY 19th *[Across the South Pacific]* The fog broke up and day ended with a slow, smooth ride and clear skies, though the air has a cold bite to it still.

Spent a little time with Samuel Evans. His progress is considerably slower than *Endeavour*'s.

MONDAY 20th TO WEDNESDAY 1st MARCH *[Lat. 38°44' S, Long. 111°43' W]* The Marines drill often, led by Mr Monkhouse, in anticipation of making a Landing. Captain is precisely on course, according to Isaac, and we shall reach King George's Land in ample time to take the measurements required by the Lord High Admiral.

Mr Banks insists there is another continent, an undiscovered continent, somewhere in this sea, but Captain says if there were such a continent, we would experience currents to indicate such, and we do not.

The weather improves. It's much better than London is having now. I'm warming up.

THURSDAY 2nd TO WEDNESDAY 15th *[Lat. 29°43' S, Long. 126°53' W]* Tropic birds soar above us, bright to behold against the sharp blue of the sky. The cats look interested. But not as interested as I.

Tonight Mr Green and Captain were out on deck making observations of Saturn and the Moon. An occultation, they called it. John Charlton did not know what *occultation* meant, but Isaac Smith said it means 'covering up'. Saturn was covering up the Moon.

THURSDAY 16th *[Towards King George's Land]* We make progress but it is slow. Our water is still fresh, which pleases Captain. It tastes better than it did when we first loaded it at Tierra del Fuego. Mr

Perry says that's because the red substance that was in it has now settled out. Mr Perry is surprised at the water still being so good. He said going from a cold climate to a hot one generally leads to a fast fouling.

FRIDAY 17th TO MONDAY 20th *[Lat. 25°44' S, Long. 129°28' W]* Mr Banks has been holding much discussion with the other Gentlemen about the undiscovered continent. According to a map made by a Mr Dalrymple, Captain Cook has done the impossible. He has sailed *Endeavour* across land! In the past month we have not even seen land, much less sailed atop it! Isaac said Mr Dalrymple has made a mistake. I never thought to hear someone say a grown man had made a mistake. But if a man draws an island on a map and then a real ship sails over where that man has drawn, clearly the man has got it wrong.

Every day we sail with Captain Cook across this immense Pacific Ocean, we sail in waters never charted before. I wonder what Father would say. I doubt my brothers, with all their book learning, with their perfect Latin, shall ever have such an adventure.

TUESDAY 21st *[Towards King George's Land]* The birds make Ginger Bigfoot's tail switch and her mouth water, and she makes little sounds in her throat of hunger and longing. Mr Banks had a good day of collecting out in his boat. I stole into the Great Cabin to get a closer look at the downed tropic birds. I never saw such beauty.

WEDNESDAY 22nd *[Towards King George's Land]* Some of the men spotted a bird they call the Man-of-war. They say such a bird rests only on land, never on water, so we must be close to land! We saw many birds last night, all heading at sunset towards the north-west. The men felt certain we would find land there, but the wind did not take us north this day, only west. Mr Banks tried shooting Egg Birds, small white birds that lay large eggs, and though his aim was true, the felled birds landed in the sea and he could not recover any.

My skin is always damp here and the sun piercing. I'm never so fair as I was when first I came aboard *Endeavour*, but my skin is still easily burned.

THURSDAY 23rd *[Lat. 24°43' S, Long. 130°8' W]* The Man-of-war birds soar over our heads, and we know any time now we shall sight land.

FRIDAY 24th TO SATURDAY 25th *[Towards King George's Land]* Mr Greenslade, a Marine, took his own life a few hours ago. Earlier today, while he was on Watch, he was admiring a tobacco bag being fashioned from sealskin by the sail maker's assistant. Mr Greenslade asked if he might have one of the sealskin pouches and was refused, rather rudely. When left to look after the tobacco bags for a moment, Mr Greenslade took one and tucked it away on his person. I know because I was looking after the pigsty when it happened. I saw and heard everything. And I couldn't blame Mr Greenslade for taking it. He'd been treated so rudely, after all. And he'd so admired the bag. I can't imagine anyone keeping his hands off the goods in such a circumstance.

When the bag was found missing, Mr Greenslade was asked for it. If I were Mr Greenslade, I might have said I didn't have it. But Mr Greenslade immediately returned the bag.

That should have been the end of it. But I wasn't the only witness to the affair. Mr Bootie saw it, too. And when the story got out, the Marines came down hard on Mr Greenslade. They told him their honour had been utterly destroyed because of him, because he had stolen something on Watch, something that he'd specifically been asked to guard.

When the Marines left him, Mr Greenslade moved down below deck and lay in his hammock, as sorrowful as any soul has ever been. I tried speaking with him. I don't think he heard me. He made no sign showing he even knew I was there. He was lost to everything but his own shame.

When the Sergeant came after him to bring him before Captain, Mr Greenslade followed. 'He offered no resistance,' the Sergeant said, 'only he moved so slowly.' In the dark, on his way to Captain, Mr Greenslade let the Sergeant get ahead, and as silent as ever a man could, he went overboard and sank into the sea.

SUNDAY 26th *[Towards King George's Land]* The wind goes round in a circle. From minute to minute no one knows which direction it will come from. The men call this weather the trolly-lollys.

MONDAY 27th *[Towards King George's Land]* We see logs of wood float by, and seaweed, and the water is smooth in this place. Mr Pickersgill, the Master's Mate, says all these things add up to land. I see nothing but vast ocean spread everywhere around us. Even the birds have deserted us. I dreamed of Mr Greenslade last night. He stood at my hammock, shaking me. 'Hurry, Nick,' he said. I woke to find John Charlton calling me to my watch.

TUESDAY 28th TO SATURDAY 1st APRIL *[Towards King George's Land]* Mr

Banks is not well. He has a soreness in his throat of which he makes much. He told Surgeon Monkhouse he believes he is suffering from scurvy. We eat fresh foods whenever possible, but it has been some time since we've been in reach of greens. Mr Banks has a swelling in his mouth and pimples, and Dr. Monkhouse agrees, scurvy it is. He has Mr Banks putting lemon in everything, and the poor Gentleman walks and talks with his mouth puckered, but he says he's feeling better.

SUNDAY 2nd *[Lat. 19°0' S, Long. 135°33' W]* A glorious day of wind and sun and speed. We had birds overhead, crying and dipping and fishing for their supper. Not even a moment for Samuel Evans and his letters.

MONDAY 3rd *[Towards King George's Land]* Monday, Wednesday and Friday are Banyan days. On these days we get no meat. Today we had portable soup with pease instead. I prefer Meat days. I'm not overly fond of portable soup, with pease or without, though many of the men find it palatable enough.

TUESDAY 4th *[Lat. 18°42' S, Long. 139°29' W]* Land! Peter Briscoe spied it first. It was during the forenoon watch when Peter's cry came. The men in the topmast head called out what they saw. Something they called cocoa nutt Trees, upon which were big, hairy nuts. And natives. They saw natives! The natives carried clubs, as if they meant to fight us. They were dark-coloured with long black hair, and they went naked but for a piece over their privy parts.

The island appears on no chart in Captain's knowledge, and so he has charted it himself and named the place for a water hole in its centre. Lagoon Island. I cannot say how it feels after so long with nothing but sea in our eyes to look upon land and trees and Natives and huts! We watched longingly as we passed without stopping.

WEDNESDAY 5th *[Nearing King George's Land]* Today we sighted another island. It is shaped like a bow, and that is what Captain has named it. Bow Island. There must be inhabitants, for there were signals of smoke coming from three spots.

Lieutenant Gore said he saw natives walking in and out of the trees, unmoved by the sight of our passing ship. Why are they not as excited by the sight of us as we are by them?

THURSDAY 6th *[Nearing King George's Land]* Two more islands. We sailed directly towards them until we found they were surrounded by many large rocks joined all together beneath the surface of the sea.

Some of the natives walked along the shore, following the path of our ship. When they reached the island's tip, they set out in canoes. Captain brought *Endeavour* to and held her, waiting for the natives to approach, but they would not come out beyond a certain point.

These natives, like the first, were of a deeply browned colour. They carried poles and wore no clothes that I could tell. Their hair was dark and long and loose. They made signs to us, drawing us towards them, and yet they waved their poles at us and shouted. We waved our hats at them and shouted back.

FRIDAY 7th *[Lat. 17°48' S, Long. 143°31' W]* Now we see where the Man-of-war birds go. We passed by a small island with no natives but hundreds and hundreds of birds. They deafened us with their noise, the air exploding with sound as we passed, and I could not contain my excitement at the sight and call of so many.

SATURDAY 8th TO SUNDAY 9th *[Approaching King George's Land]*
Samuel Evans is the most unpromising student. Yet still he will not give up. Nor will he give up digging about in my past.

'You're such a lucky lad to know all this,' he said. 'What ever made you walk away from it? What trouble drove you to the docks, boy?'

I shrugged and looked over the rail, remembering the indifference of my father, the cruelty of Reverend Smythe, the bite of the Butcher's whip.

'Nick,' Samuel asked, calling me back.

I turned to leave. 'Lesson's over.'

'Ah, never you mind, Nick. Just teach me to read, then.'

MONDAY 10th TO TUESDAY 11th *[Approaching King George's Land]*
King George's Land! We can see it in the distance!

WEDNESDAY 12th *[King George's Land]* What a day, hot and sticky. Natives put off from King George's Land in Canoes, but they did not come aboard. They only wanted to take a closer look at us. The Natives traded fruits and cocoa nutts, which are delicious, the taste I had of them. We sent the Natives down beads in trade. And they called us *Taio*, which Francis Haite says is 'friend.'

THURSDAY 13th *[King George's Land]* Here we come at last into King George's Land!

Captain and Surgeon Monkhouse are extremely pleased, for

we've come all this way and not lost one man to scurvy.

King George's Island is beautiful, so green with ridges that build until they meet in the distance in a high range of mountains.

We have strict rules to follow while we are here. We are to be friendly to the Natives and treat them with respect.

Captain took a party ashore as soon as *Endeavour* dropped anchor. I was not picked as oarsman and had to watch from the deck as the Natives approached Captain waving green boughs.

Mr Thompson has land food to work with again, fresh and new grown. The Natives came out to us with cocoa nutts, and a large globe called breadfruit, and fish and apples.

And Captain has made me part of the crew, to draw pay like any boy in the employ of the Royal Navy! Captain said nothing to me about the change in my position on board. He gave the order to Lieutenant Hicks, who passed the word to Surgeon Monkhouse, who passed the word to Mr Perry, and Mr Perry told me. Francis Haite, Samuel Evans and John Ramsay drank to my health tonight.

PART VI

OTahiti

APRIL 1769

FRIDAY 14th *[King George's Island]* This morning found our ship surrounded by Natives in their canoes. I cannot get used to the sight of so much green land and the smells coming off it, so rich and thrilling to my nose, and these strange natives so full of goodwill.

They climbed up into our ship with the ease of spiders. Amongst them were two chiefs. One chief came to Captain. The other to Mr Banks. The chiefs wrapped Captain and Mr Banks in cloth, embracing them as they would their dear brothers.

In exchange for this friendship offered, the chiefs were each given a hatchet and some beads, which pleased them very much. But before long there was complaint made. Dr Solander had a spyglass picked from his pocket by a Native. Dr Monkhouse admitted his snuffbox had also vanished. The chiefs saw to the return of the missing items and all ended happily.

SATURDAY 15th *[King George's Island]* Today was a bitter one for us all. Captain picked the site where he would make his observations of the Transit of Venus for the Royal Society. He brought a tent with him and a Company, including John Charlton. I was not amongst those chosen to land.

We had the story on dog watch from John. He said Captain explained to the Natives that our Company would need to live here for a certain period of time. Then Captain and the Gentlemen went to walk in the woods. But as soon as they were out of sight, the Natives pushed down a sentry and stole his musket. The order was given by Mr Monkhouse, who is in charge of the Marines, to stop the Natives. Mr Monkhouse himself shot the Native who stole the musket and killed him.

By the time Captain's party heard the shots and returned, the deed was done.

Captain did his best to make peace with the Natives before returning to *Endeavour*. He had a private interview with Mr Monkhouse and the Marines, and they are not to be punished.

But a Native is dead tonight because we've come. I understand the theft of a firearm is a serious offence. Yet so severe a punishment as death, does it truly equal the crime?

SUNDAY 16th *[King George's Island]* Captain brought the Ship closer to Shore. Not a single canoe came out to us today. The Natives fear us. The Gentlemen are very sober about the events of yesterday.

And the artist, Mr Buchan, suffered a fit, his body overtaken by it. Surgeon Monkhouse and Mr Perry are doing what they can. It seems he may not survive.

Worked with Samuel Evans on his letters, but there was little time and less will than usual.

MONDAY 17th [King George's Island] Mr Buchan died during the night. Mr Banks and Captain decided to bury him at sea rather than amongst the Natives, whose customs are unknown to us as ours are to them. Dr. Solander, Mr Sporing, Mr Parkinson and some of the officers attended the funeral, going off in the pinnace and the longboat. Surgeon Monkhouse and Mr Perry were there, and I was given an oarsman's seat in the Pinnace.

I shall miss Mr Buchan. He had a wonderful skill with the brushes and pens. Now it is all up to Mr Parkinson to do the drawing. Mr Banks is in great despair. He brought the artists along so all of England could see with their own eyes what we have seen.

Perhaps watching us take leave of Mr Buchan has changed the Natives' opinion. After our return the chiefs came aboard with dressed hogs and breadfruit, and Captain gave them a hatchet and nail each, and all seems right again between us.

TUESDAY 18th [King George's Island] I am ashore! Though my legs can hardly make sense of it. The solid ground of King George's Land rises up and falls back again in a way it should not do. John Ramsay says I shall get over the feeling soon. More than half the Company has come off the ship. Goat, too. She is well pleased to be eating fresh greens again.

We have brought off Mr Banks's Baggage and some

Astronomical Instruments. Captain has landed as many of us as he can spare from the work on *Endeavour* to erect a fort in which he can set his tents and equipment without fear of their being disturbed. The Natives brought breadfruit and cocoa nutts enough, there is a pile to last us for days. In exchange they were paid in beads.

WEDNESDAY 19th *[King George's Land]* Captain cautioned us to take nothing from the island without making payment, not even wood. We are to treat the Natives as if we were guests in their home. The Natives are glad to cooperate with such treatment.

Today Surgeon Monkhouse took a small group of us out in the woods. There I saw a dead man's body stretched out on a staked wooden frame with a little roof above. This was the Native shot dead by Mr Monkhouse several days ago. He had many things around him – a hatchet, a cocoa nutt shell filled with water, some hair. Surgeon Monkhouse went close, but I kept my distance.

THURSDAY 20th *[King George's Island]* Worked on the Fort in the rain today. One Native brought a Hog around to sell but would only take a carpenter's axe in payment. We had none to spare, and the Native went away with his Hog. My stomach grumbled as they vanished into the woods. I do like fresh pork. Lieutenant Gore and Master Molyneux said when first they were here on the *Dolphin*, the Natives did not know the worth of an axe. They happily traded a hog for a spike Nail two years ago. Now they want more.

FRIDAY 21st *[King George's Island]* Showers all night, but fair during the day. Mr Thompson's Copper Oven is come Ashore and with it Mr Thompson. The fort Captain ordered for our protection and the protection of our property is coming together. We've built three sides up and our fourth wall is the river, where we float our empty casks as a sort of barrier. I am just coming into my land legs. It has taken me days to be at ease ashore after the endless roll of the sea.

SATURDAY 22nd *[King George's Island]* The Armourer is at work at his portable forge, making hatchets. One of the Chiefs brought a hatchet he got from the *Dolphin*. It was wanting repair.

The flies are in our eyes and in our sweat all day. And always buzzing in our ears. They eat the paint as fast as Mr Parkinson can lay it on the paper. They light on the specimens Mr Parkinson draws, so that he can't make out the shape for the covering of flies upon it. We have rigged up a net over Mr Parkinson and all his business, but still the flies eat his colours.

Mr Banks ordered a fly trap of molasses and tar. He mixed the two on a plate and set it out. One of the Natives came upon the plate, caught some of the tar mixture in his hand, and smeared it on his backside, upon which he had a sore.

I heard the Native music today. The big Chief brought musicians and flutes, which were played by blowing into them with one nostril while the other was held closed. All their songs sounded alike to me. I was thinking we should play for them some of ours.

Mr Banks is already beginning to understand the Native language. I never saw the worth of learning another tongue before. I do now. Mr Banks has more freedom than the rest of us, to come and go amongst the Natives, because he can address them.

SUNDAY 23rd *[King George's Island]* Captain gave us our half-day off to spend ashore however we pleased! He warned us to be careful with the Natives. We should not molest them in any way, he said. We must behave in all things as if he were immediately present.

There is a boy who is near my age, a Native boy who has watched me since I've come ashore. He often moves within the fort, for he keeps close company with an old priest called Tupia, who Lieutenant Gore knows from his previous visit. The boy met me at the edge of the fort today and led me a short way into the woods. I never would have thought of such a friendship in London. But everything is different here. And the boy is so cheerful and easy to be with.

He can climb as well as I. We had a race up the breadfruit trees, which are tall, with leaves deeply green and shining. The trees are loaded with hundreds of globes all yellow in colour. The Native boy won the race, but only just. And he can swim! I took off my shirt and he saw the scars upon my back from the Butcher and traced them with his hand and said a string of words that made no sense to me. But I said they were nothing and he soon forgot them. He showed me how to move my arms and breathe air and kick my legs in a pool of clear water. He laughed, coaxing me at every new skill.

After, the boy took me to the place where the body rests. I did not come very close, for the smell was worse today than it had been days ago. The boy lifted the mat covering the body, and pieces of the body came off with the mat and maggots crawled everywhere. I ran into the bushes to be sick. The boy found me and led me along a path and out to a small beach, where we walked until I settled down.

I missed working with Samuel Evans today.

MONDAY 24th *[King George's Island]* Had a nightmare about the body. I came upon it in my dream, and when I pulled the mat away, the maggoty body rose up and reached for me. But it wasn't the Native Mr Monkhouse shot. It was Mr Bootie. This morning Surgeon Monkhouse heard I'd spent a restless night. When he asked, I told him about the maggoty body. Surgeon Monkhouse told my story to Mr Banks, and Mr Banks left immediately with his collection jar and gathered up the maggots for his observations.

When I worked on the fort today, I felt things crawling all over me.

My native friend, the boy, came and watched me work for hours. I pointed him out to John Charlton, but John has little interest in the Natives.

TUESDAY 25th *[King George's Island]* More work on the Fort. We must be mindful always of our tools, for the Natives would very much like to possess them and will take them if we leave them unattended.

WEDNESDAY 26th *[King George's Island]* Breadfruit, breadfruit, breadfruit. It was nice in the beginning, but I would be glad of some other refreshment. More Fresh Pork, for instance. I never grow tired of that.

THURSDAY 27th *[King George's Island]* Six of the ship's guns were mounted at our nearly completed Fort. When my Native friend saw the guns, he covered his ears and ran away.

FRIDAY 28th *[King George's Island]* Natives came in canoes from other parts of the island to have a look at us. Master Molyneux called out excitedly to a Native woman, who made her presence known by her great size and loud voice. She was brought, with the priest Tupia, my Native friend's grandfather, and presented to Captain Cook by Master Molyneux. The woman was Queen of the island when Master Molyneux was here last. Sometime in the past year the Queen had lost her power. Captain showed her great respect and offered many presents. The one she most favoured was a doll in the likeness of Mrs. Cook, Captain's wife back home in England.

SATURDAY 29th *[King George's Island]* Captain brought all of us on deck to witness justice. Mr Jeffs had stolen a stone hatchet from the island's chief and threatened to kill the Chief's wife. Mr Jeffs was stripped and fastened to the rigging and was given two dozen lashes with the cat-o'-nine-tails. He cried and begged for mercy, but Captain would not suffer a stroke less than the full lashing.

SUNDAY 30th *[King George's Island]* So much grows here without effort on the part of the Natives. They but go out and gather from the wild plants to keep their families fed and healthy. They have fish, too. But the fish is much prized, for it is difficult to catch here, and what finds its way to the table is savoured.

I talked with Samuel Evans today after his reading lesson. 'Something has me puzzled,' I told him. 'No Native locks anything away here on this island. In England locks are everywhere, and we have such exact laws about theft, but no one is content. Yet here, on this island, they leave their goods where anyone could take them, and things are taken, but no one is punished. I can't seem to make it come clear in my mind.'

Samuel Evans agreed. 'It is an odd state of affairs,' he said, 'isn't it? I hadn't thought about it, Nick. You are a one for using your head.'

MONDAY 1st MAY *[King George's Island]* I've kept an eye out for my Native friend, but there has been no sign of him in days.

The Fort is complete, with walls of Turf and Mud, and guns to protect us at the water and at the walls. Inside is Mr Banks's tent, the Observatory, the Armourer's Forge, the Oven and Cook Room, a tent for the Ship's Company, a tent for Captain, a tent for the officers, a tent for the Cooper, and a tent for the Sail maker; a regular little city all setting upon island sand.

Captain Cook has us moving his instruments to shore, confident of their safety within the confines of our Fort.

TUESDAY 2nd *[King George's Island]* When Captain and Mr Green went to assemble their Quadrant this morning, they found it had vanished. The success of *Endeavour's* entire journey depends upon that single instrument. First our own Company was searched, in the full belief that a Native could never slip in and out of the Fort with such a heavy instrument. But once it was determined the Quadrant was truly vanished, the Gentlemen and Captain went off in pursuit of it.

The Marines took two of the chiefs into custody until the safe return of our Property, and the two were much distressed and feared for their lives, judging by the way they wept.

Captain and the Gentlemen returned late in the day with the Quadrant, which had been damaged during its adventure. Mr

Sporing has taken the Quadrant and with watchmaker's tools from Mr Banks's possession is certain he can make the necessary repairs.

Captain was not pleased when he discovered the chiefs had been held prisoner, for he had given orders only that they should be prevented from leaving in their Canoes. The Chiefs were released, and though silent at first, they were so relieved to have their lives spared, they delivered two hogs in gratitude, which Captain Cook reluctantly accepted.

WEDNESDAY 3rd [King George's Island] Fair breeze and pleasant. On board the men worked on the rigging. On shore Captain and Mr Green prepared their Instruments for the Observation. Mr Banks and Dr. Solander went out Botanizing.

I saw a child today who looked much like a Native blended with an Englishman. The father was aboard the Dolphin, the child's mother said. I looked upon this child with wonder, that it should be of both British and Native blood.

We also met with Tupia again today. I wish the boy would return, but it has been ages since I've seen him. I don't even know his name to ask. Tupia came to recover the old Queen's canoe, taken from her yesterday when the Quadrant went missing. The old priest speaks our language better than any other Native. He and Mr Banks get on together quite well.

The Natives must be unhappy with us for holding their chiefs hostage. Before we had so many cocoa nutts and bread-fruit, we could not begin to eat it all. Now we are brought very little, not nearly enough to feed the ship's company. How could I have dismissed breadfruit? I am longing for a taste of it now.

THURSDAY 4th *[King George's Island]* Mr Sporing is hard repairing the damage to the Astronomical Instruments. Mr Banks manages to get fish himself when he cannot trade for them. But he will not let anyone eat of the fish until it is fully studied and recorded.

FRIDAY 5th *[King George's Island]* Captain brought a Chief who had been held prisoner back to the ship today. No sooner did the chief board and safely leave again than the Natives poured from the woods bearing Breadfruit and Cocoa Nutts in plenty to trade with us.

SATURDAY 6th *[King George's Island]* Captain is employed at surveying in preparation for a small Garden at the Fort.

SUNDAY 7th *[OTahiti]* The boy returned today. At last I came to know his name. He is called Tarheto, and I gave him to know I am Nicholas, but he calls me Nit. He took me to his house, and I sat with his family and they fed me. '*Maa,*' they said, giving me things to eat. They themselves ate nothing whilst I was there. Tarheto's people cook in a sort of oven that is a pit filled with hot stones. The food, wrapped in leaves, is placed over the stones, covered with more leaves and dirt, and left till it's fully roasted. Tarheto's family dipped each bite of the cooked food into a cocoa nutt shell filled with saltwater before presenting it to me.

After I ate, I went again with Tarheto about the island. This time we did not go back to the tent of the dead man, who I fear may have been Tarheto's father. This suspicion dragged at me and I hung back from my friend. But Tarheto came after me and took my hand and pulled me forward. We compared the colour of our skin and our hair in our reflections in the pool. I remembered standing beside my brother Charles, whose hair, like mine, is red, as our mother's was. I told Tarheto about Charles and my other brothers and my sisters. I told him about life in England, though he understood little. I found the courage to ask if the dead man was his father. *'Ima,'* Tarheto said. No.

I tried to explain that we British call his island King George's Land. Tarheto pronounced 'King George' as 'Kihiargo.' He laughed and told me, *'Ima Kihiargo. OTahiti!'*

MONDAY 8th TO TUESDAY 9th *[OTahiti]* We work now every day on the ship, overhauling it from stem to stern.

WEDNESDAY 10th *[OTahiti]* Captain planted his garden just outside the walls of our fort. He planted seeds carried in glass bottles all the way from England.

THURSDAY 11th *[OTahiti]* We have so many cocoa nutts now, Mr Banks has lowered the price he is willing to pay for them. The natives traded today six cocoa nutts for a bead of amber colour, ten cocoa nutts for a bead of white glass, and twenty cocoa nutts for a single fortypenny nail. In this way is the value of a thing determined. There is such abundance here. No one need ever go hungry, nor struggle to fill their belly. If it were so easy to get enough in England, would we be always jovial, too? Would Father, and Reverend Smythe, and the Butcher, I wonder?

FRIDAY 12th *[OTahiti]* Such a peculiar sight I beheld today as I worked upon the ship. On shore, which was in easy sight, Mr Banks engaged in his trading until a canoe arrived with a native man and two native women. One woman in particular came forward. She walked upon a piece of cloth spread between herself and Mr Banks, and dropped her lower clothing, revealing her privy parts. I should have looked away, but I could not. Mr Banks did not look away, either. The woman turned in a slow circle, three times. Then she presented a great roll of cloth as a gift to Mr Banks.

I must have blushed, for Mr Bootie teased me cruelly.

SATURDAY 13th TO MONDAY 15th *[OTahiti]* Spent my half day with Tarheto. Asked John Charlton if he would come with us. He would not.

TUESDAY 16th TO FRIDAY 19th *[OTahiti]* I try to understand why the Natives behave the way they do, helping themselves to whatever of ours interests them. The men say it's because they're nothing but thieves. But I'm not certain. These natives don't need to work hard for anything, so the things they have don't hold much value to them. Perhaps that explains the Natives' thievery. If nothing has much value, why should anyone be upset at its being taken? I wish I could talk it over with Tarheto. I'm sure I should understand it all better if I could. It's easier teaching Tarheto to speak English than Samuel Evans to read it. But Tarheto's English is not yet good enough to ask such things.

SATURDAY 20th *[OTahiti]* Thunder and lightning last night. Heavy rains today. A fruit similar in taste to our apple begins to come in for trade. Tonight Mr Thompson prepared apple pie.

SUNDAY 21st *[OTahiti]* Fine weather. Divine Service at the fort. The old Queen and her company attended. Spent the day with

Tarheto. I am learning a little more of his language, he a little more of mine. But we understand each other, even without words. Tarheto took me to a beach where the waves come in with a height and power that would make it impossible to land a boat. And yet several Natives swam out beyond where the waves begin to break. Once out, they began paddling back towards shore until they caught up with a forming wave and rode it in, rising to stand on a plank of wood, coming almost all the way back to shore before turning to paddle out again. I must be a much better swimmer before I try such sport.

Fresh Pork for dinner.

MONDAY 22nd TO SATURDAY 27th *[OTahiti]* The men, when they are off duty, are out shooting. They like the rats of this land in particular because they make good eating and are easy to kill. Captain had the longboat pulled ashore, for she was leaking. When she was turned about, it was found her bottom nearly eaten out by worms. The Carpenters set straight to work repairing her. Mr Banks set straight to work as well, for this is a species of worm new and unknown.

SUNDAY 28th *[OTahiti]* Tarheto did not come today. I went out with John Charlton instead. I showed John how to climb a breadfruit tree and how to float. He would have no part of either.

Samuel Evans can read and write his own name at last.

MONDAY 29th TO FRIDAY 2nd JUNE *[OTahiti]* All is preparation for the Astronomical Observation.

SATURDAY 3rd *[OTahiti]* The day dawned clear and hot, becoming hotter than ever it has been here, with not a cloud to block the Observation of Planet Venus passing before the Sun. Isaac Smith said though the weather proved perfect and the Natives stayed out from underfoot, Captain fears the readings are not exact enough. Isaac said the atmosphere of Venus made it impossible to fix the two moments, the beginning of Transit and the end of it, for the true edge of the planet was not distinct. Isaac said Captain was disappointed. He said these circumstances shall not come again for one hundred years, and Captain did not carry out to his satisfaction what he'd been sent to do.

SUNDAY 4th *[OTahiti]* All the boats came back from making their Observations, and all were of great cheer for the clear skies at the appointed hour. Only Captain is glum. Many thefts took place at the time of the Transit, when so much attention was turned towards the heavens and not on the ship's stock. Not a single person in high command remained aboard the ship.

Mr Bootie might have prevented the thefts. But I think he's partly responsible for them. I told John Charlton so, and he said I should be careful. Mr Bootie harboured no goodwill towards me and had spoken against me to Captain on many occasions. I found opportunity, while Mr Bootie was off on his half-day, to get into his journal. It revealed he has a rough hand, and a slow mind, and he often writes the most unkind and untruthful things about the men aboard. I came across an entry where Mr Bootie wrote that John Ramsay was lazy and a shirker. In another entry Francis Haite was called feeble. John Ramsay is no such thing as lazy, and Francis Haite may be one of the oldest men aboard, but he is certainly not feeble. Reading such lies about my friends, I felt a black rage rising in me, and before I knew what I was about, I wrote across Mr Bootie's journal, 'Evil communications corrupt good' and signed my name under. I don't know what possessed me to do so. I shall certainly pay.

MONDAY 5th *[OTahiti]* I did not sleep at all last night. Mr Bootie made complaint to the Captain, and Captain ordered me whipped before the Company. When my shirt was taken from me, the men stared at my scars. Still I was not spared.

I am sore tired tonight, but I have survived and Mr Bootie seems satisfied, at least for the moment. What sleep I can manage shall be on my stomach. Curse Mr Bootie.

TUESDAY 6th *[OTahiti]* Captain had Surgeon Monkhouse check all the men for infectious disease before we made land in OTahiti so we might not bring European illness among the natives. Only one man had suspicious symptoms then and has remained aboard ship since our arrival. But now other of our men are showing signs of disease. Raspberry-coloured swellings on their skin. So far twenty-four seamen infected and nine of the eleven Marines. Surgeon Monkhouse has kept me busy preparing bandages and salve for the men. He is kinder than usual to me today. All the men are.

WEDNESDAY 7th *[OTahiti]* Mr Banks has been told of two ships visiting this island since the British *Dolphin*'s departure. The Captain of the *Dolphin*, like our Captain, took great care for the natives' health. It appears the two foreign ships did not take such care, and the infections have come from them to our men, through the Natives of OTahiti.

After completing an inspection of the ship's bottom and

determining that the worms have not got in, we are working her with Pitch and Brimstone. Mr Bootie ordered me aloft to tar the mizzenmast. I have little strength in my back and arms since my flogging. Surgeon Monkhouse, who was passing when Mr Bootie gave his order, told Mr Bootie I could not be spared from sick bay today with so many ill. I was ordered down and slowly, I made my way back out of the rigging and below deck.

THURSDAY 8th *[OTahiti]* Mr Banks brought a shirt and a woollen Jacket he got from the natives to Captain Cook's attention. They are not native, nor are they made in a way the English make their clothes. Mr Banks says these articles prove that foreign ships have recently been upon the island.

It is my twelfth birthday today.

FRIDAY 9th *[OTahiti]* Mr Banks fears the island's Breadfruit crop has very nearly vanished because we have demanded so much of it. 'Have we eaten all their food, then?' I asked. 'What shall the natives do with nothing to eat?'

'Don't worry, Nick,' Mr Banks said. 'They'll get by until the next fruits ripen.'

SATURDAY 10th *[OTahiti]* The men left off the Pitch and Brimstone work because of Rain. Surveyed the provisions. Cleaning the ship Fore and Aft.

SUNDAY 11th *[OTahiti]* Spent some time with Tarheto. He likes very much when I make bird calls for him. *'Mannu,'* he says. Bird. He gave me the gift of a little nose flute today, which he is teaching me to play.

We could not wrestle nor climb nor swim as we usually do, so we had time for quieter pursuits. I showed him my back. *'Toto,'* he said. Blood. He could not understand how it came to be that way. He had seen my scars before and touched them, when first we went swimming together. But he was surprised to see wounds so fresh upon my back. 'I received a whipping', I told him. Tarheto spoke, but I could not understand what he said. Nor could I explain what had happened. Except to say Mr Bootie had a hand in it. 'And I had a hand in it, too.'

Fresh Pork for dinner.

MONDAY 12th TO TUESDAY 13th *[OTahiti]* Poor Dr. Monkhouse was attacked by a native today and beaten. When I came to understand the circumstances, I could not truly determine who to blame. Dr. Monkhouse, while out walking, plucked a flower at a sacred place, and a native punished him for such a misdeed. Certainly we have punished the natives for far less.

I carefully tended Surgeon Monkhouse's wounds, just as he did mine only days ago. Surgeon Monkhouse shall survive his beating. But neither of us will soon forget how easy it is to go wrong.

WEDNESDAY 14th TO SUNDAY 18th *[OTahiti]* Sorting through the ship's provisions. Those goods that are turning to spoil we have put in the way of Mr Thompson so we might consume them first. While Surgeon Monkhouse recovers, I am kept busy by Mr Perry, tending to the sick and preparing the surgery for the journey home.

The clouds at last have lifted. Some of the men have been out to collect Ballast to take aboard *Endeavour.*

The men found heapings of rock at a sacred burial site and thought it ideal ballast. When they began dismantling the burial place, the natives rose in protest and insisted they desist.

I wonder what the men were thinking, so soon after Surgeon Monkhouse's beating. How would they feel if the Natives hauled off grave markers from an English cemetery?

MONDAY 19th TO FRIDAY 23rd *[OTahiti]* One of the seamen came up missing. Some of the men said he'd gone off with a native woman and that he planned to remain here.

Captain Cook offered a hatchet as reward for the person who could restore the man to our Company, and before night he was returned to us. He said he had not run away, but rather the natives had kidnapped him and carried him off with his mouth stuffed so he could not yell. He said they held him hoping to get a hatchet in exchange for his release, which is precisely what they did get. Since his story could not be proved one way or the other, he was not punished, but there are many in our Company who believe he made the entire story up, and that it is only his cleverness which has saved him from hanging.

SATURDAY 24th TO SUNDAY 25th *[OTahiti]* Spent the afternoon off with Tarheto. We wandered along the paths of the island, under the Breadfruit and cocoa nutt trees. We passed the places where the natives reside in their open houses, with the breezes blowing through and the trees and thatched roofs offering welcome shade. It was so quiet, so pleasant, I am nearly persuaded to remain here.

'What reason is there for me to go back?' I asked Samuel Evans after dinner, during his lesson.

'You're not the first to think it, Nick. Quite a few seamen sign on to get free of something at home. It's simpler at sea. Simpler still here. But it isn't home, is it, boy? No books for you here. I've seen you in the Great Cabin with them books. Whatever you're running from, Nick, even King George's Island isn't far enough. You only stop running when you face your trouble head-on, boy.'

I gave him a shove with my shoulder. 'I don't like your advice tonight, Samuel Evans,' I said.

'Had an idea you wouldn't,' he answered. 'But if you value your life, you won't jump ship, Nick. Captain would send Mr Bootie after you. If he didn't kill you before he brought you back, he'd see you hanged. Believe me.'

Fresh Pork for dinner. I hardly tasted it.

MONDAY 26th *[OTahiti]* Captain and Mr Banks have gone off in the Pinnace to make a chart of the entire island. Samuel Evans did not pick me for an oarsman's seat.

TUESDAY 27th TO THURSDAY 29th *[OTahiti]* We are kept even busier with Captain gone than we are when he's here. The Officers work us hard in the heat and driving rain, making preparations, bringing wood and water aboard. There isn't time even to think.

FRIDAY 30th *[OTahiti]* Lightning last night and tonight. I might as well give up sleeping anywhere but Goat's pen. At least my presence quiets her. Otherwise she drives the men on watch mad with her bleatings.

SATURDAY 1ST JULY *[OTahiti]* At last, Captain and Mr Banks returned this evening.

SUNDAY 2nd TO MONDAY 3rd *[OTahiti]* We are emptying the fort of articles no longer needed, bringing them back aboard ship.

TUESDAY 4th *[OTahiti]* Mr Banks spent the day planting seeds he'd brought from Rio de Janeiro. He dug along the outer walls of the fort, which we are fast emptying. He has already seen the fruit of seeds he gave to natives or planted himself when first we came. The watermelons, which have ripened already, pleased the natives immensely. Oranges have been planted, too, and lemons and limes, though it shall be some time before they bear fruit.

The garden planted by Captain Cook did not fare so well. Only mustard came. Mr Banks thinks it is not the fault of Captain's planting, but the fault of the packing of the seeds for the journey.

WEDNESDAY 5th *[OTahiti]* The fort is nearly empty.

THURSDAY 6th TO FRIDAY 7th *[OTahiti]* The Carpenters dismantled the walls of the fort today. A native made off with the iron from the gate. Mr Banks, as usual, went off in pursuit. He returned instead with a scraper from the ship. Later a chief returned the stolen iron.

Getting water on board and stowing the booms.

SATURDAY 8th *[OTahiti]* The natives are now out of food, as we have either eaten or taken all that is ripe. The tables have turned and we open our supplies to help feed them. The old Queen managed to bring four small pigs to us today and some OTahitian dogs, which, I am alarmed to note, the natives eat.

'What shall they do?' I asked Mr Thompson. 'What shall they do after we're gone? They mustn't starve.'

'They won't,' Mr Thompson said. 'Their fruit will ripen fast enough. Or they'll go off and find more on another part of the island, or another island nearby. I'm more worried about us. These provisions must last until we reach land again. Who knows when that will be?'

'Aren't we going back now?' I asked. 'Aren't we off for England?'

'Ask your friend John Charlton,' Mr Thompson said. 'He's most likely to know. Or Isaac Smith. Or the Gentlemen, they might know. I certainly don't. Why should anyone tell me? I'm only expected to keep the lot of you fed.'

Are we not going home yet?

SUNDAY 9th *[OTahiti]* Spent my free time today with Tarheto as I have so often done on my Sundays. It is difficult to think this may be the last I shall have with him. I gave up fresh pork today to be with Tarheto, but my messmates saved a piece for me anyway.

MONDAY 10th TO WEDNESDAY 12th *[OTahiti]* Mr Banks has requested that Tupia be allowed to join our Company. He knows the surrounding sea well enough to act as our pilot. Mr Banks promises to take full care and responsibility for Tupia, even after we're back in England. I believe Captain Cook will grant permission.

Mr Parkinson worked late at his drawing Table. He has, since we arrived, drawn trees, plants, fish, birds, and everything else Mr Banks has requested. England shall truly see OTahiti, thanks to the planning of Mr Banks and the skill of Mr Parkinson.

JULY 1769

THURSDAY 13th *[OTahiti]* This afternoon, after three months, we left OTahiti. Our ship, surrounded by the natives in their double canoes, filled with the sound of noisome lamentations. I suspect their noise came not so much from grief over our departure as from competition as to who could be loudest.

Tupia has been granted permission to travel with us, and he brings with him a servant. Tarheto! My friend.

PART VII

Island Hopping

JULY 1769

FRIDAY 14th *[Society Islands]* Tupia steers us among the islands. It seems Captain's intention is to sail from one to another, claiming each land he sees and charts in the name of His Majesty. John Charlton says there are secret orders that Captain opened upon sailing from OTahiti, orders from the Lord High Admiral. I don't know where those orders shall take us, but we are not returning directly to England!

It's so good having Tarheto aboard. Between the work of the ship and the company, I forget for hours what awaits me at home. And now there's to be a secret mission that Tarheto and I might share together!

I thought I might regret leaving OTahiti, being under the mast again, but I was wrong. I am not sad to be leaving, nor am I

sorry I did not jump ship. It's good to hear the sea once more part-
ed by the Larboard bow and the wind whipping the sails and
Endeavour grizzling over the water. If only I can stay on Mr Bootie's
good side and keep Tarheto safe from his foul temper, all will be well.

SATURDAY 15th *[Society Islands]* Tupia prays to a wind god to fill our
sails.

SUNDAY 16th *[Society Islands]* Came close upon the island of
Huahine. Tupia had a native dive under the ship and call out the
depth of the bottom so that he might safely bring us to harbour.
This is a method I have not seen before. It is rare to find an
English seaman who can swim, let alone dive. I am not
volunteering my new skill to Captain. It is a dangerous job.

The natives of this island seemed shy of us at first, but when
they saw Tupia and Tarheto, they brought out their canoes and
rowed to us, boarding us easily and with curiosity. Upon arriving
on shore, Tupia bent his knee and offered up a prayer. Then he
spoke with the natives and presented them with gifts.

These natives are much like those of OTahiti in appearance.
They use the same speech, dress in the same folds of cloth, are
marked with the same tattoos. Tupia says the natives of this island
are different from the natives of OTahiti in one particular way.
They will leave our possessions alone.

Captain found a good harbour later in the day and went
ashore with Mr Banks, Dr Solander, Dr Monkhouse, Tupia and
Tarheto. They returned well pleased, carrying a hog with them. I
did like the sight of that hog. Tarheto says the hog was given for a
gift to our gods, but Mr Thompson intends it should be a gift to
our stomachs.

MONDAY 17th TO TUESDAY 18th *[Society Islands]* Tarheto accompanied Mr Banks on his botanical explorations, for Tupia was busy with the Natives. Tarheto said he did his best, but he could not explain everything Mr Banks asked. I told Tarheto no one could possibly answer all of Mr Banks's questions.

Tarheto said the natives of this island prefer cocoa nutts to breadfruit. They seemed unwilling to trade either. We did take eleven pigs on board.

WEDNESDAY 19th *[Society Islands]* Trade a little better today. Surgeon Monkhouse was at it most of the morning. The people of this island are so different from the Natives of OTahiti. On OTahiti they were more eager to please. The people of Huahine are less timid and less curious about our things. They seem to neither need nor want what we have, but are content as they are. Were the natives of OTahiti once as these natives are now?

Captain gave the Chief of Huahine a plate engraved by the armourer with the date of our landing and the name of the island. This shall be proof that we were the first Europeans to come ashore here.

THURSDAY 20th *[Society Islands]* Sailed to the next island with Tupia as our pilot. Captain ordered the Pinnace hoisted and Master Molyneux, with caution, led *Endeavour* into this new harbour.

The natives did not hesitate but came directly on board. Tupia informed us that this island is under the rule of the chief of Bora Bora and we must leave before his warriors come to defend what is theirs. I have never seen Tupia so fearful.

Captain Cook had the English Jack planted and claimed this land for His Majesty King George, along with three other Islands in sight.

FRIDAY 21st *[Society Islands]* No sign of the dreaded Bora Bora. Tupia and Tarheto seemed most relieved. Tarheto says Tupia once was chief of this island, but the Bora Bora defeated him and he came to live on OTahiti. Tarheto says this is the island of great builders of canoes.

They have tools that an English Carpenter would refuse to use, made of stone and bone, for there is no iron available. But the Natives manage with those inferior tools to create canoes of astonishing quality.

Captain Cook and Master Molyneux set about in the rain to chart the harbour.

I am kept busy. Though the sick men have responded well to the arsenical injections, Captain requires we see the Company completely healthy before we enter the colder seas on the next part of our expedition. Captain says we are to go in search of the Great Southern Continent, Terra Incognita, the very Continent I have heard Mr Banks speak of. Our orders are to find the Great Continent and claim it for His Majesty!

SATURDAY 22th TO MONDAY 24th *[Society Islands]* Under sail this morning, but unexpected Shoals and a light wind made our departure slow and careful. I asked Tarheto if we should see the Bora Bora warriors now, and he said we were in danger of them at every moment. I watch out for them, though the men say I'm foolish. They say no native could come near harming us. We're British.

TUESDAY 25th TO FRIDAY 28th *[Society Islands]* Sailing from Island to Island.

SATURDAY 29th *[Society Islands]* Captain tried coming in close to Bora Bora, but the wind and sea were not with us. Tarheto says Tupia was praying for precisely that.

SUNDAY 30th *[Society Islands]* Caught sight of an island that Tupia says is fertile and rich with provision, but it is surrounded by reefs and *Endeavour* cannot make her way safely there.

Of late we have not been given our half-day off. There is too much to be done. I hope Samuel Evans won't forget what he has worked so hard to learn.

MONDAY 31st TO TUESDAY 1st AUGUST *[Society Islands]* Tupia is a fine pilot. Under Captain's command he brought us to harbour at the south end of an island called Raiatea. We have a leak in the Powder room that cannot be easily repaired at sea. We also must take on ballast, for *Endeavour* is too light should we catch a good wind. Traded while in harbour, taking on pigs, fowl, plantains and cocoa nutts.

WEDNESDAY 2nd *[Society Islands]* Tarheto and I accompanied Dr Solander and Mr Banks on shore, Botanizing. We met not one new plant but were consoled by the hospitality of the natives. We met there a Native girl, not much younger than I. She sat on a long mat upon which crowds of natives dared not tread. She wore a gown of red and plaited her hair round and round and round her head, and when Mr Banks gave her beads, she extended her hand the way a princess might, but she looked away from Mr Banks and his beads and rested her eyes upon me. I was brought over to sit before her, and she gave me the beads from Mr Banks as a sign of favour. She had me lower my head. Then her fingers were in my hair. The men teased me after. Tarheto joined them.

THURSDAY 3rd *[Society Islands]* Captain located a supply for ballast and fresh water and set the men to bringing both aboard. The Carpenters, meanwhile, worked on the leaks.

We returned to shore later and saw a performance of some native dancers. Back on *Endeavour*, Tarheto and I showed the Company how the native men danced out their story. Then we showed how the women danced as well, with quick flicks of their hips. But we could not move our bodies in the way the women had, and we looked so funny in our attempt that the entire Company rolled on the deck laughing at us until tears came to their eyes.

I received a rough kick from Mr Bootie, who claimed he did not find our antics amusing, though I saw him laugh, I know I did.

FRIDAY 4th TO TUESDAY 8th *[Society Islands]* The Carpenters have finished repairing the leaks, and we are waiting only for a good wind.

WEDNESDAY 9th *[Society Islands]* Picked up a breeze before midday that carried us from the harbour. Brought our boats aboard and made for the South. We've got fruit and livestock enough to last us until next we see land, Mr Banks's lost Continent, Terra Incognita!

PART VIII

Land Ho!

THURSDAY 10th *[Leaving Society Islands]* We are full sail again in an active sea. Mr Banks and some of the others are seasick in the way they were when we first began this journey. I am not feeling sick as some of the others, though I have not much appetite. Tarheto does not fare well, but Tupia is content.

FRIDAY 11th *[Lat. 18°59′ S, Long. 151°45′ W]* We have a good wind and fine weather, my sea legs have been restored, and the Company is well pleased to be under sail. Tupia and Tarheto talk about a land to our south where demons live who dine on men and are violent in all things. I do not believe there are such demons. There were no monsters at Cape Horn, nor did the warriors of Bora Bora ever show their faces. I am not afraid.

SATURDAY 12th *[Leaving Society Islands]* I kept half an eye out for Tupia's demon land, but he says we have passed it.

SUNDAY 13th *[Leaving Society Islands]* Tarheto is learning English, though I still can say only a few words in his tongue. Reverend Smythe was right. I have no gift for languages.

MONDAY 14th TO TUESDAY 15th *[In Search of Undiscovered Continents – Lat. 24°1' S, Long. 150°37' W]* We've crossed the Tropic again. This makes the third time.

WEDNESDAY 16th *[In Search of Undiscovered Continents]* Thought we had land off to eastward, but after we followed it for hours, found it only to be Clouds. Everyone was fooled, even Tupia.

Returned to our Southerly course. The hogs we took aboard have begun dying. They need vegetables, food they are accustomed to. The fowl also grow sick.

THURSDAY 17th *[In Search of Undiscovered Continents]* Had to throw the sweet taros overboard. Spoiled. Mr Thompson's mood was foul when I came to help with the buckets.

Rode all day on a heavy swell from the SW. Captain says that is clear indication there is no continent to our South. But Mr Banks, studying Mr Dalrymple's map, believes we shall find land.

This afternoon I helped Mr Thompson with inventory. We are still good with beef, pork, pease, flour, oatmeal, portable soup and sour Kraut. The water is still good. But the ship's bread is nearly inedible. Before we eat, we must shake out thousands of vermin from a single biscuit. The Officers and Gentlemen heat their bread in an oven, which drives the little beasts out. But we must eat the biscuit, vermin and all, taking a mouthful of the little, fiery weevils with each bite. It takes a great hunger to chew and swallow them down. I'd rather do without . . . but Captain gives lashes for not eating. If not for Mr Bootie and the stripes already on my back, I'd almost think a whipping better. But I don't think I could endure another. And Captain would make me eat the bread in the end anyway.

I asked Mr Thompson if there wasn't anything we could do for the dying livestock. 'Eat them or throw them over,' Mr Thompson said. 'Or bundle them in boots and jackets. Those island beasts won't bear the cold. What don't starve to death will soon freeze. Mark my word.'

Mr Perry was not much more help. 'Forget it, Nick. You can't save everything.'

FRIDAY 18th TO SATURDAY 19th *[In Search of Undiscovered Continents]* Still the swell comes at us from the SW. Still we search for a continent Captain Cook does not believe exists.

SUNDAY 20th *[In Search of Undiscovered Continents – Lat. 28°24′ S, Long. 148°25′ W]* An Albatross flew with us today. High swells. The rolling makes Tarheto green. I do what I can to help.

MONDAY 21st *[In Search of Undiscovered Continents]* We exhausted the Plantains today. Not one went to rot. They were eaten before they had a chance to go bad. But they were not eaten by the People. I fed them all to our pigs. The pigs have eaten only Plantains since we set sail. They will not touch our English food. I'm grateful Goat's not so fussy.

When Mr Bootie discovered what I'd done with the

Plantains, he went directly to Lieutenant Hicks to report me. After an investigation Lieutenant Hicks learned I was only following orders. Mr Bootie gives me looks blacker than tar.

TUESDAY 22nd *[In Search of Undiscovered Continents]* When we are on duty, Tarheto and I rarely see each other, except in passing. But when we are off, we spend much time on deck with Goat. Tarheto is delighted with the cats, though they'll have little to do with him. He cannot at all understand my attachment to Lord and Lady Grey, who simply look like supper to him.

I tell Tarheto about London and the wonders of Bartholomew Fair, with its magicians and acrobats and wire walkers. I tell him about the menagerie at the Tower, about the lions and leopards and bears, and particularly about the elephant. I don't think Tarheto understands or believes half of what I say. And yet I haven't half begun to tell him what he should know before we get home. I tell him of men like Reverend Smythe and the Butcher. And how, of all things in this world, I want least to spend my days slaughtering and cutting up beasts. Tarheto laughs. 'Do not,' he says. It is so easy for Tarheto. He does, has always done, only as he wishes. Will it be so even when Mr Banks brings him to England?

WEDNESDAY 23rd *[In Search of Undiscovered Continents]* The hogs and fowl are perishing at an alarming rate. They are starving to death and freezing, just as Mr Thompson said they would. It grows colder with each day we travel south.

Saw a great, dappled whale this afternoon. Tarheto sang out in wonder at the sight of it. He did not stop speaking of it for hours.

THURSDAY 24th *[In Search of Undiscovered Continents – Lat. 32°44' S, Long. 147°10' W]* Watched a Waterspout off to the NW. It was about the width of a tree trunk. Mr Banks seemed unimpressed. I suppose he could not shoot it, nor bag it, nor stick it in a glass bottle, and felt it not much to consider. But Tarheto and I thought it a thing of wonder.

FRIDAY 25th *[In Search of Undiscovered Continents]* Main Topsail split. We had to replace it with another. All the birds we see are birds that come great distances from land.

It is a year since we've been gone from the south-west coast of England. In the Great Cabin they shared a cheese of wonderful odour – Cheshire, I think – and wine. We had no such celebration among the ship's People.

What I have seen and learned in a year I cannot begin to tell. I have gained in height and weight, and I'm certainly greater in strength. My hair has grown long, my skin weathered brown. I wonder if they'd recognize me back home.

SATURDAY 26th *[In Search of Undiscovered Continents]* Barely any distance did we cover today. Several grampuses played about the ship. What big, wonderful creatures they are. Tarheto and I watched them surface and blow, then dive again. We made a game of being first to spot the next one up for air. Tarheto shivers in the cold, even when he's bundled in the foul-weather clothing from Mr Banks.

SUNDAY 27th *[In Search of Undiscovered Continents]* Good breeze today and birds doing great feats of flight above our heads. Tarheto and I met on deck. He is learning our language well. I tell him about my apprenticeship to the Butcher and picking up live-stock at the River Thames, with its forest of masts. I tell him how I asked after the different ships and where they were going and how long they'd be gone. How I offered money to Samuel Evans, John Ramsay and Francis Haite if they would hide me aboard *Endeavour*, for she was going farthest, would be gone longest.

'You do what you like,' Tarheto said. 'Yes, Nit?'

'Yes,' I answered.

In the Great Cabin, Mr Banks and the Gentlemen were drawing, reading, discussing their observations.

MONDAY 28th *[In Search of Undiscovered Continents]* Tupia is not well. I think it is the cold, for he is always ashiver.

Mayhap it was the cold that drove poor John Reading to drink so much.

Some men go down and siphon wine from the Madeira casks, emptying the barrels and replacing the wine with seawater. However he came by it, Mr Reading was found this morning so far gone there was barely a flicker of life in him. We did what we could, but within an hour of our finding him, Mr Reading was dead. I suppose I'm growing accustomed to such things.

TUESDAY 29th *[In Search of Undiscovered Continents]* Been watching something approach in the night sky these last two or three days. Mr Green thinks it is a Comet.

Mr Bootie caught me at the side and sent me aloft to fit a strip round the main topmast head. He thinks I'm afraid to go aloft. But I don't mind. Except when I can't feel my fingers and toes.

WEDNESDAY 30th *[In Search of Undiscovered Continents]* 'Twas a Comet passed over us last night, faint but great.

A swell continues from the SW, tossing us rudely and washing our decks with saltwater.

THURSDAY 31st *[Lat. 39°28′ S, Long. 147°0′ W]* Violent wind and seas, with the ship bowing severely before the waves. The birds are all around us in the storm. Mr Banks was out in the blow trying to catch them with a hook. A whole morning at this activity got him one Pintado, which he spent the remainder of the day studying.

FRIDAY 1st SEPTEMBER *[In Search of Undiscovered Continents – Lat. 40°12′ S, Long. 146°29′ W]* Frothy weather, gales and squalls. The sea rises to the size of mountains. The ship is tossed about like a toy. Nothing remains where it is put. Everywhere is crashing and banging about us.

John Charlton says Captain has reached the Latitude required by command of the Royal Society in pursuit of Mr Dalrymple's Continent, yet there is no sign of land. How much longer can *Endeavour* stand these seas tearing at her? Mr Bootie has me aloft at every opportunity. The wind pushes and pulls at me, and my hands go numb, so that I must secure my arms in the rigging to keep from falling.

SATURDAY 2nd *[In Search of Undiscovered Continents]* It is the same as yesterday. This is a place of violent, evil weather, unrelenting. Everything movable has been spilled and tossed and rolled from its keeping place.

Captain decided to take us out of it. He has given all effort to discovering Mr Dalrymple's Continent, but the sea is wild and Captain is certain there can be no Land near with a sea of such demeanour. So we are turning and heading out of this tempestuous latitude before our sails and our rigging and ourselves are completely destroyed. 'But where shall we go now?' I asked Isaac Smith.

'We proceed West, Nick,' Isaac said, 'and search for Mr Dalrymple's Land still. But in a somewhat more hospitable latitude from now on, I think.'

The comet is brighter than we have yet seen it.

SUNDAY 3rd *[Turning West]* The sea continued its torment until noon, when the weather began to moderate. The ship begins to gentle down.

MONDAY 4th *[Turning West]* The sun set into a bank of clouds and lit its edges with fire. Tupia says there will be more gales tomorrow. Calm tonight though. Sat with Tarheto and Goat and Ginger Bigfoot in silence and watched the comet. I am exhausted from fighting Mr Bootie. I am exhausted from fighting the sea.

TUESDAY 5th *[Heading West]* Blowing sheets of rain. No good sleep to be had anywhere.

WEDNESDAY 6th TO SATURDAY 9th *[Heading West]* 'Tis like sailing through an endless, dark hall.

SUNDAY 10th *[Heading West – Lat. 35°19' S, Long. 150°46' W]* The sea's colour is changing. Captain sounded for depth, but we are still in deep waters. Fooled by a cloud bank. Pursued it briefly in hopes of finding land, but it was only illusion. Another visit to Cape Fly Away.

MONDAY 11th TO TUESDAY 12th *[Heading West]* Helped make Wort for the sick men and tended to their needs.

WEDNESDAY 13th *[Heading West]* It's been nearly a week since we left the churning mountainous waters of the Southernmost latitude. It is only now, as Tarheto and I talk of it, that I realize how close we came to losing *Endeavour*.

THURSDAY 14th *[Heading West]* The winds blow from all round the compass today. But mostly we are becalmed. The marines drilled at the great guns and small arms. Tarheto and I watched two very large albatross winging atop the waves.

'Birds like Nit and Tarheto,' Tarheto said. 'Friend birds, go home.'

Tarheto shivered in the chill winds. He misses the warmth of his own home. I wonder if he misses anything else? What do I miss of my home? I should like to say nothing. But the truth is I miss quite a bit. The sights and sounds. The food. The moving about on land. And the opportunity to become a man of learning, like the Gentlemen, like my brothers. I think I miss that most of all. And of all things, that is the hardest to admit.

FRIDAY 15th *[Heading West]* Mr Banks complains of feeling ill. There has been much of it aboard, keeping me and Mr Perry and Dr Monkhouse ever on our toes.

SATURDAY 16th *[Heading West]* Large swells continue to reach us from the South. But the winds blew well today, and we sailed a good distance. Mr Banks still complaining of sickness.

SUNDAY 17th *[Lat. 30°14´ S, Long. 159°6´ W]* Mr Banks has recovered.

MONDAY 18th TO WEDNESDAY 20th *[Heading West]* Becalmed. Tarheto treats Mr Banks as if he were a god. It matters not to Tarheto that this god gets seasick or behaves as a spoiled child at times. Tarheto worships everything Mr Banks touches. It seems Mr Bootie and Tarheto have this in common. This awe of Mr Banks.

THURSDAY 21st TO SATURDAY 23rd *[Heading West]* Now it is Dr Solander who is not well. Dr Monkhouse has suggested Essence of Lemon Juice. Mr Banks also saw to the baking of a pie from his special stock of North American apples. Tarheto and I dipped our fingers in the sauce left in the pie plate when the Gentlemen were done. I thought the taste quite wonderful and felt a stab of homesickness, remembering Ganny Pajet's apple pie at Grandmother's house.

Mr Thompson does a good job with the ship's beef and pork and pease. May they last, for we know not when we shall next reach land and be provisioned again. The Malt that is left is very bad and does little good for us. The bread I loathe. It tastes and reeks of ammonia. We have boiled wheat often, and both Tarheto and I look forward to that. Captain has Mr Thompson prepare it with raisins, wort, portable soup or greens. My favourite is with raisins. Tarheto's, too. 'Nenenne,' Tarheto says. Sweet. Sometimes we take our bowls on deck and steal a bit of milk from Goat. A single squirt makes a glorious difference.

SUNDAY 24th *[Heading West]* We made good speed today with a moderate breeze at our back taking us SW. Seaweed has been floating past. And the swell from the south is nearly gone.

MONDAY 25th TO TUESDAY 26th *[Heading West – Lat. 36°9' S, Long. 167°14' W]* Excellent wind and clear skies.

WEDNESDAY 27th *[Heading West]* Heavy storm last night, but clear and bright today. We continue to sail with speed, passing through heaps of seaweed. Tarheto and I spied a seal sleeping as it bobbed on the surface of the sea. And a shoal of Porpoises busily blew and dived beside us for some time. Tarheto grows as excited about these things as Mr Banks. They are a pair to behold.

THURSDAY 28th TO FRIDAY 29th *[Heading West – Lat. 38°30' S, Long. 170°14' W]* Captain spied a bird he believed to be a land bird. I did not see it, though from his description I believe he must be right. I have learned much in the Great Cabin. Mr Banks, his books and his specimens have taught me more than I ever imagined.

The weather is crisp and fine. I cannot see a change in the colour of the sea, but there are those who insist it is lighter. Captain has ordered soundings to commence. Is it possible we are soon to come upon land? Dalrymple's land?

SATURDAY 30th *[Heading West]* Captain has promised one gallon of rum to the first one who spies land by day, two if sighted at night. And that very land shall be named for the man who first sees it.

Mr Bootie says there is no eye better than his, no name as worthy and no thirst as deep. He says he shall have the rum and the honour.

Mr Bootie is not a kind man, particularly when he has rum in him. I would see the land first if only to keep Mr Bootie from getting a gallon of rum in him.

Tarheto is marvellously good in the rigging. We have races up the masts as once we had up the breadfruit trees.

SUNDAY 1st OCTOBER *[Heading West]* The wind has mostly failed. Sounded the depth, but no ground at 120 fathoms. Birds passed over us in great numbers. Another Seal asleep on the waves. The Gentlemen thought at first it was a piece of wood and determined to take it up for their studies. Our approach woke the sleeping seal and it dived before we got too close.

We see rockweed in enough quantity to suggest we are close to land indeed. Caught up a stick floating past, but it was covered with barnacles and had been at sea a good long time so was no help in our estimate of distance from land. Mr Banks took the barnacle-covered stick and preserved it and the insects feeding upon it.

Tarheto went out at the rail near sunset and watched the whales feed. Mr Perry and Dr Monkhouse kept me too busy to join him.

MONDAY 2nd *[Heading West – Lat. 37°10′ S, Long. 172°54′ W]* The Gentlemen had roasted leg of mutton and French beans for dinner last night. Just to smell such a meal carried me back to London and my father's table. I went about my work, my mouth filled with water, my belly filled with wanting.

Today Mr Banks took a boat out on a sea as quiet as a pond. He shot an Albatross. It measured close on eleven feet from wing tip to wing tip. He shot two other Birds, very much like Ducks. His killings make good stews, and we have appetite enough to eat nearly everything he takes. More Whales. Tarheto and I never grow tired of watching them.

TUESDAY 3rd *[Heading West]* Felt the force of a stiff gale, which lasted only a few minutes. Such gales are a rare occurrence out at sea. It seems more likely than ever we are close to land.

Mr Banks went out on the boat shooting and brought back seaweed he had never seen before. In the Great Cabin this afternoon Dr Solander, Mr Parkinson and Mr Banks worked tirelessly and talked without pause. Dr Solander and Mr Banks at their tables writing, and Mr Parkinson, the seaweed hanging above him, the wood with its barnacles on the table before him, drawing. And all they can think of is finding the new continent and what species they shall discover upon it.

WEDNESDAY 4th *[Heading West]* The wind returns, though light. More soundings, no ground yet. We had a show from the porpoises today, which swam in a group round *Endeavour* and leaped from the water and pierced it on their return with such energy. Tarheto and I decided it would be the most pleasure to grab a porpoise by its fin and take a ride through the waves upon its sleek back.

THURSDAY 5th *[Heading West]* Chased Cape Fly Away for several hours today before we could all agree it was nothing but cloud. A wonderful show of porpoises again. Thousands of them, slipping over and under one another. Leaping and blending back, the lot of them at times gathered together in a foaming company, at times spread in a long line end to end. They swam round us for more than an hour, and even when we could no longer see their lively bodies, the water roiled with their antics, looking like distant breakers.

FRIDAY 6th *[Heading West – Lat. 39°11′ S, Long. 176°3′ W]* The water colour continued pale and Captain sounded regularly, but no bottom, even at 180 fathoms.

But then, during afternoon watch, while I was at the masthead, I saw it. Land!

'Land Ho!'

No sooner did the words fly from my lips than they were caught up all round the ship.

'Land Ho!'

This is no Cape Fly Away. It is truly land, and I have won Mr Bootie's rum. An occurrence that has put him in a black mood. Captain has named this place Young Nick's Head. Tarheto calls it YaNitHa.

I thought perhaps I should tell Captain to name the land for my dead mother. 'Do you think Mr Bootie would be so foul then?' I asked Francis Haite.

'You're a good boy, Nick,' he said. 'You're a boy to make a father proud. I don't know how to repair the tear between yourself and our Mr Bootie. He only wants to keep a tight ship. You came to us running from something and slammed straight against him. I don't know who's at fault, really. But since you ask, lad, I'd let the land carry your name as Captain recorded it. Mothers like their boys to leave such a mark.'

PART IX

Restless Natives

SATURDAY 7th *[Approaching Land]* Sailed towards the Land, easily seen by all now. There is smoke rising from it, so that I think we shall find natives.

We hope with our hearts that this truly is the new Continent. It is a vast land, with mountains riding the backs of mountains, until the farthest peaks soar into the very clouds.

I decided to share the most of my rum. The men drank a toast to me, then licked their lips and wiped their mouths. I brought the rum over and poured up to the rim of Mr Bootie's cup.

'Cheers, sir,' I said.

He studied me hard. I turned and proposed the next toast, to my mother.

'To Nick's mother,' the men cried.

The sound of it quite cheered me. And then they all drank to her, even Mr Bootie.

SUNDAY 8th *[New Continent]* Captain Cook and Mr Banks went ashore with the Marines late in the afternoon, in search of fresh water. I had hoped for a seat in the Pinnace but was not taken.

The first natives our men encountered ran away. But more natives, who had been hiding, attacked our people.

The Bosun saw first the mischief of the natives and fired warning shots, which the natives ignored. The aim was lowered, and one of the natives was killed. His mates dragged him off but then left him.

Mr Banks examined the dead body. It was shot through the heart.

Tonight Tarheto and I heard the natives meeting alongshore. Their voices, loud with excitement, carried out to us on *Endeavour* as we stood in the dark. Tarheto said it was difficult to make out, but he thinks he understands their language.

MONDAY 9th *[New Continent]* The Captain, Mr Banks and Dr Monkhouse, with Tupia along, attempted another landing today with the marines. It did not go well. Tupia, who could understand their language well enough, told the natives we wanted only water and provisions and would trade Iron in exchange. The natives agreed but would not put down their arms. Tupia warned our people that the natives were not our friends and meant us ill, and we must be on guard.

Captain offered presents, and at one point he met face-to-face with a single native and they touched noses in greeting. But the natives wanted everything in our Company's possession, particularly the firearms. They came at our people with long pikes and stone weapons. Mr Green's small sword was snatched from him. The native could not be persuaded to return it and, fearing the others would become as bold, Captain Cook ordered the thief to be shot.

One of our men fired directly at close range and the native was killed. Rather than run, the remaining natives attempted to take the sword from the dead man and carry it away, but Dr Monkhouse thinks it was a green stone they were after more than the sword.

Captain, feeling the situation could only grow worse, ordered the men to set off. A Canoe of natives pulled up beside Captain's boat and pelted our men with stones and beat them about with paddles. Again the order was given to fire, and four more natives were killed.

Three native boys were taken unharmed. They were brought on board with great effort, where they were treated well.

TUESDAY 10th *[New Continent]* During the night one of the native boys was overcome with grief, and Tupia and Tarheto comforted him. The boy sang a strange song, which made a chill of yearning climb my spine. When the two other boys joined him, I found their music so complicated and beautiful, tears came on my cheeks.

Captain Cook took a party to shore to return the three young natives today. For all their resistance yesterday, today they did not wish to leave the Company of our ship. They told Tupia their enemy lived on this part of the bay and if they were captured they would be eaten. I did not believe that. No more than the monsters of Tierra del Fuego or the demons of the South Seas.

A party of many, many natives gathered with their spears and pikes, and Tupia parleyed with them and gave them to understand we meant only friendship. The three boys trusted none of the gathered natives and came back to the ship with Captain Cook, unwilling to part from him. But in the evening Captain insisted they should be restored to their own people, and they were.

WEDNESDAY 11th *[New Continent]* Tupia managed to persuade several canoes full of natives to come aboard. They did so because the boys had told of the kindness they'd met on *Endeavour.*

These are a brave and warring people. They do not run from danger but rather straight towards it. They do not understand the strength of our weapons.

They are a dark-skinned, sturdy people. Their lips and cheeks are stained with tattoos. They wear their black hair knotted atop their heads and stuck with feathers, and they wear red paint upon their faces.

Mr Bootie said we cannot expect friendship from them until they know they cannot defeat us. But is it friendship then?

We weighed anchor and left during the night when a breeze came up. Captain has named the place Poverty Bay because he could not find the necessary provisions for us here. On his chart the SW point of Poverty Bay is labelled YOUNG NICK'S HEAD. It is something to see it in writing, just the way he promised. But I am troubled knowing the sorrow attached to this place with my name. That here, with our first encounter in a new land, we brought death instead of friendship.

Captain intends to follow South along the coast, charting

what he sees as he goes. I hope this continent does not drop below the latitude we met when the sea turned to a churning tempest and the cold cracked inside our bones.

THURSDAY 12th *[New Continent]* From the ship we can see land, ploughed and planted and farmed.

Mr Banks brought only forty species of plants from Poverty Bay, but he had so little time to collect, and such trying circumstances. He seems disheartened by our experiences on the new Continent thus far.

Sailed into a rough patch where the soundings changed each time they were taken, but Captain steered us safely through.

FRIDAY 13th *[New Continent]* We continue making our way south along the coast. This country, with its hills and woods, is beautiful but unfriendly.

A Canoe filled with eighteen or twenty men came close enough to yell and shake their spears at us.

SATURDAY 14th *[New Continent]* Following the coast south. No good harbour yet. Great Canoes filled with hundreds of natives came out to us, singing together a terrifying war song. After a warning from Tupia, Captain showered the natives with grapeshot and they returned to shore.

SUNDAY 15th *[New Continent – Lat. 39°50' S]* We were able to buy fish from the natives who brought their offerings out for trade. The fish they traded had a strong odour, but Mr Thompson said it was not spoiled.

Some of the native canoes are remarkable pieces of work.

Aft, they are adorned by a tall, filigreed tail hung high with streamers. The head of the canoes are also done in remarkable filigree, with a face containing two large mother-of-pearl eyes and a tongue stuck boldly out.

Captain, in a token of friendship, passed bundles of cloth down to the natives in their canoes, for it is cloth they seem to value above all other things we have for trading.

Captain saw a native wrapped in a cloak of dark skin. He and Mr Banks were eager to have the cloak to see what animal the skin came from. A cloth of red was offered him in trade and the native agreed with much eagerness. But when our men handed down the cloth, the native departed with our wares and his own. This event led to a most terrifying series of occurrences.

For the very same Canoe returned shortly after it took off, and this time it came to steal Tarheto, who was over the side in the chains, helping to hand bundles up and down between the canoes and the deck of *Endeavour*.

The natives in the Canoe grabbed hold of Tarheto and kidnapped him.

Captain commanded our men to fire.

Tarheto disappeared in the smoke and I feared he'd been shot and was lost. But clever Tarheto, seeing an opportunity to escape in the confusion of gunfire, had jumped from the natives' canoe into the water. He swam back to *Endeavour*, where we brought him on deck. But he was senseless for hours after.

It was Mr Banks's dog Lord Grey that brought Tarheto comfort in the end by curling up with him and licking his face and hands until he began to respond again.

Tarheto said the man who held him was shot clean through his body.

This evening I went with Tarheto as he brought a fish to Tupia to sacrifice to his god Eatua in gratitude for his life being spared. Tupia gave Tarheto and the fish his blessing, and I watched as Tarheto gave the fish over the side.

The white cliffs of this new land slipped past and we sailed away from Cape Kidnappers on a gentle breeze.

MONDAY 16th *[New Continent – Lat. 40°34' S]* The sea shivers with fish all about us and the sky is peppered with birds. They swoop down and disappear into the water, only to appear again where you would not expect to see them, with their catch sparkling in their beaks.

Captain has decided to reverse our direction, for we have been dropping to lower and lower latitudes and have found no opportunity for bringing on fresh water or provisions. The hope is that we shall find a Northerly route more agreeable.

TUESDAY 17th *[New Continent]* As we sailed past the coast we have already seen, a seal floated by, cradled in the sea, sleeping peacefully. Someday I shall let go all my cares and sleep so. But for now I cannot relax entirely, particularly as long as Mr Bootie is around. I tie my hammock up as it should be, and yet when it's inspected, it's not right. I suspect Mr Bootie has a hand in the mischief, though I can't prove it. I imagine he's been into my journal as well. I know it can be done. I've been into his. At least he is clever enough not to sign his name.

Tarheto has no interest in my journal. My writing is just marks on paper. He would rather hear me make bird calls or play the nose flute or sing patriotic songs. It is Samuel Evans who envies my journal, who longs to master the art of reading.

His appetite and persistence have somehow infected me. I never saw the worth of any sort of formal education. But watching Samuel's determination to learn the simple task of reading stirs me to a book hunger I never experienced before.

WEDNESDAY 18th *[New Continent]* This evening we were approached by a boat with two chiefs and three servants. The chiefs, with human teeth hanging from their ears, came aboard, and we had peaceful exchange. They were well pleased with the presents given them and decided to stay aboard through the night, though they were told the ship might be some distance from the spot where they boarded.

The three servants ate heartily of our stores, but the two chiefs would take nothing, and Tarheto, who is still frightened of them, said it was *Tapu* for the chiefs to eat in our company.

One of the chiefs seems a man of great care and gentle manner.

It is hard to understand how we could meet with such war-like advances when last we were in this harbour, and then meet these Chiefs so open and trusting this time.

THURSDAY 19th *[New Continent – Lat. 38°44'30' S]* The Natives were sent off early this morning. Came past the spot Captain named Young Nick's Head, then past Poverty Bay. From now on everything we see shall be new to us.

The Cliffs have dropped away and have become instead fertile land, green and festive with flowering plants and tall palms. The land gives off a sweet, green odour.

FRIDAY 20th *[New Continent]* Captain pulled into a Bay, though it is not well sheltered, for we are in great need of fresh water. The natives here seem friendly enough.

Two chiefs came aboard, and the remainder of the natives traded with us what they had in their canoes. One chief wore a dog-skin cloak and the other wore a cloak of beautiful red feathers.

SATURDAY 21st *[New Continent]* Lieutenant Gore took a party ashore to begin filling the water Casks.

Mr Banks and Dr Solander were eager to set out collecting and took Tupia and Tarheto with them. They met with great success, finding many new plants and shooting birds of brilliant plummage.

Tarheto said they visited inside the houses, where the natives offered them crayfish and roasted root. The native women, Tarheto said, wear red paint on their faces and go about in skirts that smell sweet. Their dogs, Tarheto said, were small and ugly, not at all like Lord and Lady Grey. More like what they ate on OTahiti.

Dr Monkhouse said the natives are wonderful gardeners, cultivating sweet potatoes, taro and yams.

SUNDAY 22nd *[New Continent]* Put to sea before first light. We have now in our stores some fresh water, wild celery and sweet potatoes.

MONDAY 23rd *[New Continent]* Fighting the wind to make headway. Some Natives came out and directed the Captain to a calm bay where fresh water might be easily gathered. We set anchor and trading commenced immediately. I asked my messmates if we wouldn't run out of things to trade at this rate. They said no. There are barrels of things in the Hold. We shan't run out, they said.

Captain found the watering place just as promised and resolved to bring wood and water aboard until our needs were well satisfied.

Captain has us eating wild celery boiled for breakfast every morning. And we have fresh fish. Fish Tarheto and I help to catch off the side of the ship.

TUESDAY 24th *[New Continent]* Captain spent the morning with Mr Green employed in making observations and drawing charts. Dr Solander and Mr Banks went off Botanizing, taking Tupia and Tarheto with them.

Tonight Tarheto, stroking the grey-striped Smoke, sat with me and Goat in the chill air. He told us about an enormous arch through which the sea could pass. He said that Mr Banks was excited at the sight of it and many sketches were made.

WEDNESDAY 25th *[New Continent]* Tupia spoke with a native priest today. He asked if the natives truly did eat men here in this place. And the priest said yes! They did! They ate the bodies of their enemies killed in war. This is the dirtiest thing I have ever heard!

THURSDAY 26th *[New Continent]* Rain falling with great force. Mr Banks reluctantly remained on board. I don't care if I never go ashore.

FRIDAY 27th *[New Continent]* Captain brought on board scurvy grass enough to keep us well for some time.

SATURDAY 28th *[New Continent]* Continue to bring Wood on board. Some of the men have gone ashore to cut stiff grasses for making brooms. Another party gathers wild celery. Mr Sporing came back with a story of a bird with a tail so great it appeared to have a flock of small birds flying behind it. Tarheto and I watched for Mr Sporing's bird until it grew quite dark, but we never saw it.

SUNDAY 29th *[New Continent]* Hauled anchor and set sail, but the wind was so disagreeable, we ended the day not far from where we started.

MONDAY 30th *[New Continent]* Finally caught a good wind. A number of canoes put off and tried to catch us, but Captain was unwilling to wait. A fog settled over much of the land, so we could see little more than the shore.

TUESDAY 31st *[New Continent – Lat. 37°32′ S, Long. 181°50′ W]* Came round the Easternmost point of the land, so Captain thinks, and now we head NW.

WEDNESDAY 1st NOVEMBER *[New Continent]* Many canoes approached this morning, prepared to trade.

We took on eel and mussels. Some of the men ate of them and got sore ill. We have been busy this evening, Dr Monkhouse, Mr Perry and I, seeing to the sick.

THURSDAY 2nd *[New Continent]* Captain had planned to keep sailing last night but changed his mind and had us weigh anchor. It was a good thing he did, for in the morning we discovered we were directly before a ridge of underwater rocks eager for a taste of *Endeavour's* hull. Those rocks surely would have satisfied their appetite had we sailed among them in the dark.

Today, in the light, Captain carefully led us through. We pass villages and plantations; some towns have upward of five hundred houses, Isaac Smith says.

FRIDAY 3rd *[New Continent – Lat. 36°58′ S]* Came this morning, while the Gentlemen were at their breakfast, on a series of rocks poking up out of the water like needles of various thickness. Mr Banks decided they looked like a court of Aldermen, and he and the other Gentlemen entertained themselves for a goodly time naming the various needles after men in real life whose shape and form most fit the rock upon which their eyes fell.

It's a rugged, barren land, with the hills rising every which way. No plantations to be seen here. Later we passed an island where houses clung to the steep sides of the hills, and I could not see how a person could get to and from the house other than on the back of a bird.

This afternoon three canoes paddled out to us. They are not finely made like the ones at Cape Kidnappers. These instead are tree trunks hollowed by fire with not even a washboard to keep the easiest sea out. By now we know the war song of these natives, and these coming sang it as lustily as any so far.

Captain found a fine bay this evening. Coming out to meet us was yet another series of canoes filled with yet another complement of natives who told us they'd be back to kill us in spite of our entreaties of friendship. I asked Tarheto why these natives speak the same language as he, wear similar clothes and yet are so different from the people of OTahiti. He says this is not OTahiti. That is his only answer.

SATURDAY 4th *[New Continent]* This is a place of many birds, much fish and a good supply of wild celery. Mr Banks is eager to get ashore and Botanize.

SUNDAY 5th *[New Continent]* The natives came again this morning, but they are most changed in manner towards us. They did not cheat and were genuinely friendly. An old chief came aboard and Captain gave him presents of English cloth and nails. This is much better than the killing.

MONDAY 6th *[New Continent]* We are having little success at fishing in these waters. It is fortunate that the natives begin to favour us. They brought fish that I do not yet have a taste for, but at least they are offering fish for trade and not fists. Mr Banks went ashore, taking Tupia and Tarheto. Tarheto said these natives sleep under bushes.

There is not a crop of any sort growing here. How barren this part of the new continent is.

TUESDAY 7th *[New Continent]* Brought on much wild celery. The weather is dirty with rain.

WEDNESDAY 8th *[New Continent – Lat. 36°47'43" S]* Worked on the ship, scrubbing her sides while a party went ashore for Wood and another for water. Natives came today to trade after their absence yesterday in the hard weather. They traded fish for cloth. This fish they brought today is much tastier than what they brought last.

Captain took many Observations and measurements today. Mr Banks spent the day Botanizing. He gathers his specimens with delight, exploring this new country. And he comes away with ever and ever new plants.

Tarheto says the natives here cook as they do in his home, in a pit with leaf-wrapped food covered by dirt and baked on heated rocks. He says they mourn for their dead in a similar way, with the living cutting the flesh of their own body until they bleed. And yet he speaks of the natives as 'them,' and he speaks of the English as 'we.'

John Charlton cannot understand my friendship with Tarheto. To John, Tarheto is a native and nothing more. All natives are alike to him, be they from OTahiti or this new land. But John is wrong. Tarheto is not simply a dark-skinned native of OTahiti. Calling him thus is no more complete a description than calling me a red-headed runaway from Butcher Row.

THURSDAY 9th *[New Continent]* Mr Green, the astronomer, went ashore to make his observations. How fortunate to find the weather clear after so much rain. Captain and Lieutenant Hicks also were busy at taking their measurements when *Endeavour* was approached by canoes we had not yet seen.

The new natives in their canoes offered to trade their arms for our cloth from OTahiti, and one native offered a cloth he wore in trade. He was young, this native, and well built. Yet when he got hold of our cloth, he refused to send up his own and his canoe paddled away, once again with the strains of a war song rising up to taunt us.

Lieutenant Gore, who was in command while Captain was

about his Observations, shot and killed the native dead. I do not think he had to do so. If Captain had ordered such a harsh punishment for every native who had served us so, there would be none left with which to trade.

I dread these people not so much because of what they might do to us, but because of what we are led so quickly to do to them.

PART X

Stormy Weather

NOVEMBER 1769

FRIDAY 10th *[New Continent]* Captain, Mr Banks and the Gentlemen went out in the boat to study the Bay. They take Tupia and Tarheto everywhere because they speak the language of these natives. I am of no use to Captain in that regard. Nor am I the strongest oarsman in case of trouble.

I am always eager for Tarheto's reports when he returns. Particularly when Dr Monkhouse or Mr Perry has also gone along. It is interesting to hear how the stories part and come together again.

The party went ashore and found nests of Shags in the mangroves, shot and killed them, and ate of them for lunch. Mr Banks says Hunger is the most excellent sauce. I cannot believe what we will eat. Back in London I had rather starve than eat such things as I have eaten on this journey.

Captain's party returned this evening, well sodden with rain. Mr Thompson gave Tarheto work to do that kept him close by the oven until he was warm again.

SATURDAY 11th *[New Continent]* Again a day of dirty weather. Rain and wind. Captain sent out the Longboat in hope of finding natives with which to trade. Whilst out, the men discovered an oyster bank and returned loaded with rock oysters. The entire company sat contentedly eating oysters the long day until our supply was exhausted.

SUNDAY 12th *[New continent]* Worked with Samuel Evans.

MONDAY 13th TO TUESDAY 14th *[New Continent]* Mr Banks, restless, went ashore with Dr Solander in spite of the dirty weather. Dr Solander found a new cove and studied the natives at their employ of bringing in lobster, that which Mr Parkinson calls crayfish. This is a fish most delicious. It is of excellent size, and the natives gather it by walking in the surf up to their middles. When they feel a lobster with their feet, they immediately dive down and grab hold of it. Blisters, I shouldn't like that job. I place too great a value on all ten of my toes.

WEDNESDAY 15th *[New Continent – Lat. 36°47' S, Long. 184°4' W]* Made sail this morning out of the Bay, Mercury Bay, so named by Captain because of the observations of the planet Mercury he made there.

Before leaving, Captain had *Endeavour's* name and the date carved into a tree. Then he set the English colours in the soil and claimed the place for His Majesty.

THURSDAY 16th TO FRIDAY 17th *[New Continent]* Heading North into Foul Weather.

SATURDAY 18th *[New Continent]* The wind came at our backs after a restless night and blew us, for a time, north-west along the coast. Lost the good wind and came to anchor.

SUNDAY 19th *[New Continent]* Approached by canoes. The natives today knew of us already by word of people from a part of this country we have already visited. They called Tupia by name and came aboard and received presents from Captain and went away well pleased.

Evening found us thick in fog, surrounded by land on three sides.

MONDAY 20th *[New Continent]* Captain, Mr Banks, Dr Solander, and Tupia set out with the Pinnace and the Longboat to explore some of the interior of this land. I taught Tarheto a drinking song to take his mind off Tupia's absence, and learned a tune from him on the nose flute he gave me on OTahiti. They are most deeply attached, Tarheto and Tupia. There are times when Tupia loses his temper with Tarheto and calls him all manner of unpleasant names, but there is such affection between them, and such trust and good humour, I sometimes feel a black envy wash over me. Times like that I seek out Mr Perry or Mr Banks and ask how I might make myself useful. That's something I've learned aboard. The best way to banish the darkest mood is to lose myself in a useful pursuit.

TUESDAY 21st *[New Continent]* Captain and his party returned this morning near seven o'clock. Tupia told Tarheto they'd sailed in the Pinnace, entering a river Captain called the Thames after our river at home. Much mud and swamp was found and trees of enormous height and girth, which were measured and recorded by Mr Banks.

The wind blew against Captain's party, preventing them from returning last night. They fought the gale again this morning, pulling through an uneasy sea, but managed at last to regain *Endeavour.*

Captain took advantage of a change in weather this afternoon to take up anchor, but still we've made little headway out of this bay.

WEDNESDAY 22nd *[New Continent]* Many canoes came out to us today. I wonder what they think of us in our ship, towering over their rough canoes. Where do they think we've come from? And what a lot of things we must appear to have. A group of natives climbed aboard while Captain and Dr Solander were out surveying in the Pinnace. All went well until the Half-Minute Glass was stolen by one of the natives. He was caught as he made away with the piece. The Half-Minute Glass is used to measure our speed and is necessary to the ship's operation. Lieutenant Hicks, in Command, ordered the native to the gangway, where he was dealt twelve lashes with a cat-o'-nine-tails. The natives who witnessed this were much outraged and raised a deafening cry of protest. They were prepared to attack us, until Tarheto got them to understand the reason for the punishment and the fact that the thief would not die. At that they settled down, and in fact an old native beat the thief when Lieutenant Hicks was done with him, with more ardour than he had been dealt by the Lieutenant.

THURSDAY 23rd TO FRIDAY 24th *[New Continent]* Picked up a wind early and got out of the bay at last.

SATURDAY 25th *[New Continent]* Saw fires during the night. Captain is in a fine mood and calls the islands by names most surprising, like Poor Knights, after a supper of fried bread.

SUNDAY 26th *[New Continent – Lat. 35°11′ S]* Proceeding Northward.

MONDAY 27th *[New Continent]* Tarheto and I welcomed a young native boy aboard from the endless canoes that come out to us. Whilst I saluted the boy in the manner of his land, by rubbing noses, he picked my pocket. Tarheto caught him and made him return the little nose flute.

TUESDAY 28th *[New Continent]* Sailed with the wind in our mouths today, losing ground.

WEDNESDAY 29th *[New Continent]* Foul wind blows us back and ever back. Captain felt it would be good to come in at anchor and see what we could of this place instead of fighting against a wind that would not carry us where we would go. We were almost instantly surrounded by canoes.

THURSDAY 30th *[New Continent]* Hove anchor as we changed to morning watch to take advantage of a light breeze out of the east, but we soon lost it to a calm. Matthew Cox, Henry Stephens, and

Manoel Pereira received twelve lashes apiece for going ashore during the night, deserting their duty, and digging Potatoes at one of the native Plantations. Captain's anger is understandable. How can he take action when the natives steal from us if our men behave so?

FRIDAY 1st DECEMBER *[New Continent]* Wind still too contrary for sailing. I went with a party ashore to cut grass for Goat and the sheep. There was a bit of trade. The natives here like our glass bottles as much as they like the cloth from OTahiti.

Tarheto does not trust even these kinder natives. 'I hear all they say,' Tarheto says.

SATURDAY 2nd *[New Continent]* Mr Banks and Dr Solander went out in hopes of discovering something they had not yet seen. All they discovered was how very wet a Gentleman can get in the driving rain.

SUNDAY 3rd TO MONDAY 4th *[New Continent]* We have filled our water casks and brought aboard much wild celery. Tarheto does not care for it and Tupia likes it even less. I know Tarheto does not eat his share. I don't say anything. I would not bring Captain's wrath down on Tarheto for all the world. Still, I worry after his health.

TUESDAY 5th *[New Continent]* Weighed anchor this morning, but the wind was not with us. Dropped our hooks and lines instead, hoping to catch some fish, when suddenly the ship caught in an eddy tide that rushed us fast towards land. We dared not drop anchor, for the bottom was so foul. Captain ordered the

Pinnace out instead, to hold us off the rocks. But the Pinnace, in being lowered, caught on one of the guns, and in our haste to get it free we nearly spilled the oars. The natives stood cheering the tide and hoping for our destruction upon the rocks. They would no doubt have eaten us if we'd wrecked.

At last someone thought to pull the gun in, which allowed us to get the Pinnace free and into the water. Then began the labour of our best oarsmen, towing the ship away from shore.

By the grace of God a light wind lifted the sails, aiding the men at their towing. With the breakers roaring and natives chanting their war song in our ears, we began to pull away.

Tonight we all give thanks that we are under sail rather than under leaves being roasted in a native's pit oven.

WEDNESDAY 6th TO THURSDAY 7th *[New Continent]* The wind is against us.

FRIDAY 8th *[New Continent]* Southerly breeze. By evening we were carried so far off land that we can make out nothing but water in all directions.

SATURDAY 9th *[New Continent – Lat. 34°44' S]* We have come upon islands that Captain calls the Cavalles. The natives here did not come near at first, having heard from other natives of our guns. Tupia was able to calm their fears and spent a good time talking with them. They said that we were close to a place where the land turns and goes no more North. When Tupia asked about other countries, they said there was a big country to the Northwest and that their ancestors went there and ate hog.

'But we have seen no hogs here,' Tupia said.

The natives answered Tupia that their ancestors did not bring the hogs back.

Tupia says they lie, for no one would do such a thing. And now he believes nothing of what they say and encourages us to do the same.

SUNDAY 10th *[New Continent]* We are come to a place where the land is only white sand lifting in small hills.

MONDAY 11th TO TUESDAY 12th *[New Continent]* Tacked all day. The sails are taking it hard.

WEDNESDAY 13th *[New Continent]* Weather foul with gales and rain, and ever the wind blows against us from the North.

THURSDAY 14th *[New Continent]* Caught a glimpse of land today, bearing south. The sail makers are hard at repairing and drying the damaged sails.

FRIDAY 15th *[New Continent – Lat. 34°10′ S, Long. 185°45′ W]* Kept in with the land as much as possible given the wind. We have reached the northernmost part of this land. It would seem doubling any Cape is fraught with weather, danger, and hard work.

SATURDAY 16th to Monday 18th *[New Continent]* Most of the sails were split by the blow round the Cape. The sail makers work steadily at their repairs. Mr Ravenhill certainly can use colourful language.

TUESDAY 19th TO WEDNESDAY 20th *[New Continent]* Thunderstorms came with great exploding claps. Mr Bootie kept me too busy to comfort Goat and the dogs. They had Tarheto instead and seemed satisfied enough.

THURSDAY 21st TO FRIDAY 22nd *[New Continent]* I can see no land. Swells come from the West, making poor *Endeavour* pitch and groan.

Christmas will be here soon. How is London, I wonder? And my family? I suppose the Butcher is up to his ears in goose feathers about now. There's some comfort in that.

SATURDAY 23rd *[New Continent]* Mr Green has begun training some of the men to take astronomical readings. Mr Clerke, who sailed on the *Dolphin*, Mr Saunders, and Mr Monkhouse all had a turn with the Quadrant. None did particularly well. Mr Green told them not to worry, that they would improve with practice. I'd like to have a try at it. I did better with my numbers than my Latin. But I'm only 'the boy'. It would never occur to Mr Green to give me a chance with his instruments.

SUNDAY 24th *[New Continent]* We are mostly becalmed today, though land is in sight and I think we are clear at last of the troubled weather surrounding the Cape. Mr Banks went out on the boat shooting birds today with much success, killing several geese, which Mr Thompson says we shall have tomorrow as our Christmas dinner. Now it is Nicholas Young up to his ears in goose feathers.

MONDAY 25th *[New Zeland – Lat. 34°12' S, Long. 188°5' W]* Captain has known for some time that this is not a totally new and uncharted Continent. In fact, this land was discovered a very long time ago, Mr Banks says, 150 years to be exact. By a Dutchman named Tasman. This land has a name after all, New Zeland.

What a Christmas party we had – to take the disappointment out of not discovering Dalrymple's continent. With the sweet, good taste of the goose pie, and the men reeling drunk and singing, I remembered last year, on our way to Cape Horn. I was the stowaway then, not even the official 'boy.' I'm older now. I shared my rum with my messmates, taking just enough to warm me. Tupia drank far too much. Tarheto spent the night watching over him.

TUESDAY 26th *[New Zeland]* Tupia holds his head and looks out through bloodshot eyes. He is not the only one.

WEDNESDAY 27th *[New Zeland]* The wind came in such gales we were blown back out to sea. We are all grateful the wind blew us out and not in, for it is blowing powerfully, so powerfully we could not have held off the rocks.

THURSDAY 28th *[New Zeland]* Wind. Rain. Towering seas. This is hurricane!

FRIDAY 29th *[New Zeland]* Cannot keep up with the damage.

SATURDAY 30th *[New Zeland]* Land in sight after being blown around for days. Captain says this is the Cape again and that the storm has driven us back in sight of it. The wind still blows, but the back of the storm is broken.

SUNDAY 31st *[New Zeland]* I tend the sick and injured. Even now the wind would drive us to our destruction if the men would let it.

MONDAY 1st JANUARY *[New Zeland]* We begin a new year not very far from where we spent a long stretch of the old one. It is hard to believe it has taken us so many days to move so little distance, but the winds and storms have conspired against us. At least we still have a ship to sail. A lesser bark, a lesser Captain, and we would long ago have been swallowed by the deep.

TUESDAY 2nd *[New Zeland]* Captain does his best at making careful observations, but the weather and our distance from land make it a trying task. It's safer to stand to sea with the winds coming so violently against us. When we did see land this morning, it was only sand we saw.

WEDNESDAY 3rd TO SUNDAY 7th *[New Zeland]* The weather gentled as the Carpenters and sailmakers made their repairs.

Mr Banks and I went out in the boat shooting birds. There was no time for Samuel Evans to practice his letters.

MONDAY 8th TO TUESDAY 9th *[New Zeland]* Making good progress south along the Western coast, keeping land in view all day, though it looks little more than a bank of clouds.

WEDNESDAY 10th *[New Zeland – Lat. 38°4' S, Long. 184°42' W]* This morning we have come close to land, and what we see is an end to the sand and a return of green. What a welcome sight.

We passed a rock crowded with birds. They made the most outrageous squawking. In the evening we caught the first glimpse of a mountain, very high, way off in the distance.

THURSDAY 11th *[New Zeland]* Becalmed this morning. Dropped our fishing lines and brought in some bream. Caught a light breeze near midday and made sail to the South, towards the great peak that sometimes we see floating above the clouds.

FRIDAY 12th *[New Zeland]* Winds coming at us from all round the compass, with the sky low and dark and heavy. The mighty peak was hidden from us by blackened sky and sheets of rain, except for a moment when snow, upon the side of the mountain, was revealed to us. Tonight there is a fire burning onshore. This is the first sign of natives we have seen in days.

SATURDAY 13th *[New Zeland]* Storms with thunder and lightning during the night. Watched the sky lighting up, huddled with Tarheto and Goat on deck. It was not much drier belowdecks with the rain running down through the grates.

Early this morning the mountain, which Captain has named Mount Egmont, emerged briefly from its veil of clouds, at least the top of it, and it is covered with snow. Tarheto is fascinated by snow. He should like to touch it, he says. I am disturbed by the sight of it. This date is the equal of mid-July back home in England. If there is snow in this place now, in the height of summer, how bitter it must be in July, the depths of its winter. And besides, it reminds me too much of Tierra del Fuego and my friends left behind there.

SUNDAY 14th *[New Zeland – Lat. 40°27' S, Long. 184°39' W]* Traveled across Murderers Bay. It is very deep and broad. I shudder to think why Tasman, the first to discover this place, chose such a name for it.

MONDAY 15th *[New Zeland]* We saw a sea lion with a snout that hung down several inches from its face. By afternoon Captain had brought us into a fine cove where he intends to work us very hard, *Endeavour* being most foul, needing repairs and a replenishing of our supply of wood, water, and provisions. We had visits from the natives, who threw stones at us. But Tupia spoke with them and brought several on board. And perhaps it will be all right with them.

Captain went ashore with most of the Gentlemen, where they found the water fresh and cool and excellent and the wood plentiful. Our seine net brought up hundreds of pounds of fish.

Only Mr Banks and Dr Solander came back disappointed. They found but two new plants to catalogue.

TUESDAY 16th *[New Zeland]* All of us are engaged in scraping *Endeavour* and scrubbing her clean and smearing her with oil and tar to keep her watertight.

The Gentlemen took a boat out after dinner and rowed into a cove. They saw the body of a dead woman, dead some time, floating in the water. They had from some natives they met onshore the story that it was tradition to tie a stone around the body of the dead and set the weighted body into the sea. In this case the stone had come loose. These same natives were in the process of cooking a dog in their pit oven, and in a basket bones were seen that could be nothing other than human bones. There were still bits of roasted human flesh left. Gnaw marks were everywhere upon the bones.

Tarheto could speak of nothing else when he returned to *Endeavour* tonight. He said when Mr Banks questioned the natives, they told him an enemy boat had come and seven men had been killed. The bones in their provision basket belonged to one of those men. When Mr Banks asked why they had not eaten the flesh of the woman floating in the sea, they said she was a relative and they did not eat their family, only those they killed in war.

The men who went ashore say this place shall always be Cannibal Bay to them, and none of them wanted anything but Rum for supper, and a lot of it.

Part XI

Lost Continent

JANUARY 1770

WEDNESDAY 17th *[New Zeland]* In the midst of night a song woke me. It came from shore. It was the song of birds. Their call has a light ringing sound, like the soft chime of bells, and it is a music so beautiful. I doubt I shall ever copy it well enough. The birds sang from sometime after midnight until sunrise. Tarheto slept through it, but Mr Banks woke and we stood at the rail, listening. He nodded and smiled at me when they settled down quiet for the day as our nightingales do at home.

How can there be such beauty on this Cannibal shore? In spite of the birds, I have no desire to remain here any longer than is necessary.

Natives came with a human arm to show us they did not mislead us. They ran it through their mouths and smacked their lips to let us know how much they enjoyed it. Perhaps because I was so tired from staying up all night, I threw a reefer nut at them to drive them away. Lieutenant Hicks sent me to Mr Perry, and Mr Perry put me to work below deck.

THURSDAY 18th TO FRIDAY 19th *[New Zeland]* The Forge is at work, repairing the braces of the Tiller and other Ironwork. Natives traded Mackerel for cloth, paper, and nails (it has not taken them long to learn the use of nails). These natives were fair; they never once tried to cheat.

SATURDAY 20th *[New Zeland]* Natives came by with four human heads with hair and skin and eyes still attached as further proof of their Cannibalism. Mr Banks bought one of the skulls, broken at the Temple by a blow. He intends to return with it to England to show that such a thing really does occur and that we are not spinning this story out of moonlight. The flesh looked soft but did not stink. I got a look at it when Dr Monkhouse and Mr Perry examined it, trying to determine how the natives preserved it so. 'Twas horrible.

Captain, Mr Banks, and Dr Solander took the Pinnace to survey the Bay. Mr Banks returned to say there is no sign of cultivation whatsoever. It seems these natives live entirely on fish, dogs, and one another.

SUNDAY 21st *[New Zeland]* Captain gave us all leave to go ashore at the place where we are filling our water casks. Tarheto and I would have liked taking a good walk, but we were both too frightened to venture far from the safety of our Company.

MONDAY 22nd *[New Zeland]* While Mr Banks and Dr Solander Botanized, Captain took a small party and climbed one of the many hills to get a better view of the Inlet. I was tapped to come and felt safe enough with the Marines and their arms. 'Twas a steep hill we climbed, deeply wooded, and difficult to ascend. But at the top Captain made a discovery that pleased him more than I can understand. I know only this, that he is excited in a way Captain rarely is. He discovered a strait utterly separating the island we have just charted from the land we are upon now. Captain piled loose stones into a sort of monument, within which we left Musket balls as a marker that Europeans had been here.

While the Gentlemen were Botanizing and Captain making his discovery, Dr Monkhouse went ashore and found hanging from a tree a great hank of hair, enough to make a full wig. He cut it down and brought it back with him to the ship. Tupia and Tarheto showed extreme alarm. They said Dr Monkhouse would have lost his life for such an act had he been caught.

TUESDAY 23rd *[New Zeland]* Rain through the night. Clouds and haze this morning. Captain went out again in the Pinnace to continue his survey.

WEDNESDAY 24th TO THURSDAY 25th *[New Zeland]* Bringing on fresh grass, wood, and water. The Caulkers have finished with the entire ship, and now we are applying the last coating of tar and oil for protection of the keel.

Captain accompanied Mr Banks, who returned to shore to collect plants. They were invited to a village and treated with great courtesy and fairness, trading beads for fresh, good fish.

FRIDAY 26th *[New Zeland]* Captain is resolved to travel the passage that runs between the west sea and the east, the passage dividing the north island, which we have just sailed around, from the south, which we are now upon.

SATURDAY 27th *[New Zeland]* On board, the men secured the newly repaired Tiller. The Carpenters completed work on the transom. We've brought a load of stones into the bread room to shift the balance of *Endeavour*. And we are still happily pulling in great supplies of fish.

SUNDAY 28th *[New Zeland]* Mr Banks and I find we are not alone in our early-morning attendance at the concert of the bell-throated birds. There are others of the ship's company who come to listen before morning watch ends and it is time to scrub the deck.

Though it rained hard, the rain kept neither the birds silent nor the listeners away. Only sunrise silences them.

Rain continued all day. No time for Samuel Evans's lesson.

MONDAY 29th *[New Zeland]* Captain went out this morning and erected another tower of stones, in which he placed a silver coin and some Musket Balls and Beads, with a pendant flying over all.

Tonight Tarheto and I disagreed over an incident. An old native who has come often to us came out to *Endeavour* today to tell us that a young native is dead of a wound he received from our people. The old one has brought no evidence, and no one aboard has confessed to the act. Tupia says the old man is lying. That no one was even hurt. Captain accepted Tupia's judgment and took no action. I am not certain what to think.

Tarheto believes Tupia entirely. I should like to also. These natives are cannibals, after all. But what if they are telling the truth?

Tarheto says, 'Don't worry, Nit.'

But I do worry about such things.

TUESDAY 30th TO WEDNESDAY 31st *[New Zeland]* Our Carpenters took timber to use for the ship and some to erect marker posts. One post was set at the watering place with the Union Flag hoisted upon it. Captain, Dr Monkhouse, Tupia, Tarheto, and I, along with four Marines, took the second post and traveled with the old native to the highest point of all the islands here. Through Tupia, Captain asked permission to set the post. Permission was granted, along with a promise that the natives would not pull the marker down as soon as we leave. The post was set with the Union Flag flying from it. Captain called the place Queen Charlotte's Sound and took possession of all he stood upon and could see around him in the name of His Majesty. A bottle of wine was lifted in celebration of His and Her Majesty's health, and the empty bottle was presented to the old native. Tupia and Tarheto were in high spirits throughout the entire ceremony, remembering with a certain mirth such ceremonies on their own island, I suppose.

The water and wood is now all brought on board. I worked this afternoon with a party of men cutting and making brooms, whilst others worked still on the rigging and a good many continued with the fishing.

THURSDAY 1st FEBRUARY *[New Zeland]* Much rain. More than ever before perhaps. So much that the birds with the beautiful bell sound in their throats did not ring in the day. Or perhaps the rain beat too loudly for us to hear them. We dropped three anchors to hold the ship against the wind. The water runs freely down the hatchways and through the grates, and we are soaked no matter where we go.

FRIDAY 2nd *[New Zeland]* The rain came with such force it flooded the brook where we had filled our water casks, carrying away many of the smaller ones that were freshly filled and waiting to come on board. Though Captain had us looking for them, we did not find even one. I hope we shall have water enough for the next leg of our journey, whatever that may be.

SATURDAY 3rd TO SUNDAY 4th *[New Zeland]* We have everything from the shore but our hay, which came so sodden in the last weather that we cannot bring it on board. We are ready to depart this place, but the weather does not work with us, and so we remain. Tonight, sitting with Tarheto and Goat, I wondered about these people, how even when they come at us to fight, they bring their women and children. Tarheto said if they did not, their enemies would steal the women and children and eat them while their men were engaged in war.

MONDAY 5th *[New Zeland – Lat. 41°0' S, Long. 184°45' W]* The entire time we have been in this bay we have had only fish, not beef, nor pork, nor flour, nor even many pease, except for breakfast with our portable broth and wild celery. Today Captain split the remainder of the fish amongst us, and we ate the last of it. We spent the better part of the day in warping *Endeavour* into a better position for sailing.

TUESDAY 6th *[New Zeland]* We are under way, in the straits that Mr Banks has persuaded Captain to call Cook Straits.

These natives were not like the others we met on the North Island. They liked to trade for paper very much at first, until they found it came apart once it got wet. Then they would have nothing to do with it. Where the others liked the cloth from OTahiti, these natives preferred English broadcloth. They liked nails, where the others had no use for them. But those few details, which would indicate they might be more like us, could not stand up in the face of the detestable custom they share with their North Island brothers, the custom of eating their enemies.

Near evening, with the wind gone, the tide began to carry us towards land. We dropped the lead anchor, but still we drove towards the sound of breakers at great speed. We were within a cable's length when we dropped a second anchor, which held us as the tide roared around us.

WEDNESDAY 7th *[New Zeland]* At midnight the tide slacked. We brought up our anchors and sailed on a light breeze out of the path of danger.

Came past a point of land today Captain has called Cape Campbel. Cape Campbel forms the southeast entrance to the straits, and Cape Pallisser, on the Northern island, forms the northeast entrance. Captain, checking the old charts against the charts he draws as we sail, seems certain the North Island is little more than what we have already seen. But there are some Officers who believe the North Island is not an Island at all but connected to Dalrymple's continent. They press to sail the part of the coast of the northern island we have not seen already, the land south of Cape Turnagain. They think we shall turn sharply to the east and there discover the Southern continent in its entirety.

THURSDAY 8th *[New Zeland]* There is no sign of Dalrymple's great continent extending east into the sea. But the weather is all ahaze, and we cannot say with certainty that such a body of land does not exist, not even with the spyglass. Because this is a matter of great importance to His Majesty and the whole of civilization, Captain continues with the wind at our back to the NE, following the coast.

A group of natives rowed after us for some time, caught us, and came aboard. We made presents to them and they to us, something that has not happened yet here. They asked to see the nails, and we showed them, but they had never seen nails before. Captain thinks they must have spoken with the natives from Cape Kidnappers, for that is the most southern point at which we traded nails.

FRIDAY 9th *[New Zeland – Lat. 40°55′ S]* At eleven this morning we saw Cape Turnagain off to the NE. The Officers then consented that this body of land was indeed an island and not their Continent. And so we turn yet again, this time to explore the land South of Queen Charlotte's Sound.

SATURDAY 10th TO WEDNESDAY 14th *[South of the Straits]* So much haze we can hardly make out land at all.

THURSDAY 15th *[South of the Straits]* Last night some of the men caught sight of Cape Fly Away, and we sailed for it some distance before we knew we were once again deceived. We so much wish to discover Mr Dalrymple's Continent that we are quick to imagine what is not there. Today, in the calm, Mr Banks was out after Albatross, shooting six in less time than it takes to drink a pot of tea.

He'd have kept at it, but the wind came up and he had to come aboard so we might sail.

FRIDAY 16th *[South of the Straits]* Saw a fire on this land, where there are few signs of habitation, so we know there must be some natives present.

Lieutenant Gore said he saw land to the SE.

'Do you think it's Mr Dalrymple's Continent?' I asked John Charlton as we stood watch together. Mr Bootie was below, off watch.

'Captain doesn't think so,' John said.

'Blisters. What does he think?' I asked.

'Says this is just another island,' John Charlton said. 'Says all our heads are filled with Cape Fly Away and nothing more.'

'But he keeps looking,' I said.

'And he shall. Until every man is satisfied.'

Mr Banks shall never be satisfied.

SATURDAY 17th *[South of the Straits – Lat. 44°7' S]* We are ordered to sail to the east and see if Lieutenant Gore's sighting was another Cape Fly Away or not. We came around a high, peaky island Captain has named after Mr Banks, and headed East in search of Lieutenant Gore's land.

SUNDAY 18th *[South of the Straits]* There are many who still believe we shall find a continent, though Lieutenant Gore's land, everyone agrees now, must have been clouds.

We are sailing back towards the land we know to exist, the land South of Queen Charlotte's Sound.

Had a good show from the Porpoises tonight. Lord and Lady Grey barked and barked at them, which only encouraged the Porpoises in their antics.

Samuel Evans makes small strides with each lesson. He can write his birthplace and date of birth now, along with his name and position aboard *Endeavour*.

MONDAY 19th *[South of the Straits]* We had an alarm during the night when the Officer of the watch sighted land straight ahead, but Captain, upon Observation, found the Officer's land to be only a cloud. This morning caught sight of a large body of true land extending SW as far as the eye can see, and once again we are filled with hope that this is the Continent we seek.

TUESDAY 20th *[New Continent? – Lat. 44°44′ S]* Tacking towards the Land, which has no sign of human habitation.

WEDNESDAY 21st TO FRIDAY 23rd *[New Continent?]* We cannot seem to make any way to the south. Captain kept us busy with examining the wear on the ropes and cables, waiting for conditions to improve.

Sometimes days go by and I forget who I was before all this. In a way it seems as if my life began on *Endeavour*. I forget my father and my brothers at their schooling, and the Butcher and my obligations to him. I am simply a sailor, an explorer, and I am happy. Happier, in a way, than I have ever been in all my life. But then Mr Bootie trips me up so I spill my supper, or I see the Gentlemen, heads bowed over their books, and all the past comes rushing back, the good and the bad of it. And I wonder what I shall do when we sail into Plymouth.

SATURDAY 24th TO SUNDAY 25th *[South Island – Lat. 46°0' S]* Picked up a breeze and sailed SSW, along the coastline, though at too great a distance to make observations. We see no sign of smoke, which makes us think there are no natives living in this place. Only Mr Banks, with Mr Bootie's support, feels strongly that this is still Dalrymple's Continent. I agree with Captain. There is no one who knows the sea better than this Captain of ours. If Captain Cook says this is not a continent, it is not a continent. But little does my opinion matter. What matters at the moment is how much I wish Mr Thompson would serve roast pork.

MONDAY 26th *[South Island]* Heavy rain. Deep seas. Cold wind in our teeth.

Mr Parkinson applies colours to some of the line pictures he's made, though I don't know how he keeps his hand steady enough in these wicked waters.

TUESDAY 27th *[South Island]* The seas are still so heavy we cannot move about the ship without holding on. We lurch to and fro as if we had a Christmas drunk on. We are blown where the wind wills us, far from where we wish to go.

WEDNESDAY 28th *[South Island]* A Cask of Cabbage was opened and served today. We are not quite as blown about, and we found we could eat and enjoy this dish as we have not enjoyed any food for some time.

THURSDAY 1st MARCH *[South Island – Lat. 47°52' S]* On OTahiti this date marks a new season. Tarheto and I celebrated last night under the New Moon. Captain gave best wishes to Tupia and Tarheto today.

FRIDAY 2nd TO SATURDAY 3rd *[South Island]* We are completely out of sight of land and have been now for some days.

Yesterday particularly heavy swells rolled in. *Endeavour* bucked and pitched in the monstrous seas.

Captain told Mr Banks we shall find no land based on this swell. The No Continent party rejoiced in this prediction. The Continent party, however, is going about rather glum.

We were entertained by whales, seals, and a very noisy Penguin, a species Mr Banks and Captain think we have not seen before.

SUNDAY 4th *[South Island]* The wind blew fair today and carried us back within sight of land at last.

John Charlton called me to see a pair of Penguins that swam at our side. They kept perfect pace with us, squawking noisily as they went.

MONDAY 5th TO TUESDAY 6th *[South Island]* There is much in debate. Captain says this land is most definitely an island. Mr Banks is of full confidence that we are sailing along the shore of the New Continent. Tarheto cannot understand what all the fuss is about. I do not have words enough to explain British Gentlemen to him.

WEDNESDAY 7th *[South Island]* Captain takes observations and measurements with great frequency. We can make out land, but we cannot see well enough to reach any reliable conclusions about what we are seeing.

THURSDAY 8th *[South Island]* Thought today that the Continent group was right and felt a bloom of excitement that we had come upon the long-sought land after all, but this afternoon we saw our mistake. The land we thought we saw was nothing but clouds.

FRIDAY 9th *[South Island]* Sailed all last night under a full moon. Come morning we found ourselves close upon a rocky ledge where the waves broke toweringly high. Immediately Captain took us on a tack away from the danger, exercising great care and speed. Not long after, the wind came in and blew us clear of the trouble entirely. It could have gone very bad for us.

Captain has called this place the Traps, for they wait, eager to catch the unsuspecting sailor.

Today was the birthday of one of the Officers, and Tupia instructed the men in how to kill one of the OTahitian dogs bred on board *Endeavour.* They roasted the dog and made a pie of it in celebration. Though I was offered a morsel, I would not have it. Neither did Tarheto partake of the dog meat.

SATURDAY 10th *[South Island]* There can be no doubt, this is not the Continent we'd come in search of. The dreams of five months dissolved as land gave way to sea.

SUNDAY 11th *[South Island]* The wind holds us back from a northerly course, but we come close upon the shore and are able to see the remarkable high hills, snow peaked and much wooded. No sign of natives.

MONDAY 12th *[South Island – Lat. 47°40' S, Long. 193°50' W]* It is a hollow sea that surges towards us from the SW and a fickle wind that blows. And still Mr Parkinson, through storm, through hollow sea, through damp and chill, paints on.

TUESDAY 13th TO THURSDAY 15th *[South Island]* Continue our slow way N up the west coast of this land, keeping only two leagues or so from shore. Steep hills, lightly clad with trees, and great patches of snow. In the sea around us floats debris, leaves, twigs, grass. Above us we have Albatross every day, journeying with us.

FRIDAY 16th TO SATURDAY 17th *[South Island]* Mr Green tried not to show his agitation, but his latest pupils in navigation, Mr Forwood, Mr Bootie, and Mr Monkhouse, are some disappointment to him. Samuel Evans has proven a better pupil at reading words than they at reading quadrants. I am interested in Mr Green's instruments and feel certain I could learn.

SUNDAY 18th *[South Island – Lat. 43°4' S]* Picked up a breeze during the forenoon watch and rode a swell from the WSW, which came to us during the night. Onshore we see great blankets of snow upon the hills.

Samuel Evans has begun learning the days of the week. His progress fills me with wonder.

MONDAY 19th *[South Island]* Foul wind breeds foul humour.

TUESDAY 20th *[South Island]* Laboured all day against rain and a wind that sought to pull us from our course.

Tonight blows better.

WEDNESDAY 21st TO THURSDAY 22nd *[South Island]* We are close upon the land, but we can see little for the fog. Captain cannot make charts to his satisfaction when there is such a soup in the way.

At sunset the clouds went to every colour, even faint strokes of green. How remarkable.

FRIDAY 23rd *[South Island]* It is comfortably warm here after the cold near the southern reaches of this lower island of New Zeland. Sailed on a light breeze.

SATURDAY 24th *[South Island – Lat. 40°19′ S]* As light came we observed the land had lost its cloud-catching peaks and was now low and hillocky and went no more north but turned and rippled into the mouth of Cook Straits, the very straits we first entered nearly two months ago.

John Charlton, with his beaming grin, slapped me on the back. 'I told you so,' he said. 'It's nothing but an island.'

He said no such thing.

SUNDAY 25th *[Entering Cook Straits]* We attempt to enter the West side of the straits, but an Easterly wind blows against us.

MONDAY 26th *[Entering Cook Straits]* The wind has shifted from East to North, and the Captain makes what he can of it. We have come again nearly to Queen Charlotte's Sound, traveling full circuit round the North Island and the South Island of this country.

TUESDAY 27th *[Entering Cook Straits]* Captain took a boat at dawn to find water and a good berth for *Endeavour*.

We are now at anchor and the collecting of fresh water to fill the empty casks has begun. Mr Banks and Dr Solander placed their feet upon land and happily went about their botanizing business.

And Tupia and Tarheto and I took a boat out and brought back fish aplenty.

WEDNESDAY 28th TO THURSDAY 29th *[Cook Straits]* Mr Banks is sick with a violent stomach and blinding headache. We have seen these symptoms in some of the others, who then suffer a fever as well. And then there is the scurvy showing up amongst some of the men. Kept busy tending all the ill, while the healthy dropped their fishing lines out the cabin windows. It is something to look up and see a fish on a line sailing by.

FRIDAY 30th *[Cook Straits]* Captain prepared *Endeavour* for departure, then took the Pinnace out to do some final exploration of this place. Mr Banks is much better but for a tender stomach after its violent exercise yesterday. He went ashore and to his great joy found three new plants never seen before, which he brought with pleasure to Mr Parkinson.

The water and wood are all replenished, and we are ready to set our sails for home! Captain consulted with the Officers about the best course to take. If we go back the way we came, by Cape Horn, we could eliminate for all time the idea of a southern con-

tinent. But that would bring us across the southern latitude during the heart of its winter. The men all agree *Endeavour* is not up
to the storms and beatings she would take on such a course.
Travelling directly from New Zeland to the southern reaches of
Africa and around the Cape of Good Hope, we have the same
dangerous winter weather and slim chance of discovering anything new along the way. Therefore it is decided we shall return
by way of the uncharted East coast of New Holland, which
Captain has determined to be directly WNW of our present
location.

We did not find Dalrymple's Continent. We did not get a
perfect measure of the Transit of Venus. But for the first time
ever, all of New Zeland, north and south, is fully charted. And
there is still the East Coast of New Holland, unexplored, waiting
to be conquered, before we turn *Endeavour* towards the Cape of
Good Hope and bring her home.

PART XII

Over a Looking-Glass Sea

MARCH 1770

SATURDAY 31st *[Towards New Holland – Lat. 40°35′ S, Long. 185°6′ W]*
Got under sail as the sun rose and said farewell to the Islands of
New Zeland. Mr Thompson's inventory shows a desperate want
of sugar, salt, oil, tea, and tobacco. Our cook has done well in
keeping us from starvation, but he shall be glad to replenish his
stocks at the earliest opportunity. So shall we all.

SUNDAY 1st APRIL *[Towards New Holland]* Heading West with a
good wind behind us. The place we are heading, John Charlton
says. no European has ever seen before. The Dutch have
explored only the West Coast of this land. It is for us to chart
the East.

MONDAY 2nd *[Towards New Holland]* Dr Monkhouse has been working with Mr Thompson in devising uses for the malt we have on board. The best is when Mr Thompson boils our breakfast wheat in it. Makes a good, tasty meal, and we are fitter for the having it.

Today Dr Monkhouse sent me to Mr Thompson to help with the preparation of a batch of Wort. I carried it up from the Bread room, where it has kept reasonably dry. Mr Thompson boiled the Wort into a panada with dried fruit. Dr Monkhouse said I'm to serve this mixture to the scurvy patients twice a day.

TUESDAY 3rd TO WEDNESDAY 4th *[Towards New Holland]* The sea comes from the south in vast hollows.

Showers of rain chill us.

The Sail makers work on the Main Topsail, which split during the night.

THURSDAY 5th *[Towards New Holland]* The weather has turned mild. The wind has less bite and is somewhat gentled. Captain says this has happened every time we have passed between the latitudes of 40° and 37° south, with the 40° latitude cold and fraught with strong winds and storms, and the 37° latitude gentling down. No question which latitude I prefer.

FRIDAY 6th *[Towards New Holland]* It is pleasant on deck. Tupia told us he spied a flying fish and a kind of bird he never saw before, and Mr Banks and I have kept a watch for the sight of more, but we were not rewarded.

SATURDAY 7th TO SUNDAY 8th *[Towards New Holland]* Sunlight and gentle breeze. This is what I imagined when I gazed upon the forest of masts bobbing on the Thames. This is what kept me alive at the Butcher's, this dream.

I do not regret stowing aboard *Endeavour* nearly two years ago. I know I should not have stolen the money from the Butcher to buy my way on, but the coins I gave Francis Haite, John Ramsay, and Samuel Evans, no one can convince me that money was not well spent.

MONDAY 9th *[Towards New Holland]* We are kept busy in this slow and pleasant weather, setting upon this looking-glass sea, with the tasks of maintaining *Endeavour*, working up Junk and picking Oakum. The Sail maker is at work on the Mizzen Topsail, the Carpenters repairing the Yawl.

I sighted a Tropic bird!

TUESDAY 10th TO WEDNESDAY 11th *[Towards New Holland]* It is almost too hot after all the cold of the past months. And it is certainly too still. Since we were becalmed, Mr Banks went out shooting. He got one of the birds Tupia saw last week, the new one. Mr Banks brought on board an Albatross whose stomach contained the remains of a Portuguese man-of-war. How could anything eat such a stinging mass of blubber without its throat and stomach being burned through?

THURSDAY 12th TO SATURDAY 14th *[Towards New Holland]* The mornings drip with the heavy dew.

The sails are coming all to pieces, worn out by the wind and salt. Ever is the Sail maker at his task of saving what can be saved.

I don't believe in all this time I've ever seen the sail maker sober. Not once. But he is good at his craft and makes whole what seemed impossible to repair, out of pieces no one else could find the good in.

A wind has begun building. Coming with it a great field of Porpoises, playing in the sea about the ship.

I've had precious little time with Tarheto. When I am below deck, Dr Monkhouse has kept me waiting table, polishing boots, washing and repairing shirts, assisting Mr Thompson, and ministering to the sick and injured. I am never idle but for the four-hour stretches we're given for sleep. I have little time for Lord and Lady Grey, though Mr Banks relies a great deal on me for their care. I have even less time for Goat and the remaining live-stock and Smoke and Ginger Bigfoot. I have not given Samuel Evans a reading lesson in a month. And Tarheto, when I meet him, is as tired as I. We sit together under the stars, too weary to speak.

SUNDAY 15th *[Towards New Holland]* Mr Bootie caught me teaching Samuel Evans to read today. It put him in a fury such as I have never seen to see us so engaged. He grabbed me and threw me down upon the deck. I thought my chest would shatter under the weight of his boot. Then he unlatched and threw back the lid on the wild hogs' pen and pushed me inside, slamming the lid back down and locking it. The hogs have been on ration for some time. Mad with finding me locked in with them, they attacked. I thought I would die. But Samuel got me out as soon as Mr Bootie went off.

'You should report this to Captain,' Samuel Evans said.

'Mr Bootie would see me dead if I did.' I wiped at a trickle of blood on my cheek.

'Perhaps we should stop the lessons awhile,' Samuel said. Hard words to say. Hard words to hear.

I thought I was strong enough, alert enough for Mr Bootie. I was wrong.

MONDAY 16th *[Towards New Holland]* We begin to see land birds about the ship, and Tupia saw a float of seaweed. A butterfly was spotted by the Second Lieutenant. Captain had us taking soundings, but we are still in deep sea. A little sparrowlike bird came aboard this evening in the rain, and I nearly took hold of it, but I am so bruised. The bird flew up into the rigging and I could not get it.

Dangerous seas tonight washing over our decks. I helped move Goat to a safer berth. Stayed with her through the Thunderstorm, though the ship tossed and the sea made every attempt to pull me overboard. Stayed out of Mr Bootie's way.

TUESDAY 17th TO WEDNESDAY 18th *[Towards New Holland]* After a perilous night the weather has cleared. The men say judging by the weather and the sightings we've had, we're not far from land. Captain makes more than his usual number of observations.

THURSDAY 19th *[Towards New Holland – Lat. 37°50′ S, Long. 210°29′ W]* Saw land at daybreak! Captain named the place Point Hicks, for Lieutentant was first to spot it.

In the afternoon we witnessed the formation of a waterspout. The column, which began on the underside of a dark cloud, reached towards the water. The sea was greatly disturbed beneath the cloud and rose up in a tube, transparent, like glass, so that the column finally reached from sea to cloud. The spout did not hold straight very often but twisted in one direction or another. Tarheto and I watched as the column moved towards another, more distant, and when the two joined, the spout dissolved to nothing.

We've kept Point Hicks in our sights all day, sailing straight for it.

PART XIII

Charting the Coast

APRIL 1770

FRIDAY 20th *[New Holland]* Though there are hills, New Holland is, by far, a flatter country than the mountainous New Zeland. What we see is very green but for the seashore, which is very white. The land trends North in one direction and SW in the other. Captain sails North along the coast.

There are signs of natives. We saw smoke during the day and more this night.

SATURDAY 21st *[New Holland]* At sunrise we were abreast of a great mountain looking somewhat like the hump of a camel, which Captain has called Mount Dromedary. Captain and Mr Green are busy at their observations and charts, and we are regularly taking soundings. Mr Banks is undistractible in his eagerness to get ashore.

More shore fires seen this night.

SUNDAY 22nd TO MONDAY 23rd *[New Holland]* Lost the wind. Mr Banks took the boat out but brought no birds back with him. He did bring some samples from the sea for Mr Parkinson to draw. They were got with his dipping net.

TUESDAY 24th TO WEDNESDAY 25th *[New Holland – Lat. 34°22′ S, 208°36′ W]* Made sail during middle watch to the North, having the wind at our backs. Spotted several large fires.

Captain named the North point of the bay we've just come past Long Nose because of its appearance. He might have called it Long Face, for that is what Mr Banks wore as we sailed past.

THURSDAY 26th *[New Holland]* Becalmed last night. Picked up the breeze again near the start of middle watch. After noon we came upon a series of white cliffs rising from the sea. They put me greatly in mind of England. The sail maker is putting the tents from our fort at OTahiti to use in repairing the Main Topsail.

FRIDAY 27th *[New Holland]* We saw some natives along the shore carrying a canoe, but they did not put to water. At last some of the Gentlemen hoisted out the boats in order to land. Mr Banks seemed most pleased with Captain's decision. But the Pinnace, when lowered, leaked very badly and could not be used.

The men tried the yawl next to better success. Captain, Dr Solander, Mr Banks, Tupia, and four rowers made up the party. I was not amongst them. Tarheto and I stood watching the departure of the yawl from deck, whilst the natives sat watching the approach of it from shore. But when Captain's party came close, the watchers sprang up and vanished.

In the end the surf made a landing impossible. When they returned, Mr Banks could speak of nothing else but the treasures waiting for him to gather.

Many fires onshore tonight.

SATURDAY 28th *[New Holland]* The carpenters worked on the Pinnace through the night, so that by dawn, when Captain sighted a safe harbour, Master Molyneux was able to take the Pinnace out to sound the entrance.

Endeavour sailed into an inlet near noon. There were natives in canoes fishing with long, pointed poles. They paid no attention to us, and I wonder, busy as they were and with the pounding of the surf in their ears, whether they even knew of our presence.

An old woman came out of the trees followed by three children. They had been gathering sticks, for their arms were full. They arrived at a group of six or so huts. The old woman looked out at us from time to time, but she didn't seem frightened. She lit a fire, and the fishermen came ashore and dressed the fish, also unbothered by our presence. All these natives, men, women, children, wear not a stitch of clothing, not even a leaf to cover their privy parts.

These people paid no attention to us until Captain landed. Two natives rushed at the landing party with lances and short sticks. Tupia tried speaking with them, but they did not understand his words, nor he theirs. The natives were outnumbered, two of them against thirty of our men, but they kept menacing and shaking their weapons though our men tossed nails and beads to them.

The party tried to express in gesture that they meant no harm and only wanted water. But the natives in turn expressed very clearly they wished Captain's party to leave.

Captain had a musket fired over their heads, which startled the younger of the two natives for a moment, but he quickly recovered, and Captain was answered with the throwing of a rock. Small shot was fired next at the elder native, and after the second round he ran to a hut and returned with a shield. It was a pathetic but valiant battle on the natives' part, their pikes and shields against our firepower. Finally the two warriors ran away.

Tupia and Tarheto found children hiding behind a shield in one of the houses. They did not go to them nor remove the shield, but left them where they huddled and instead tossed beads and cloth to them and then departed, gathering as they went all the lances and weapons they could find.

I got a look at the native weaponry after it came on board. Some of the spears were stained with a slimy green stuff that Mr Banks suspected was poison. But Dr Monkhouse concluded it was no such thing.

Though the skin of these natives is very black, Mr Perry says they are not Negro judging by their features and the soft texture of their hair.

After dark, lights moved near shore with great regularity in a slow dance as the natives did their night fishing.

SUNDAY 29th [New Holland] A party went ashore and found fresh water for the Company. The beads and presents left for the children yesterday were still on the floor of the hut this morning, though the hut was deserted. Are we so frightening?

Water and wood were brought on board today, and Captain busily charted the bay.

Mr Banks and Dr Solander had great luck in finding plants but no luck in finding people.

MONDAY 30th *[New Holland]* The natives' spears are not made for battle but for fishing, that's what John Ramsay says.

The grass cutters were separated from the rest of the landing parties, and they were approached by some natives who shouted at them and then left.

Mr Banks went off to a small island collecting shells this evening. He, too, saw natives, but they ran before he could get close.

What a shy people these are.

TUESDAY 1st MAY *[New Holland]* Forby Sutherland died last night of the consumption that has plagued him since we rounded Cape Horn. We buried him onshore this morning at the watering place, and Captain gave the spot his name to honour him.

Captain went ashore with presents, which he left where the natives have often been seen. He left cloth, looking glasses, combs, beads, nails, and other sundry things. Then Captain, Dr Solander, Mr Banks, Tupia, Tarheto, and a company of others went off to explore the country. I was left behind to tend the ill. Tarheto said Captain's party saw but one native in a full day of walking, and he disappeared long before they reached him.

Tonight Tarheto sat with me and Goat and Lord and Lady Grey, Smoke in Tarheto's lap, Ginger Bigfoot in mine. Mr Bootie safely below. Tarheto described what he saw with Captain's party.

'Many houses,' he said. 'Many places in the grass where people sleep. And animal,' he said, 'the size of rabbit. Lord Grey wanted to chase.'

In answer Lord Grey whimpered in his sleep, his paws
twitching and his side heaving with his dream chase.

Mr Banks found the dung of an animal that fed on grass and
must be the size of a deer. He also found prints of a clawed animal, a dog or perhaps a wolf. And something like a cat. And many,
many birds.

How I wish I had seen those things, particularly the birds.
Being Surgeon's boy keeps me out of Mr Bootie's way more than
not, but it does have its disadvantages.

WEDNESDAY 2nd [New Holland] Rain this morning. The
Gentlemen, after their success in gathering yesterday, were well
content to spend the early hours in the Cabin making their
observations. However, as soon as the weather cleared, Mr Banks
resumed his collecting. Tarheto and Tupia accompanied him
ashore. Tarheto said he and Tupia caught sight of perhaps nine
natives, but they ran as soon as they saw our people.

Tarheto and I watch the natives as carefully as they watch us.
They catch oysters, mussels, and cockles with their hands, picking
them out of the sand and mud, whilst still remaining in their
canoes. Sometimes they even roast their catch and eat it in the
canoe over a fire they keep there.

Isaac Smith read this last entry in my journal, as I came to
him requesting more supplies to continue.

'You have a good eye, Nick,' Isaac said. 'And a good way with
words.'

So there, Reverend Smythe!

THURSDAY 3rd *[New Holland]* Captain went ashore in the Pinnace with Dr Monkhouse and Dr Solander. They came upon a place where fishermen had been only moments before, roasting mussels by their fire. Captain's party ate of the mussels and left presents in trade.

Mr Banks has discovered so many new species that he is concerned they will not be properly recorded and preserved. I believe Mr Parkinson has given up sleeping entirely. He is at work in the Great Cabin day and night. And still he cannot keep up.

So today Mr Banks went ashore, spreading every specimen upon a sail so it might all dry in the sun. And I went ashore with him! It was so good to feel the sand under my feet and between my toes. And though my sea legs had me unsteady, I can't say how much it brightened me to smell and feel land beneath me again.

It was my job to turn Mr Banks's plants throughout the day to dry evenly. I brought them back aboard this evening before the dew and dampness wet them again, reluctant to return to *Endeavour* until the last possible moment.

There is a new fruit discovered and brought back to ship. It resembles a cherry, but it is not sweet. Pity. I would have loved a taste of cherry pie.

FRIDAY 4th *[New Holland]* Captain sent Mr Monkhouse out to see if a connection could be formed with the natives. Mr Monkhouse returned reporting he came suddenly upon an old man and woman with two small children and offered them a bird he had shot. They would not accept the bird and showed great fear of him. They were naked entirely.

Mr Banks went off botanizing without the least fear of these natives. How different from New Zeland.

Lieutenant Gore caught a stingray weighing more than 240 pounds with its guts out.

SATURDAY 5th *[New Holland]* Dr Solander and Mr Banks continue to find success in their botanizing and are excited each day with their discoveries. The insects are bad here, and we constantly work with the whine of mosquitoes in our ears and the bite of them in our flesh. Lieutenant Gore took more stingrays today, this time bringing one in at 336 pounds.

SUNDAY 6th *[New Holland]* Captain has named the place where we have spent these past days Botany Bay, for the Gentlemen have found so rich a treasure here as they have found nowhere so far.

We left our inscription carved into a tree near the watering place, recording our claim to this land.

Back at sea with a fair wind, we passed one good harbour after another. Ate Lieutenant Gore's stingray and his tripe for dinner. The ray was not very good, but the tripe excellent. Mr Thompson also served a boiled leaf, much like spinach, which met with good success.

MONDAY 7th TO TUESDAY 8th *[New Holland]* We are in with the heavy dews again. The sails drip with it. No wind. *Endeavour* sits well offshore.

WEDNESDAY 9th *[New Holland – Lat. 33°37′ S]* What a rainbow appeared today! It formed a full arch and was so vivid its colours were reflected in the sea. John Charlton came up beside me on deck and reached to tousle my hair. But I'm taller now than when

I came aboard, taller than John Charlton. He punched me lightly in the arm instead.

'What a show, eh, Nick?' he asked.

'Aye,' I answered. ''Tis.'

THURSDAY 10th *[New Holland]* The wind came up from the SW this morning. We sailed past many likely harbours, but we rode the wind whilst we had it and did not stop.

FRIDAY 11th *[New Holland]* Kept up our soundings through the night. Green the hills are and green are the hills behind them.

SATURDAY 12th *[New Holland]* Mr Parkinson concluded the drawings from the many plants gathered at Botany Bay. He is quick and he is skilled and he is also very tired.

SUNDAY 13th *[New Holland – Lat. 30°43′ S, Long. 206°45′ W]* The wind brought us in closer to land. A group of porpoises came along, laughing their porpoise laugh. Lately I have found them at *Endeavour*'s side when I'm emptying pails.

'Am I that funny?' I called out to them.

The men in the rigging above me sniggered.

'They always do come by when you're topside,' John Ramsay said.

'Well, I could do worse than be good for a porpoise's joke,' I called back to him.

We might have continued longer, but Mr Bootie showed up and I moved below deck.

MONDAY 14th *[New Holland – Lat. 30°22′ S, Long. 206°39′ W]* Rain, heavy wind, and crashing thunder kept me by Goat as much as my duty permitted. After a time, though, the wind calmed, then turned, blowing from the south and fair. The more Northerly we travel, the higher the land becomes. Everywhere, from Botany Bay to this point, is a green verdure.

TUESDAY 15th TO THURSDAY 17th *[New Holland]* Had a close call with some breakers these past days.

The sea is a paler colour here, changed from the transparency we are accustomed to seeing to the colour of grey clay. Mr Banks says that means there is a great river feeding into this part of the ocean, but Captain's soundings bring up white sand from the bottom at thirty-four fathoms, and that could be the reason for the colour.

There are mountains that mark this place, shaped like glasshouses.

FRIDAY 18th *[New Holland – Lat. 25°34′ S, Long. 206°45′ W]* The land here has lost the green blanket we have before seen. Sand is everywhere, and it shifts to bury trees still green with their leaves on and to reveal the stumps of trees it has already smothered. We had water snakes, two of them, swim past the ship. Mr Banks went out in the small boat and brought back a bird and two bones from the cuttlefish, which he found different from the European variety.

SATURDAY 19th *[New Holland]* Still sand wherever there is land. The sun set on the barren shore, turning it pink.

SUNDAY 20th *[New Holland]* We were kept company in our course today with many large fish, Sharks, Dolphins, and one enormous Turtle. A wonderful, grand grampus lifted entirely from the sea and entered again with a great, explosive splash. This he did several times to the pleasure of all aboard.

We have smooth sea now after a high swell following us all the way up the coast.

MONDAY 21st *[New Holland]* Picked up land again this morning, nicely green and wooded, and smoke from fires upon the shore. From half hour before sunrise to half hour after, we had birds steady flying over the ship to the SSE. I asked Isaac Smith if they were heading for New Zeland. He said it was more likely they fed during the day in a place south of us and would return, flying over us tonight. I listened for them all afternoon but did not hear them come back.

We set anchor for the night rather than risk accident, sailing along this uncharted coast. Another water snake. They are beautifully marked, these snakes, and they move with a liquid grace, but they make a chill run up my back when I see them. Tarheto likes them no more than I.

TUESDAY 22nd *[New Holland]* Weighed anchor at sunrise on a gentle wind from the South and made our way closer to shore. The Gentlemen with their glasses can see Palm nut trees, something Tarheto recognized even at a good distance. How strange it is that something so plain and ordinary as a tree or a bird can bring us comfort when we are so alone and so far from home.

Two natives were out along the shore, but they neither looked up nor took any notice of us. It is unnerving to be ignored by these people. Mr Perry says they have never seen anything like our ship before and they are not able to recognize it and react in a civil way.

WEDNESDAY 23rd *[New Holland]* Mr Orton, Captain's clerk, had great mischief acted upon his person during the night. He was dead drunk, and someone came and cut the clothes off his body and the ends off his ears. It was Mr Bootie brought him to us.

Helped patch poor Mr Orton's ears together and ease his misery by finding more drink to dull his pain. Mr Bootie's eyes followed me as I went about my work. Gave me an odd chill to have him watching, but when I dared look up at him, there was no malice there.

Much suspicion has fallen on Mr Magra, who is no one's great favourite. He is held in far worse regard than I ever have been, even when I first came out of hiding. And he has made mischief regarding Mr Orton before. Captain suspended Mr Magra from duty, which will not inconvenience the rest of us in the least, for Mr Magra does as little as possible on his shifts.

Captain does his best to maintain good humour and peaceable relations upon *Endeavour*, but we are crowded in this small ship and sometimes short-tempered, some more often than others. Never is there a place where you cannot see or smell or hear another man. And we have been thus with few exceptions for nearly two years.

Captain went ashore with the Gentlemen, Tupia, and Tarheto this morning. Samuel Evans put me in an oarsman's seat. We found small oysters clinging to Rocks and Mangrove trees. We saw Mussels and Pearl Oysters and Cockles, too.

It was cold when we set off to shore, and the Gentlemen wore their cloaks to protect them against the chill wind. I wasn't cold at all once we started rowing. The day warmed to a hotter than pleasant degree.

In the Mangrove trees reside Ants in enormous nests hanging from tree branches, built of leaves glued together. When disturbed, these Ants rush out, biting. Tarheto was stung. Such a sting he said he hoped never to feel again. There were also caterpillars, many of them, all lined up upon the way, and if the gentlest touch of human flesh came upon them, they stung with every little hair on their woolly backs. I did what I could for Tarheto and Samuel Evans, who fell victim to a caterpillar, by using a plant with curative properties confirmed for me by Mr Banks.

This evening, on deck, Mr Banks discussed our Latitude with Captain. Mr Banks is disheartened by the fact that we are leaving the southern zone. 'Though we must go South again to round the Cape of Good Hope,' Mr Banks said, 'the plants I come upon now will most likely be plants seen before by Europeans.'

I was surprised at my reaction to Mr Banks's words. I felt a thrill as he spoke of rounding the Cape at the southernmost tip of Africa, returning home. I'm ready to leave the southern hemisphere, with all its strangeness. And I begin to turn longingly towards England. How curious to feel so.

PART XIV

Pierced Through

THURSDAY 24th *[New Holland – Lat. 23°52' S, Long. 208°37' W]* Left the Bay this morning before sunrise, catching a fair breeze from the south. Tarheto and I ate cold Bustard left from the Gentlemen's dinner, shot by Mr Banks yesterday. We were to feed the scraps to Mr Banks's greyhounds. We asked permission of the dogs and shared the Bustard four ways.

FRIDAY 25th TO SATURDAY 26th *[New Holland]* Crossed the Tropic of Capricorn again. This makes our fourth time. Two more times to go.

The soundings have been coming up irregular, some quite shallow. Captain has sent Master Molyneux in the boat ahead to guide us.

Caught sight of smoke from native fires a good distance inland. Mr Banks went out shooting in the small boat. The Gentlemen brought in crabs of a most beautiful blue colour.

SUNDAY 27th *[New Holland]* We are anchored with barely any clearance from the bottom. Master Molyneux went out with two boats at first light in search of a safe way out of these shoals. He returned with the report of no safe passage.

MONDAY 28th *[New Holland]* It is delicate going. Captain had the boat back out taking soundings. We have rocks, small islands and shoals between *Endeavour* and the Mainland, and larger islands between *Endeavour* and the open sea.

We pick our way slowly up the channel between the ever present danger. Master Molyneux, taking soundings from the small boat, signaled we were coming upon dangerous shoals a little before noon, and we dropped anchor just as a strong tide rushed round us. The soundings revealed we were anchored upon the worst of it, so we picked up *Endeavour's* skirts and tiptoed through. Anchored at dark.

TUESDAY 29th *[New Holland]* Captain found a good flow and ebb, and considered laying the ship ashore to clean her bottom. He and Master Molyneux went looking for a place convenient for such work and for fresh water. Mr Banks brought me along with the rest of his Company. To his satisfaction, Mr Banks found several new plants, and I saw with my own eyes a fish that went on land as happily as in the water.

We were troubled by mosquitoes and burrs that clung to and stung our flesh as we walked. Even so, we were not deterred and came upon a grove so filled with butterflies that we needed to part them as we walked. Butterflies rested upon every twig and stick, and filled the air with the sound of their soft wings. Mr Banks brought a Pupa back with him, and it opened during the night and let out a butterfly of velvet black with edges of brimstone.

WEDNESDAY 30th *[New Holland – Lat. 22°05′ S, Long. 210°24′ W]* Captain could not find water, nor fish, nor any other good thing to eat here. He has named this place Thirsty Sound.

THURSDAY 31st *[New Holland]* Put out at dawn with a good breeze at our backs and our faces full of mist and rain.

Forced to set anchor early, surrounded every which way by islands, rocks, and shallows!

FRIDAY 1st JUNE *[New Holland]* The weather has gone fine again after some dirty wind last night. Not many slept well in the storm knowing the cable might break in a moment and leave us to founder in the shallows. What have we gotten ourselves into along this coast of New Holland? This entire way is pimpled with danger. If Captain gets us through this, it will be nothing short of a miracle.

Kept along the rocky and barren coast until night, when we dropped anchor. Tupia complained that his gums were swelled and he'd been sore about the mouth for nearly two weeks. I brought him immediately to Surgeon Monkhouse, who began treatment for scurvy that moment, giving him Lemon extract to add to his drink.

SATURDAY 2nd *[New Holland]* We had a brief respite from the danger, a bit of smooth sailing. We could still see islands sprinkled across the face of the sea before us. But for some time we had a good channel. Then at noon the soundings became irregular again.

SUNDAY 3rd *[New Holland]* At the end of morning watch we took a passage between the Mainland and a group of Islands that Captain has called Whitsunday Passage for this day. The Mainland looks inviting here and green.

MONDAY 4th *[New Holland]* There were many places for safe anchor, but the moon was with us and the wind, and Captain did not wish to wait, so we sailed through the night. Early this morning we passed, on the Mainland, hills of great height. We are ever watchful for shoals. Seaweed drifting past makes our job more difficult. Passed a place where a mountain rose straight up out of the sea. Captain called it Cape Upstart.

TUESDAY 5th TO WEDNESDAY 6th *[New Holland]* We have tried our hand with our lines and hooks, but there has been not much fish about lately. Mr Banks took the small boat and returned with his hair and clothes plastered with perspiration.

THURSDAY 7th *[New Holland]* We spied something that looked like a Cocoa nutt tree, and several of the men urged Captain for permission to go ashore. To our disappointment the party discovered not Cocoa nutts, but a Cabbage Palm instead. Mr Banks did not waste the trip, though, gathering perhaps fifteen new plants. They are spread now before the ever wakeful Mr Parkinson.

FRIDAY 8th *[New Holland – Lat. 17°59' S, Long. 213°57' W]* As we passed by one of the Islands today, a group of natives stood together looking out at us. They were all naked, their skin dark, their hair short. We had grown accustomed to the natives ignoring us. This was a diverting change.

There are more fires onshore; they have a good smell to them. Lord and Lady Grey lift their noses to the scent.

I turned thirteen today. I wonder if anyone at home even thought of me.

SATURDAY 9th TO WEDNESDAY 13th *[New Holland]* Thought we might spend a day or so at anchor, but there was no fresh water or provisions to be found, so we set sail at midnight.

We were in water littered with coral reefs. But the moon came so bright and the ship ran so light and we were sounding continually.

At supper *Endeavour* sailed over top a bank only seven or eight fathoms from her bottom. Once we cleared that, we imagined ourselves past danger. Captain went about as usual, giving instructions and making certain all was well, and then retired for the night.

He had not been abed long when something went very wrong. I sprang from my hammock, with all the others, at the cry of 'All Hands'. We raced on deck to find we were stuck fast upon a rock. All through this voyage we had feared such a thing. The sound *Endeavour* made, I can still hear it. Her creaking and groaning had become so familiar, so comforting. But this, this was like a scream of agony, that went on and on.

We were not near shore. We had been running on a good wind about three hours off the coast, too far from land for any of us to have hope of reaching it.

Captain came on deck in his drawers and calmly took a measure of our circumstances, and with quiet confidence he directed us as to what we should do. The men spoke softly. We hoped it was not coral we had run upon, for coral has teeth to chew the bottom out of the best of ships. Let it be some rock or shoals that we might get clear of, we prayed.

The Officers did not yell nor make a flurry of confusion. I went aloft with the best climbers to take the sails down immediately, and all boats were hoisted out. Master Molyneux went out in one of them and sounded all round the ship. 'Twas his voice called out the readings. Each time he called out worse news. We were upon coral. And there was shoal water all round us.

Immediately we began lightening the ship. Casks went over. Our guns went over with buoys attached so we might retrieve them if we came out of this trouble. Iron and stone ballast went over. Hoops and staves and oil jars went over. Decayed stores went over.

Poor *Endeavour*, she was in agony without the buoyancy of the water to hold her up. Our hearts stuck in our throats and stayed there, listening to her labour. In the brilliant moonlight we saw pieces of *Endeavour* floating away.

As the tide ebbed, *Endeavour*'s agony increased as she settled hard down on her rock. There came such a groaning from under her starboard bow. It echoed throughout the fore storerooms. It made tears come to my eyes, to listen to her.

When day broke, we saw the land eight leagues distant. There was no land nearer. All this time we had been dogding around islands, and now there was not a single one in sight. To the good, the sea calmed and flattened and the wind died, so that we sat still, waiting for high water. We all worked with a quiet willingness. Not even the sail maker cursed.

High water came at eleven in the morning. We hoped with it to heave *Endeavour* off her reef, but she would not float. We threw more weight overboard. Anything to lighten her. But it was no good. She remained impaled on the coral.

Some of the men said the high tide at night came in greater than that during the day, and so we waited again in the hope that the sea would lift *Endeavour* from the spike of coral.

Two pumps could hardly keep up with the sea coming inside *Endeavour*. We all took turns manning them, changing hands every quarter hour. Mr Banks, Captain, all the Officers, Tupia and Tarheto, everyone pumped.

At Noon we were heeling to Starboard. The Pinnace touched bottom and lay useless beside *Endeavour*.

But then the tide began to rise. Our hearts beat hard to see the water level climbing, but poor *Endeavour*, the strain of being lifted doubled her pains. She groaned and shuddered and filled with seawater. We had three pumps working now, just keeping her clear. The fourth pump we could not get to work.

The tide almost floated her free, but she held to her reef. Mr Banks went quietly to his Cabin and began making preparations to abandon ship. We all looked upon one another knowing full well that death of some sort awaited us. Our only hope was to get off the rock and heave to shore before we sank. Then, perhaps, we could piece together a ship out of what was left of *Endeavour*, a ship seaworthy enough to get us all back to the East Indies for repairs.

The tide continued to rise, lifting our hopes of raising *Endeavour* off, but just as the tide rose outside of *Endeavour* and righted her again, so did it rush inside her, so that even with the three working pumps we could not keep up with the water coming in. If we did get her off this rock, once free she would take water on so fast we could never save her.

Now I knew I should not see home again.

And then I felt it. We were floating. She was free. And the boats were pulling her into deeper water.

We were exhausted. But no rest would be ours yet, for now the pumps were our only hope of survival.

When my turn came to pump, I relieved Isaac Smith. Mr Bootie had the job of keeping a measure of the depth of water rushing into the ship. We worked together. I stayed on longer than my quarter hour, for no man came to relieve me. When at last I was relieved, Mr Bootie came off, too, and Mr Monkhouse took over the measurement, whilst three new men laboured at the pumps.

But Mr Monkhouse's figures brought the worst news. The leak was gaining at an alarming rate. We would never reach land if *Endeavour* continued taking water so fast.

We were a sinking ship. Mr Bootie and I, hearing the cries, knew the worst at the same moment.

Captain called Mr Bootie back and I followed. Captain asked Mr Bootie to show Mr Monkhouse how he had taken his measure. And when this was done, it was discovered there was a mistake made. The men measured the amount of water coming in from two different points. It was proved she was taking no more water in than she had before we were relieved.

Once we knew that, we felt as if the hands of God were preserving us. And our entire Company stayed on those pumps and pumped with all our hearts, all our strength, all our hope, while Captain led us slowly to shore.

But it was a long way, and before another hour had passed, the leak truly was getting ahead of us. That's when Mr Monkhouse proposed fothering the ship. Some of the company had heard of such a practice but had never used it before, except for Mr Monkhouse. Fothering required the creation of a sling. We were to mix Oakum with wool and place the mixture upon an unused sail. The sail was to be sunk and wrapped under the belly of *Endeavour*. Because the ship was sucking seawater in, it should suck the Oakum-and-wool–covered sail in as well, plugging the hole.

We continued constantly working the three pumps as preparations were made for the fothering. Whilst most of us laboured to keep *Endeavour* from sinking, Captain led the remainder of the men to work the sails and run us towards land.

When the fothering sail was ready, it was taken over the side. With careful cooperation and delicate maneuvering, the men managed to apply the sail to the bottom of the ship and fasten it by ropes at each corner till it was drawn tight.

One half hour later we found only a single pump was needed. I could have fallen at the feet of Mr Monkhouse.

I am grateful to be on this ship with such men. Never did anyone step out of line nor speak regrettably to another. Captain, through all of this, remained calm, as did his Officers, and so did we all. We could have lost not only our lives before the ship went down, we could have lost our dignity, too. We lost neither.

We made our way slowly to shore, picking a course between the shoals, with the boats ahead guiding us.

At 9 A.M. today we passed two small islands with not much more than bush and sand to commend them, but they would have been salvation. And so Captain called them Hope Islands, for our Hope was to reach them before we perished. But he did not bring us in there. He continued to search for the best location for our repairs.

Mr Magra, who Captain suspected of doing the mischief to Mr Orton's ears, was restored to duty. He had been released to help save the ship in her greatest peril and then voluntarily returned to confinement after. Captain cleared him of all charges.

Dropped anchor at dark. The Pinnace went ahead and came back in the night with the news that she had found the place for us to repair. I am grateful, for it is disagreeable, at best, knowing there is only a ball of wool standing between our life and our death.

PART XV

Between a Rock and a Hard Place

JUNE 1770

THURSDAY 14th *[New Holland – Lat. 15°26′ S]* Halfway through morning watch we sailed, our small boats going ahead and pointing up to us the shoals we must avoid as we inched our way in. The wind soon had us boxed in by the shoals. Had this wind been blowing whilst we were hung up on the coral, we would not have survived. Even with all our sails furled, the wind would have battered and sunk us, without doubt.

Captain dropped anchor and called the boats back and went out himself, with an eager Mr Banks. They took the measure of the Channel. When he and Mr Banks returned, they were clearly pleased. They had discovered a river that enters the harbour near here, the measure of which is perfectly suited to our needs. In all our travels, Captain said, a more commodious berth has not been seen.

FRIDAY 15th *[New Holland]* Rain through the night. Wind too fresh to navigate the shoals today. Spent our time slaking our weariness and lightening the ship forward in order to bring her gently to shore to repair the leak. One single pump is still keeping well above the water coming in.

Spotted a single fire where we intend to rest the ship. It is Mr Banks's hope that we shall at last have a chance to better know these shy natives.

SATURDAY 16th *[New Holland]* Tried again to weigh anchor and sail to shore, but the wind was not with us. More natives sighted, more fires. I wonder if these fires are not for food and warmth but are signals to other natives along these shores. I wonder if they are each telling the other of our appearance in this harbour. Tupia has not responded to the lemon extract in his drink. Nor to any other medicine Surgeon Monkhouse has given him. He has bad spots upon his legs and every other symptom of scurvy. He is desperately ill. Tarheto will not leave his side. I do what I can for him. Mr Green is also showing signs of the disease. We must get to shore as soon as possible, Dr Monkhouse says, or we shall lose them both and more.

SUNDAY 17th *[New Holland]* We've done it. We've brought *Endeavour* ashore. Dr Solander and Mr Banks wasted no time but were off at a run collecting plants.

We have *Endeavour* close by the beach and are emptying her so we might get her out of the water to do the necessary repairs.

MONDAY 18th *[New Holland]* Erected a tent for the Sick and got them ashore. Later I was sent with a party to gather what fresh greens could be found. Brought back something Captain called Sea Purslane and a kind of bean I found growing on a creeping Vine. We have eight who are ill now with various disorders.

But Tupia is completely recovered. He began eating fresh food the moment we got here, and he is now well as ever before. Mr Green, however, is still in a bad way.

TUESDAY 19th *[New Holland]* The Purslane and the beans are working to good effect for the ill.

Captain had the Marines bring the remaining four guns out and mounted on the quarterdeck.

The hold is empty of stores, the Smith's Forge assembled, and the Armourer and his mate hammering out nails.

Mr Banks was out shooting Pigeons and crows today. Some of the Pigeons he brought back were beautiful.

Hard rain tonight.

WEDNESDAY 20th *[New Holland]* Emptied the Officers' stores out of *Endeavour* today. Nothing remains in the Fore and Main holds now but Coal. Brought the Powder out, and the stone ballast and wood still remaining aboard. Mr Banks is busy drying his new plants on a sail in the improved weather. The ship is satisfactorily lightened of her burdens.

THURSDAY 21st *[New Holland]* All Hands were at work today clearing ship's hold of Coal. Tonight, with the high tide, we pulled *Endeavour* out of the water and onto shore. She's out just enough, we can get her off again when the time comes. But how forlorn she looks, half out of water, rolled onto her side like a beached whale.

FRIDAY 22nd *[New Holland]* The tide went out halfway through middle watch, and we got our first look at the damage. The hole is a big one. The coral bit *Endeavour* a little forward, Starboard side. It made its way through four Planks and damaged three more. We were hit at a place particularly solid built or we would have seen more destruction. Most amazing was that sticking in the hole in *Endeavour* was still the chunk of Coral. The very thing that nearly finished us became the thing that saved us, for had the coral not remained embedded in *Endeavour's* hide, we should surely have sunk from the water pouring into the unobstructed hole.

By the forenoon watch the Carpenters had begun their work. I helped dig a well for fresh water.

Some of the men who went out after more Pigeons came back with stories of an animal they saw larger than Mr Banks's greyhounds, mouse coloured and very fast.

SATURDAY 23rd *[New Holland]* The men went out with the seine and tried all day to catch fish but came back with only three. We know there are fish about. We see them leaping around us, but they will not be easily taken.

The Carpenters have finished their work on the Starboard side. At high tide tonight we heeled *Endeavour* over the other way, careful to set her down where we can get her back off again.

SUNDAY 24th *[New Holland]* The Carpenters began work this morning under the Larboard bow.

Lieutenant Gore took a party inland in search of provisions. They returned with some Palm Cabbage and small Plantains.

Isaac Smith said Captain saw one of those animals this morning. It had a long tail and it jumped like a deer. Another man came back with the report of a devilish creature of flight, a very strong black in colour with horns upon its head.

The Carpenters worked all day on the Larboard side until the tide came up to stop them.

MONDAY 25th *[New Holland]* I saw the leaping creature today that they talk about! It is not so much like a greyhound. It is unlike anything ever seen. It goes very fast, somewhat like a rabbit, covering six or eight feet in a single hop.

The Carpenters finished their work at low water this evening. We lashed casks under *Endeavour's* bows to get her floating, but the casks were not lashed well enough and we were unable to get her out.

TUESDAY 26th *[New Holland]* Prepared to float *Endeavour* off again this morning.

Mr Banks took a terrible blow today. Many of the plants he had stored in the bread room were discovered underwater from the shifting of *Endeavour* during her repairs. He brought out and dried what he could, but some of his plants have been lost for ever. I have not seen Mr Banks so distressed since the death of Mr Buchan. What a foul turn.

WEDNESDAY 27th *[New Holland]* The Armourers are kept busy with repairing Iron, whilst the Carpenters caulk *Endeavour* and put a fresh stock on one of her spare anchors. Captain took the

Pinnace and tried fishing with the seine net again, taking only twenty to thirty pounds of fish. He gave the catch to us, and we are using it to feed the sick.

A new source of food was discovered yesterday during one of the marches into the woods. It is a kind of taro root, which we tried. The root was too acrid to eat, but the leaves, boiled, are not much different than spinach. There is also a sort of plum, too hard and sour to eat at first, but easier after a few days.

THURSDAY 28th *[New Holland]* Tupia showed us how to cook the Taro roots in his pit oven, and they certainly tasted better. But the roots are so small as to make them a poor choice to bring aboard. Instead we are gathering the greens that grow at the top of the Taro plant, which some of the men call Indian Kale.

Tonight Captain and Mr Green, who is entirely recovered, spent a great deal of time taking observations and making calculations.

FRIDAY 29th TO SATURDAY 30th *[New Holland]* We have not seen a single native since we made landing here. The men are having luck getting fish, though, and gathering greens.

Captain went into the hills to take a better view of the Sea. He returned to the ship more stern than usual. The tide was low and he saw much in the way of sandbanks and shoals wherever he looked.

John Charlton said Captain has decided that we shall stay along the shore, heading in a Northward direction, for this seems the only possible channel. Retracing our way south is impossible. The wind is not with us in that direction.

Lieutenant Gore spotted some small dogs, fast and straw

coloured.

The men took the nets upriver and brought back 213 pounds of fish. Captain had Mr Thompson prepare the Greens boiled up with Pease. Served together with the men's catch, it made a very satisfying meal.

SUNDAY 1st JULY *[New Holland]* One party went fishing, meeting again with good success. The rest of us were allowed to explore this place, for Captain has no fear from the natives here. And Mr Perry said I could be spared for the afternoon.

It was hot today and many of the men were lazy, but Tarheto and I had a wonderful time. He took me to a place where ants had built enormous hills as far as one could see. We explored, looking for more of the leaping creatures, but only spotted some of the small dogs, which are not quite dogs.

The ship is ready for departure. Tomorrow the tide is at its highest, and we hope to haul *Endeavour* off.

MONDAY 2nd *[New Holland]* Dew heavy this morning, which it has not been since we stopped here, and wind off the land, something else we have not yet encountered in this place. Lashed empty casks to the Ship's underside at low water in the hopes of floating her off tonight.

The men in the fishing party brought in another good catch.

We have harvested the leaves from the Wild Plantain trees for Mr Banks. Tupia and Tarheto are in charge, and some of the men are weaving baskets to keep Mr Banks's plants from going to rot until he can make his studies of them. The plants are also being dried on paper, exposed to the sun during the day, but they must be safe away before the damp of night comes and until the damp of morning has left. Mr Banks has appointed one man to be responsible for the watching and turning and covering of the leaves. He asked Dr Monkhouse if he might have me for the job since I did it so well last time, but Dr Monkhouse said he could not spare me.

The tide did not come up high enough, not as high as we expected, and *Endeavour*, looking every bit the half-beached whale, could not be brought off.

TUESDAY 3rd *[New Holland]* Master Molyneux came back with the Pinnace this morning after taking the measure of our situation all yesterday and last night. At low water the shoals are so high he got out and walked upon them. There he found an empty shell so enormous he could climb inside of it. He also brought shell-fish stranded upon the shoals back with him in the Pinnace. In his explorations the Master came upon a group of natives who fled at his approach, leaving behind their supper of fresh Sea Eggs. Master Molyneux says he sees a way we can come past many of the shoals, but not all.

Tonight the tide came up high, and we floated *Endeavour* and hauled her offshore. We had an Alligator swimming with us for some time and Garfish all about us, leaping from the sea. Several landed on deck and we were glad of them.

WEDNESDAY 4th *[New Holland]* We spent the morning in search of a place to lay the ship ashore again in order to work on her Larboard side. John Ramsay said she sat for too long out of the water and has sprung a plank between decks. We brought her in again tonight in high water.

THURSDAY 5th *[New Holland]* Mr Banks took advantage of this new development to explore the beach, finding many fruits, many plants, we had not yet seen.

Captain had the Carpenters under *Endeavour* to see what damage they could. Even at low water she was too wet to make repairs. The Master Carpenter said she has some sheathing gone and the Main plank is a little rubbed, but she is seaworthy.

Captain had us heave her off her side at high water and moor her beside the beach, where we've sheltered our stores and provisions.

FRIDAY 6th *[New Holland]* Carried the stores back on board along with fresh water, which we hauled down to the after hold. Several of the casks we threw overboard in our attempt to get off the coral have returned to us on the tide, but most, Francis Haite says, are lost to us forever.

'Can we get home without them?' I asked.

Francis Haite nodded. 'As long as we've got a ship, we can.'

Mr Banks and Lieutenant Gore took Tupia and Tarheto and headed up the River after some of the animals we have observed. We shall not see them for several days.

SATURDAY 7th *[New Holland]* The day goes fast, for I am ever employed with the work of Dr Monkhouse and the ship. He is a good man, Dr Monkhouse, though hopelessly disorganized. I must remind myself at times that he and Mr Monkhouse are brothers. I have never seen a man more precise, nor more good looking than Mr Monkhouse, nor have I seen a man more intelligent or careless in appearance than the Doctor. But they are both fine men, and caring brothers. I wonder if my brothers would have been the same with me if we had not been separated after mother's death?

SUNDAY 8th *[New Holland]* Master Molyneux and Mr Bootie were out most of the day and brought back three turtles captured with the boat hook. Another party hauled in eighty pounds of fish. I worked beside Dr Monkhouse, for it was no fun for me to have leave without Tarheto along. Mr Banks and his party returned as afternoon watch ended.

Tarheto had so much to tell. Samuel, who had come in hope of a lesson, went away again. Tarheto said the insects never left them alone the entire time. They lit fires, even in this baking heat, to keep the mosquitoes off, but the mosquitoes came right through the smoke nearly into the fire to reach them. The first day they stayed in the canoe, passing mangroves and land much as we have seen here at the watering place. The second day the party went on foot in search of game. Lord and Lady Grey chased after two of the beasts, which were so fast they outleaped the dogs. Tarheto said they fairly flew over top the tall grass.

'They go on two legs,' he said. 'Not four.'

The only animal I know that goes on two legs is man.

MONDAY 9th *[New Holland]* Mr Banks and Master Molyneux went out again this morning with proper gear for taking turtles but found none. Master Molyneux refused to come back. He, like Mr Bootie, is a stubborn man, and Mr Banks grew impatient with him. Finally Lieutenant Gore went out in the yawl and ordered Master Molyneux back.

The Carpenters, Smiths, and Coopers are all at their work, and the rest of us bring stone ballast aboard.

Captain put out in the boat when two natives came down to shore near our mooring, but immediately they ran away.

We had yesterday's turtle for dinner. It is nearly as good as roast pork. And a particular treat on a Banyan day.

TUESDAY 10th *[New Holland]* Four natives brought their canoe to the water near our mooring to fish this morning. Mr Banks wished to go out immediately to them, but Captain said no. Leave them alone. Ignore them and see what it brings us. What it brought were two very shy natives who came close enough to our Ship that we could hear them, though we could not understand a word they said. We threw some presents to them – cloth, nails, paper. They took these things without much enthusiasm. We signalled to them to come closer, which after some time they did, and we gave them more presents. They held up their weapons from time to time, shaking them at us, a warning, I think, that they would defend themselves if we treated them wrongly.

By accident a fish was thrown to them, and this they received with great pleasure. They landed their canoe close to the ship. Tupia came to them and sat with them. Captain joined him with more presents, beads, cloth. They seemed comfortable with this meeting, unless someone came close to their Arms.

At dinnertime Captain invited the natives by way of signs to join him at Table, but the natives declined, and when Tupia and Captain left them, they quickly departed in their canoe.

We examined the bread stores today. A good part of it was in such bad condition we had to discard it. About the same amount was very damaged, but we must eat it anyway.

WEDNESDAY 11th *[New Holland]* We had another visit from the natives today, two from yesterday and two new men. One wore a piece of bone in a hole through his nose. I don't think the bone was human.

They brought a fish, which they gave as a present. But some of our Company came too close and these shy men retired without taking leave, paddling away.

THURSDAY 12th *[New Holland]* Master Molyneux brought turtle back during the night, so Captain sent him out again in the yawl this morning. More natives came today, seeking out Tupia in his and Tarheto's tent whilst I was there. This time seven – five men, a woman, and a boy. The woman and boy did not come close to us but stayed instead on a point along the shore. The woman was naked everywhere women are supposed to be covered. They were all naked but for red and white paint upon their bodies. They seem to give no thought to wearing a stitch of clothing, though sometimes when they stand, their hands cover their privy parts. Tupia gave them a gift of fish, but they did not want raw fish, they wanted Tarheto to cook it for them, which was done. They ate part of the offering and gave the rest to Mr Banks's greyhounds.

These natives are a small and slender people. They are dark in colour, but I think in part that darkness comes from smoke and dirt upon their skin. Some have curl to their hair, some have straight hair, soft like European hair. They follow everything with their eyes, which are bright and alert.

They have only a few ornaments they wear upon their arms, and the bone they wear in their nose is fishbone, John Ramsay says, not human. Their language is not like Tarheto's, nor is it like ours, but I think it is more like ours. Their lances resemble those we have seen before in this country, with the sting of the stingray upon their tips. We asked, using gestures, about the leaping beasts. The natives called these Kanguru.

FRIDAY 13th *[New Holland]* All the water is got on board now and the bread we could save. Master Molyneux and his turtlers went out again this evening.

SATURDAY 14th *[New Holland]* Lieutenant Gore, out in the country, shot one of the marvelous Kangurus that go on two legs. It's a little one. Its head and neck and shoulders and front legs are very small in proportion to the rest of it, with a tail near as long as its body and thick close to the hind end, tapering as it stretches out. The fur is short and the colour of mouse. And never in my entire life have I seen nor imagined a creature anything like it.

SUNDAY 15th *[New Holland]* With leave today Tarheto and I went about the land hunting turtles. I am afraid of the alligators, but Tarheto laughs at me. We had the Kanguru Lieutenant Gore shot for our dinner today. I liked it even better than roast pork.

Worked with Samuel.

MONDAY 16th TO TUESDAY 17th *[New Holland]* As Captain prepared to leave, he was much occupied with observations and measurements. Tupia and Tarheto, onshore, were approached by three natives who offered them long roots, about the thickness of a finger and good tasting. Captain, Dr Solander, and Mr Banks joined them and brought presents of beads, but when they followed the natives in hopes of learning more about them, the natives signaled for the Company to leave them go.

WEDNESDAY 18th *[New Holland]* Mr Banks and Captain climbed for a view of the Seacoast. They are an odd match, these two men. Mr Banks, young and handsome, his eyes warm, his hair untamed. In contrast, Captain is old, stern, with cold eyes, his hair and clothing in perfect order. They have not always agreed on this voyage. Living so close, there are often misunderstandings. But we have all reached a certain agreement. All of us. Captain and Mr Banks are no exception.

The two returned to *Endeavour*, their faces wearing a look of melancholy. John Charlton said Captain cannot see a clear way out of this place, only channels threading through the reefs.

Whilst they were away, several natives came aboard who were very much interested in the turtles we had captured.

THURSDAY 19th *[New Holland]* A group of natives came aboard this morning desiring that we should give them two of our turtles. This, Captain would not do. The natives grew unhappy. Angrily, they pushed Mr Banks. We offered them bread, which they scorned. It was turtle they wanted and nothing else.

They left the ship, and taking some fire from under a boiling pitch pot, they set the grass to flame around everything we had left ashore, which was one of Mr Banks's tents still left up from when Tupia was sick, the forge, and a sow with a litter of piglets. One piglet was scorched to death in the fire, but Mr Banks managed to save the tent.

The natives then moved to a place where our nets and our linen were drying in the sun, and they set fire to the grass again. Captain shot off a musket to stop them, and they ran off, one native slightly injured. We managed to save the nets and the linen and put out the second fire, but the first spread back into the woods. Later today they set part of the inland wood afire. Tonight it burned and burned.

In spite of the destruction, it was a beautiful sight. I did not imagine a fire could burn so fast or so hungrily as the fires the natives have set today. We are lucky that so little of our supplies remained onshore.

FRIDAY 20th *[New Holland] Endeavour* is as prepared as she can be to set sail. She is taking on water still but at a rate we can survive. We are ready to leave this place. We are ready to go home.

SATURDAY 21st TO SUNDAY 22nd *[New Holland]* The wind blows dirty and we cannot depart. The turtlers brought back a turtle today with a wooden lance stuck through its shoulder. The natives must have tried to strike it on land, maybe when it came up to lay eggs. But the turtle got away long ago, for the wound was healed over. The creature, however, did not get away from our turtlers.

John Charlton was out gathering Indian Kale when he became lost from his group and encountered natives, who frightened him very much. He said they were in the act of roasting part of a Kanguru, and he feared they might roast him next. But they were civil and seemed interested only in examining and touching his body, rejecting his gift of a knife, which was all he had with him to give. They let him go after some time, directing him towards *Endeavour.* He was never so glad to catch sight of the old girl, and we were never so glad to catch sight of him.

MONDAY 23rd *[New Holland]* Mr Banks, out Botanizing, discovered a pile of all the clothing we had given the natives as presents. He did not wonder that if he looked beyond that point, he would find all the other presents made them, for they wanted nothing from us but food. But if we are to survive the next part of our voyage, that is the one thing we cannot afford to give away.

TUESDAY 24th TO THURSDAY 26th *[New Holland]* The weather continues foul. We spend the days making rope, caulking the ship, and fishing.

FRIDAY 27th *[New Holland]* More fish caught in the Seine, and Lieutenant Gore shot one of the Kangurus, a big one.

SATURDAY 28th *[New Holland]* Mr Banks has many plants from this place, and though he looks for new ones, he is unsuccessful.

Mr Thompson served the big leaper Lieutenant Gore shot yesterday. It did not taste the least bit good. In fact, it had no taste at all. Maybe it was too old.

How we all wish the wind would change and we could sail away from this place and start in earnest on our journey home.

SUNDAY 29th *[New Holland]* We had hope of sailing today, for the wind calmed and then picked up from the land. Captain sent a boat out to test the depth on the sandbar, but there was not depth enough. Not even for our shallow-draughted *Endeavour*.

The turtlers went out. We've nearly exhausted our supply of that good meat. The fishermen went out, too, to haul the seine, but they came back with only twenty pounds. And then the wind shifted, from the sea again, and we had not moved a bit.

Mr Banks took Lord and Lady Grey out, and they brought down a Kanguru. It was a little one. The big ones are far too fast even for the speedy greyhounds.

MONDAY 30th *[New Holland]* The winds are more moderate, but they are from the SE, which is no good to us. Mr Thompson said today as I worked with him in the Galley preparing a mixture for Dr Monkhouse that though we are on ration, Captain eats no more, no less, than any man on the ship. He has the same amount served him as I am served. Captain is a wondrous man, I think. I did not have a very high opinion of certain men when I came aboard. Captain has taught me that a man might be stern, even harsh, and still be fair.

TUESDAY 31st TO THURSDAY 2nd AUGUST *[New Holland]* The wind continues dirty, and hardly a fish caught in the Seine.

FRIDAY 3rd *[New Holland]* At last, halfway through morning watch, the weather moderated and we unmoored. But we could not clear the sand and had to anchor again just within the bar.

Mr Banks is impatient with us and not at all the Gentleman he once was. He's become a quarrelsome man who wishes to be away from this place. Well, we all wish to be away from this place. We are doing what we can. Each day we sit at anchor we consume our supplies, and it is yet a long journey to the East Indies before we might restock.

SATURDAY 4th TO SUNDAY 5th *[New Holland]* Captain anchored us in fifteen fathoms so that he could have a look from the mast-head at low water and see what best we could do next, whether to backtrack to the south, to try our way to the east, or to inch our way north. Any way it will be dangerous. After careful consideration Captain has chosen a course NE.

While we waited for the tide to come in high, the men ventured out after whatever turtles and shellfish they could find. They came back with a great many clams of a wonderful size, one turtle, and a stingray. We dropped our lines tonight, and several of the seamen caught shark, which now I eat. It's a wonder what the stomach will allow the mind to accept.

With the Pinnace guiding us, we got under way this afternoon, though we did not get far. Stopped before night with a shoal directly in our path.

MONDAY 6th TO TUESDAY 7th *[New Holland]* The wind is a perilous threat in this water. During the night we dragged our anchors. All sails were furled and the ship snug as possible, yet still *Endeavour* was carried by wind and water closer and closer to the shoals. We had but one anchor remaining, the sheet anchor, but before we had chance to get it out, our fortune changed and *Endeavour* ceased her drift and held.

How we long for a way out of this maze of rocks and shallows. But Captain is resolved. There is no passage to sea. Standing between us and open water is a long ridge of rocks barring our way. We have left to us only a careful winding in and out of the shoals. It is a fearful task facing us to take such a course with the winds so inconstant and no promise that the sea will ever open to us.

What if we creep northward only to find ourselves locked in by these reefs, shall we never get back? Exploring uncharted waters carries a price I never imagined.

WEDNESDAY 8th *[New Holland]* The night was very long and very dark, and we did not know whether our anchors would hold or at any moment we would feel the sickening crunch of *Endeavour* upon a reef. But with dawn came the relief of seeing we were still upon the same place as the night before.

The wind and weather kept us sitting tight until evening. Captain has just ordered the topmasts up.

THURSDAY 9th *[New Holland]* Midway through morning watch Captain had us heaving in Cable. The men are weary and disheartened. There is so much Cable out and the work so hard bringing it in again. But still they do as Captain bids. He is applying everything he knows to deliver us safe from this peril we are in.

The men had not hauled at the Anchor Cable long before the wind and sea blew with such a head that they had to let it all go again. And once more we wait with the Breakers crashing all round us.

FRIDAY 10th *[New Holland – Lat. 14°51' S, Long. 214°43' W]* Edged around four small Islands, keeping ourselves between them and the Mainland. For a brief time in our sailing we thought we had passed the danger, that the Great Reef had reached its end and the sea would open for us now. We were full of congratulations for ourselves. But we were mistaken. And then, as if in punishment for our rejoicing, the men at the masthead cried that we had land everywhere round us, in every direction. That we were entirely landlocked.

Captain set anchor and took a boat ashore to climb upon a hill and get a view of what next awaited us. To our relief our men were wrong, it was not all land, but many, many islands. Tomorrow Captain will take the boat and see if there is some way of getting past the reef and reaching the sea. But today we must live with the understanding that we are not the least out of danger's way. Captain called this place Cape Flattery, for here we flattered ourselves into believing we were free.

SATURDAY 11th TO SUNDAY 12th *[New Holland]* There is a break, a narrow channel running from inside the coral reefs out to the open sea. And so we shall be out of this danger as soon as we make our way through.

MONDAY 13th *[New Holland]* Whilst I was with Goat last night I overheard Captain discuss our situation with Lieutenant Hicks. If we stay within the Great Reef, we are in clear danger. If we are delayed in making towards the East Indies much longer, we shall not make them at all. Captain said the wind blows from the Southeast from June to October but reverses itself in November and blows from the North-west. We could not fight the strength of those winds battering against us. We would make no headway and run out of Provisions before we saw the Indies. Any longer delay shall surely prove our end.

We have three months' or less Provisions remaining on Board, have been on ration for some time, and now Captain plans on restricting our allowance even more. After considering all of our choices, Captain has decided to take us out through the passage in the Great Reef. He is disappointed to miss the opportunity of charting the part of the coast we must leave, but he puts our safety first and will sail us north, away from the coast, until such time as it is safe to come back to it again.

So at first light the Pinnace set out ahead of us, sounding, and we followed her, making our way towards the freedom of the open sea. As forenoon watch ended we relieved the Pinnace of her work, for the depth was increasing the closer we came to the Reefs.

No sooner did we sail through the channel and beyond the breakers than the soundings showed us in deep, safe sea.

Since late May, when first we wandered into this trouble, we have all worked every moment of day and night with sail and anchor, with cable and rigging, trying to keep *Endeavour* from disaster. We are a tired crew.

The sheer depth of the open sea moves my heart with a swell of gratitude.

PART XVI

Great Barrier Reef

AUGUST 1770

TUESDAY 14th *[New Holland – Lat. 13°46' S]* With the rolling sea from the East we are taking on more water, nine inches per hour, with one pump working all the time. This is a small price to pay for being free of the danger we have just been in. By Noon we had no land in sight at all, and though at times on this journey the sight of Land has been our only goal, today the sight of uninterrupted sea comforts us all.

We sailed North with the cockiness of a ship full of men given a reprieve from certain disaster.

WEDNESDAY 15th *[New Holland]* Began moving *Endeavour* back to the Westward so we do not miss the Passage between New

Holland and the land to the North of it, which is called New Guinea.

At Noon we caught sight of land from the Masthead. An hour later we caught sight of the Great Reef again. The Reef rises like a wall built straight from the sea's bottom.

How the sea must hate that wall of coral standing in its path, for the waves break upon the reef with a fury. It's as if the sea is determined to tear the reef down. The breakers are ever exploding against it, in mountain-high surges.

THURSDAY 16th *[New Holland]* It happened so suddenly. The sea itself turned against us and began drawing us from the open water, back to the Great Reef.

The wind died near the end of middle watch. We had not even the use of our sails to keep us off.

One moment we were safe and the next we were being swept towards disaster. Desperately we sounded for ground, for a place to sink our anchor and hold us off the Reef. There was no ground to be found.

The sun had not yet pulled itself up to the horizon when our ears filled with the roar of the breakers upon the Reef. At first light the sight that met our eyes filled us all with utter terror. Foaming mountains of sea broke upon the Reef before us.

We worked together with remarkable calm, but the Pinnace was under repair and the Longboat stowed well away. Yesterday we believed we would have no need of either of them for a long time. We believed ourselves to be totally out of danger.

The Carpenter hastened his repairs of the Pinnace. Desperate, we continued our soundings from the deck of *Endeavour*, but there was nothing to hold us back from calamity.

It seemed a matter of moments before only a single valley of the sea stood between us and the Breakers. On the next swell we would rise with the water and be dashed to pieces. We hoped now only for a quick end. There was no chance of getting away. The boats, had they even been out, would have been smashed along with our ship.

We all prepared ourselves, when from the air a small wind sprang. It was a wind so small we would have given it no notice if we were becalmed under ordinary circumstances. But so desperately did we need the faintest breath of air that we placed the sails, each one in a way to catch it. And we did catch it. *Endeavour* moved. She moved in a slant away from the Breakers.

With the moments this light air gained us, we got the Longboat out and sent her ahead to tow us to safety. For ten priceless minutes we sailed that faint breeze. And then it died and we were at the mercy of the waves again.

We tested with bits of paper cast into the sea to determine if the Longboat was having any effect on our direction. What we found was that we were not moving out of danger but at best holding on at the brink of disaster.

And then our little breeze returned. Again we took it in every sail and used it to carry us a little more out of the reach of the Breakers before it once again died.

Now perhaps one hundred yards more stood between us and death, when a small opening was sighted in the Reef. It was a very small opening, barely enough room for *Endeavour* to come through, but we had no choice. We must sail for it and through it if we were to survive.

For as far as we could see, to the south and to the north, the sea rose up and hurled itself upon the Great Reef but for this one place, where the sea was quiet. It was our only chance.

But how could we move *Endeavour* from here to there?

And then, for the third time, our little breeze returned and pushed us nearly there. We stood at the mouth of the opening in the Great Reef. But to our astonishment we were not being pushed through, in fact we were being pushed away from it. The Tide! The Tide was going out, rushing out through the passage.

It carried us out to sea, away from the Reef. The boats, for now we had them all out, even the Pinnace, continued towing us with all possible haste in partnership with the Tide.

And then we were off the Reef and out at sea.

But then the tide began to turn. The flood that helped us escape from death was now determined to carry us back to it. Our wind had not returned. And even if it had, we could not use it for anything but to find another passage through the reef, for it was now clear we could not escape it.

Lieutenant Hicks went out in the small boat to find another opening in the Great Reef. We struggled to hold *Endeavour* back. Sometimes we gained a little distance from disaster, sometimes we lost. We were still not under the full strength of the Tide, which would overpower our meager efforts when it came fully into its height.

The Lieutenant came back. He'd found an opening, like the last, impossibly narrow. But with good anchorage once we made it through.

Without a moment to consider, we turned *Endeavour* towards the opening and surrendered to the Tide. It carried us faster and faster until suddenly we were upon the opening. Then we were through it with such wonderful speed that we had no time to fear the narrowness.

By the first dog watch this afternoon we came to anchor in the midst of the shoals that three days before we were so desperate to escape.

Three days ago we felt blessed at our deliverance from these shoals. Today we feel blessed at our deliverance unto them.

FRIDAY 17th *[New Holland – Lat. 12°42' S, Long. 217°15' W]* Captain holds us at anchor. John Ravenhill, the sail maker, works and curses, curses and works, repairing the damaged sails.

SATURDAY 18th *[New Holland]* Got under way during morning watch with two boats ahead to lead us, bearing to the NW with soundings changing sharply from one to the next. The Tide is running strong, which makes us all hope that there is truly a water passage out. The water is smooth, though, a reminder that the Great Reef stands as a Barrier between us and the open sea.

SUNDAY 19th *[New Holland]* Headed towards an island just a little off the Main. Passed through a difficult field of shoals to reach it. But the boats and the lookout from the Masthead found us a fair Channel that brought us a little way.

MONDAY 20th *[New Holland – Lat. 11°23' S, Long. 217°46' W]* The morning brought a fresh breeze from the East, and we sailed with it, hauling this way and that through the maze of shoals. The Yawl continues searching for turtles and joining up with us and searching again. We are getting very good at spotting the shoals.

Looking towards the Mainland, we count many fires. It is best sailing close in. The shoals grow more numerous the closer we come to the Reefs, so we stay well to the Mainland side.

TUESDAY 21st *[New Holland]* The weather has been good to us ever since we escaped our death at the Reef. Francis Haite thinks we are at last upon the Passage between New Holland and New Guinea. I hope he's correct.

Tarheto has suffered through these dangerous days, clinging to Tupia. Today was the first I've heard his laugh in what seems like months.

Saw natives attired somewhat different from the others. Though some held lances, one held bow and arrows, which we have not seen among these people. Some wore ornaments around their necks that Mr Banks says are made from Mother-of-pearl shell. Captain dropped anchor and prepared to go ashore to examine whether we were in a bay or the passage itself. As the landing party came within reach, the natives walked away. The landing proved more than satisfying. We are in a strait with a strong tide this evening drawing us towards the East Indies.

We have seen the entire East coast of this land, which Captain Cook has claimed in the name of England. No European has ever seen or dared what we have. The Western Coast may belong to the Dutch. But the East Coast is ours, and we have most certainly earned it.

Captain and his party on land fired off three volleys of small arms and offered up three cheers to mark the occasion. Here aboard *Endeavour* we fired off three volleys and three cheers in answer.

WEDNESDAY 22nd TO THURSDAY 23rd *[Endeavour Strait – Lat. 10°33' S, Long. 219°22' W]* We've come out to a greater depth, losing sight of the Mainland. Mr Banks and Captain explored an Island, which they found empty but for bird dung and the birds themselves, called Boobies. They shot a few and brought them back to the ship, along with several new plants for Mr Banks's collection.

Captain returned in a rare mood. He has proved that no land connects New Holland to New Guinea.

Our discoveries, after all our trials, after more than two years, are at an end. We have one thing left to do now. We must bring *Endeavour* home.

PART XVII

The East Indies

FRIDAY 24th *[To the East Indies]* I'm not certain which is more worn through, *Endeavour* or the men that sail her. We lost the best bower anchor this morning; the cable broke as we were weighing her in. Captain set a buoy and dropped another anchor immediately. We went back and tried recovering the lost bower but kept missing it. Finally this evening we located it. Nearly had the anchor aboard when the hawser slipped and we lost the bower again.

SATURDAY 25th *[To the East Indies – Lat. 10°18' S, Long. 219°39' W]* Got the anchor on our first sweep this morning, weighed the other anchor, and got under way. No land in sight today. Met with more shoals around dinnertime, which forced us to drop anchor.

These shoals were more dangerous than any others so far, for we did not know we were upon them until almost too late. The water had the deceiving appearance of cloud shadows upon it. Once again we seem to have great fortune with us, for we surely would have wrecked the ship upon this shoal had we had low water or a moment less of notice.

SUNDAY 26th TO MONDAY 27th *[To the East Indies]* Sailed all last night, tacking four hours to one tack, four hours to the other, with even soundings all the way, heading Northward towards New Guinea. At dinner Mr Bootie sent the alarm up that we were approaching shoals again, but Captain determined the alarm unfounded, for it was only a bank of brownish-coloured scum that some of the men call sea sawdust.

'Never mind, Mr Bootie,' I said. 'We're all perked as cats on the prowl.'

Mr Bootie made no answer. But neither did he give me a blow or a cuff, as he once might have.

TUESDAY 28th *[To the East Indies – Lat. 8°52' S, Long. 221°27' W]* Land sighted from the Masthead in the afternoon.

WEDNESDAY 29th *[Through the East Indies]* Captain has identified the land by his charts as the island Saint Bartholomew. Tarheto noted with great excitement that the island had Cocoa Nutt trees upon it. Tarheto still believes that most of this world is similar to OTahiti. Wait until he's had a look at London.

THURSDAY 30th *[Through the East Indies]* Finding no way to come closer to the island, we stretched off to sea and at daylight saw land again. We've come upon what Captain thinks is Point Saint Augustine. Again our soundings proved ill favoured for an approach. We passed through several large beds of the sea sawdust. Blisters, what a stink came off it.

FRIDAY 31st *[Through the East Indies]* No land to be seen at dawn, though our soundings show us in only five and a half fathoms of water. We could just see land from the deck before sunset.

SATURDAY 1st SEPTEMBER *[Through the East Indies – Lat. 7°39′ S, Long. 222°42′ W]* During morning watch the sounding had dropped to three fathoms and we could no longer see land from the deck. But we could smell it, a fragrance brought to us from a gentle land breeze. Mr Banks stood at the rail, breathing deeply. I wish I might have had time to join him.

SUNDAY 2nd *[Through the East Indies]* Sweet smell of yesterday returned this morning but not so strong, nor so long as yesterday. The wind is nearly flat and calm, and the heat is unbearable.

MONDAY 3rd *[Through the East Indies]* Captain brought *Endeavour* as close in to land as he might, then took Mr Banks and Dr Solander in the Pinnace to this low country whose coast is naught but shallow mud.

The Gentlemen botanized along the edge of the wood while the rest of the party surveyed the beach. But before long our men were attacked by several natives running towards them, screaming with a warlike fury. Only the firing of muskets caused a retreat.

The landing party decided to return to *Endeavour* immediately. As they boarded the Pinnace, upward of one hundred natives streamed onto the beach, dogs running after them. They looked, Tupia said, like the New Holland natives, but they had something the New Holland people did not. Something that made us all wonder. They carried long pieces of bamboo that looked like firearms and gave off a flash and smoke like a small pistol might. But there was no sound of pistol fire and no projectile fired off. Still, we thought from the ship that our party was being fired upon, and we were greatly distressed until we knew all were safe. Tarheto was the worst, fearing for the life of Tupia. He gripped my shoulder until he caught sight of the old man and knew he was well.

On dog watch Tupia told us of the Cocoa nutt Trees he saw, and the Breadfruit Trees and Plantain trees. The sight of them made him melancholy, and the telling of it made Tarheto melancholy as well.

All I want at this point is to sail home to England. I have faced death more times than I can count. How much harder can it be, then, to face the Butcher? Or Father? I am as eager to return to England as I once had been to flee it.

But how must Tupia and Tarheto feel? When shall they see their home again? Dr Monkhouse said we are suffering from a disease called Nostalgia.

'How is it cured?' I asked.

'Oh, trust me, Nick. The first sight of home shall cure it,' Dr Monkhouse said.

'What hope is there for Tarheto, then?' I asked. 'Who knows when he shall have his next sight of home?'

Dr Monkhouse said, 'I shouldn't worry about Tarheto if I were you. I've never met a happier lad. He'll be fine. You'll see.'

Captain, Mr Banks, and Dr Solander are the only ones entirely free of Nostalgia. Why is that?

TUESDAY 4th *[Through the East Indies – Lat. 6°44' S, Long. 223°51' W]* Made a good race west across the sea today, sounding as we went. Captain has increased our food allowance somewhat. We've been on severe restrictions, not knowing when we might next find Provisions. The want of food has started to show on us. Mayhap we shall improve with this increase.

WEDNESDAY 5th TO THURSDAY 6th *[Through the East Indies]* After a good day and night of sailing we came in sight of land this morning. It is possibly an Island called Timor. Mr Thompson, at Dr Monkhouse's suggestion, opened a cask of Beef.

Captain keeps us busy working up junk, picking oakum, and making spun yarn to help us with our Nostalgia. *Endeavour* may be suffering from her long and trying voyage, but her decks are daily holystoned. Weary as she is, she is still sharp and trim for an old girl. Ship and Company alike, we are all threadbare and worn, but there is no lack of British pride here.

FRIDAY 7th *[Through the East Indies]* Sailed under a bright Moon last night, sounding every hour with no bottom for our answer. Flying fish everywhere around the ship. And tonight we caught two more Boobies.

Captain works at his various charts, trying to understand where we are. There are several charts through this territory, and none quite agrees with what we see with our own eyes. Nor does Captain feel any are entirely accurate, whether the fault of the earlier navigator or the publisher, who will rush through what he must to increase sales.

Captain would not release anything unless it was accurate. After the trouble we have been in, I understand why. The next ship to brave the coast of New Holland will be grateful for Captain's careful charts, for in that way their lives may be spared.

SATURDAY 8th *[Through the East Indies – Lat. 9°36' S, Long. 231°17' W]* Excellent sailing, good speed and distance. Every mile puts us closer to home. Mr Perry kept me busy today cleaning and taking stock of our medical supplies.

SUNDAY 9th *[Through the East Indies]* Caught sight of land this night to the Westward. It seemed very high and very faint, and I fear it is yet another glimpse of Cape Fly Away. We are not given our half day off, nor have we for some time. Samuel Evans says it's because Captain is afraid we shall give in to our Nostalgia. So we are kept busy every moment of the day and night.

'I'm trying to work on my own,' Samuel said as we went aloft together. 'But it's hard to stay awake, Nick.'

I know. Tarheto and I hardly have a moment with each other anymore.

MONDAY 10th *[Through the East Indies]* Land still seen this morning.

TUESDAY 11th TO WEDNESDAY 12th *[Through the East Indies]* It's a high country covered in green woods with mangroves and Cocoa nutt trees and much smoke by day, many fires by night. Captain is fairly certain this is Timor.

THURSDAY 13th TO SATURDAY 15th *[Through the East Indies]* No useful wind. Made only little progress, sailing near enough shore this morning to see houses and some evidence of cultivation. Mr Banks spent the entire day looking through his spyglass.

SUNDAY 16th *[Through the East Indies]* Passed the small Island of Rotie, which is off the SW end of Timor and more hilly. Some of the Officers counseled Captain to stop at the Dutch settlement of Concordia for provisions, but Captain refused to take this suggestion. When I asked Mr Perry, he said the Dutch do not think much of the English and would not like us upon their land. Captain says we do not need provisions yet and shall be fine until we reach Batavia.

MONDAY 17th *[Through the East Indies – Lat. 10°27′ S, Long. 237°31′ W]* Last night Tarheto and John Charlton and I watched lights in the heavens to the SSE. John said the light was something like the aurora Borealis but not as trembling. It rose above the horizon in spikes, climbing towards the heavens only to vanish and be replaced by another course of colours. We watched in silence until I fell asleep, huddled against Goat. I think Tarheto watched on with John. They have reached an understanding, these two friends of mine. I knew it would happen. Tarheto with his joyful manner and John with his beaming grin. They were too well matched to live this close and not take to each other.

We came by an island today on which we saw houses, Cocoa nutt Trees, and flocks of Cattle and sheep at pasture. Tarheto could not take his eyes off this place. He is in that way very much like our Mr Banks. Everything is an exciting discovery to him.

Our Company's health has become a concern, particularly in the number of scurvy cases. I am kept busy as Surgeon's servant most of my waking hours. Dr Monkhouse and Mr Perry are in constant conversation with Captain as to how to improve our plight. Today Dr Monkhouse convinced Captain that a diet of fresh foods was of the utmost importance for several of our patients.

Putting his misgivings aside, Captain sent the Pinnace with Lieutenant Gore to find a good landing. Lieutenant Gore carried presents for the natives, should he encounter any. He did indeed meet with natives who were not strangers to Europeans.

As we watched from the ship, we saw our men well greeted and cocoa nutts being brought into their boat. When Lieutenant Gore returned, he brought news of a good anchorage on the lee side of this Island, where we could get sheep, hogs, fruit, and fowl. My mouth watered just to hear the words spoken aloud.

Made our way into harbour and hoisted a Jack from the fore-topmast head.

Dutch Colours flew over this place Lieutenant Gore calls Savu.

TUESDAY 18th *[Through the East Indies]* Lieutenant Gore went ashore this morning and was met by natives who took him within the village to meet the King of the Island. Lieutenant Gore explained that we were British, that we had been at sea a great time, and that we had many sick aboard who needed fresh provisions. The Raja could not give us provisions without the permission of the Dutch Governor, who did not live in that town. The King had a trade agreement with the Dutch and could not trade with others as part of that agreement.

Permission was sought from the Dutch Factor in town, and he came himself, granting permission. The Dutch Factor, who could be well understood by both Dr Solander and Mr Sporing, and King Raja, who was a very fat man and spoke Portuguese, came out to *Endeavour.*

Lieutenant Gore had to leave two of our men ashore as hostages whilst they did so. John Charlton said King Raja, upon seeing everyone seated to dine, excused himself. He did not think that white men would wish to eat with a black man. Captain soon made it clear he was welcome at *Endeavour's* table, and he ate with Captain. Mr Thompson served Mutton. The Raja expressed a desire to have an English sheep of his own, and Captain, having one sheep remaining, gave it as a present to him. Next the request came for an English dog, and Lord Grey was brought forward. Could Mr Banks give Lord Grey away so easily? And would next he want an English Goat? And an English boy?

WEDNESDAY 19th *[Through the East Indies]* Captain went ashore this morning along with Mr Banks and several of the Officers and Gentlemen to repay the King's visit and to buy provisions. John Charlton said yesterday Captain was promised many things, dozens of sheep, hogs, buffalo. Today he saw not half of what he'd hoped for.

THURSDAY 20th TO SATURDAY 22nd *[Through the East Indies – Lat. 11°9' S, Long. 238°56' W]* A light breeze behind us as we sail towards Batavia. We do not go fast but still we go.

SUNDAY 23rd *[Through the East Indies]* Easy sailing with an easterly breeze. We would be wishing for a gale to carry us to Batavia if we had not stopped for Provision at Savu, but we are all much improved, even the scurvy cases, now that we are not so hungry.

It never ceases to amaze me how very sick a man can be with scurvy and with one fresh meal how that illness can dissolve. For a man near death to leap from his bed completely restored in so short a time is truly a wonder.

MONDAY 24th [*Through the East Indies*] We have a great, swelling ocean coming at us from the South. Once the West coast of New Holland is cleared, there must be nothing but a great sea. Tarheto and I made up a game with the flying fish, which are everywhere and always popping out of the water. It was good to laugh with him again. I have had so little time. It is easier now that the scurvy is not such a threat.

TUESDAY 25th [*Through the East Indies – Lat. 11°13′ S, Long. 244°30′ W*] Beautiful weather, fine sailing.

WEDNESDAY 26th [*Through the East Indies*] The trade wind slacked off a bit today, but still fine conditions. Mr Thompson served the buffalo we got from the Dutch island of Savu. It had been salted for three days and it was as good as any meat I can recall.

THURSDAY 27th [*Through the East Indies*] Wind fresh again and birds everywhere in the sky. They cried above us and I cried back to them. Closing my eyes, I felt the shadow of their wings upon my face.

Francis Haite came past. 'Are you well, Nick?' he asked.

I opened my eyes and grinned. 'Aye, aye,' I answered, and hurried back to work.

FRIDAY 28th [*Through the East Indies*] Rain through the night but an excellent wind. I don't know what Mr Thompson did to the buffalo meat this time, but it was like mush.

SATURDAY 29th *[Through the East Indies]* The weather is clear and we are flying upon the trade winds to Java.

SUNDAY 30th *[Through the East Indies – Lat. 7°34' S, Long. 255°13' W]* Isaac Smith says Captain thinks we've missed our goal, shooting too far West. Finding a good breeze, we turned *Endeavour* back towards Java. Our sails are so bad they split before the least wind.

By day's end, in a flash of lightning, we saw land.

MONDAY 1st OCTOBER *[Through the East Indies]* Spent last night with Goat under heavy skies with torrents of rain and thunder and lightning. Lady Grey stayed beside me. She mourns for Lord Grey. Tarheto and I miss him, too. I think even Smoke and Ginger Bigfoot look for him and want their old chasing games. Mr Banks says nothing about Lord Grey's absence. Only a Gentleman could have given something so dear with such ease.

This morning we found ourselves at the West end of Java with Prince's Island in sight. We keep under sail tonight, passing Krakatau, a peaked mountain of great height, revealed in the moonlight.

TUESDAY 2nd *[Through the East Indies]* Tarheto spent the night watching over Tupia, who is ill again. Captain sent a boat ashore to Java, seeking fresh fruit for Tupia and grass for the remaining buffalo.

The landing party brought back only four Cocoa Nutts, a

small bunch of Plantains, and a few shrubs.

Took what light wind we could find and, spotting two Dutch ships, came to anchor nearby. Captain sent Lieutenant Gore over for news, and the News was that England was in an uproar. People rioting in the streets, calling, 'Down with King George and up with John Wilkes,' who, it seems, has been expelled from the House of Commons. I am so hungry for news of home that even politics, in which I have never before had an interest, interests me now. We also learned the Americans have refused to pay their taxes and the King was sending a large force to put them to rights.

Part XVIII

Tent of Death

OCTOBER 1770

WEDNESDAY 3rd TO TUESDAY 9th *[Batavia]* Ever up against a Land wind these past days. At last, today, we could weigh anchor and head, with a light breeze carrying us, along the sea road into Batavia. Set anchor and were almost immediately boarded by men from another ship asking news of us. Their faces were pasty and they looked truly ill, though they had not been at sea half the time we had. We thought ourselves fortunate to be so rosy and hale, after all.

We did not send off a salute, for we have only three Guns remaining and Captain did not think that enough. There are two ships, private traders, flying the English flag. They are not Englishmen, rather they are ships from English possessions. I am still not used to the sight of another ship's sails. Nor is Tarheto. His excitement is immense. He cannot hold still but runs fore and aft, and aloft, chattering in the rigging.

WEDNESDAY 10th *[Batavia]* The Carpenter, Mr Satterley, has made his report on the condition of *Endeavour*. She is taking up to twelve inches of water per hour. Her Main Keel is wounded. The Scarf of her stem wide open. The False Keel gone beyond Midships from Forward, maybe farther. She's wounded on her Larboard side under the Main Channel. And her pumps are decayed.

It is not safe to proceed to Europe with these wounds unmended. And we still don't know the full extent of damage to her bottom. Captain has requested of the Governor of Batavia that we should heave *Endeavour* down and see what we may.

The Gentlemen went ashore in the Pinnace and found an Englishman who advised them how to manage in Batavia. They are spending the night off *Endeavour,* in a hotel.

THURSDAY 11th *[Batavia]* Mr Banks sent for Tupia and Tarheto to stay with him at a house he has rented. Tarheto was fit to burst with excitement at getting off the ship and onto land. All the things we had talked about – Carriages, Houses, Streets – all the nights we spent with me describing, Tarheto listening, made Tarheto's desire enormous to see Batavia.

I am to stay here on the ship, at least for now.

Tupia is ill and refuses to take any of Dr Monkhouse's medicine. He shall find good food and a quick recovery with Mr Banks, I trust.

FRIDAY 12th *[Batavia]* It rained last night with loud Claps of Thunder. One bolt of lightning struck a Dutch ship only two cables' length from *Endeavour.* I was on deck when it happened. We took a jolt, but the Dutch ship lost her masts. It was to our good fortune that we had just put up the Chain. It carried the lightning over our side and clear of the ship. Even so, I felt the charge through my body, and Goat and Lady Grey did not stop shivering the rest of the night.

Captain went to shore this morning and received permission to have the ship hove to.

SATURDAY 13th *[Batavia]* Tarheto came back aboard only long enough to get some of the South Sea cloth for himself and Tupia to wear. In Batavia, he said excitedly, all the different people wear the clothes of their country. Tarheto could not stop talking about all the things he was seeing. I think he has not been so happy since we left OTahiti. Dr Monkhouse was right. I needn't have worried about Tarheto's Nostalgia.

SUNDAY 14th *[Batavia]* I wish I might have spent my leave ashore. Most of the Company is not yet permitted off the ship. Worked a bit with Samuel Evans on his reading. He has made little progress on his own, but nor has he lost ground.

MONDAY 15th TO TUESDAY 16th *[Batavia]* Captain, not having the money to satisfy the charges for repairing and refitting *Endeavour,* and with no one to promise the money for us, must make an appeal for the necessary funds.

WEDNESDAY 17th *[Batavia]* John Charlton says Captain's request for money was denied because of a misunderstanding in the translation of the paperwork. The request must be made again, and it cannot be considered until two days from now, when next the council meets. Blisters! I have no patience for even an hour's delay.

THURSDAY 18th *[Batavia]* Captain weighed anchor this morning and moved us to Onrust, where, once we receive permission, we shall remove our stores and work can commence on *Endeavour*.

FRIDAY 19th *[Batavia]* Mr Perry has been to the house where Mr Banks is staying. He said Tupia grows worse instead of better. And now Tarheto is not well.

There are some on board who are not well, either. Surgeon Monkhouse, Mr Perry, and I have our work set out for us.

SATURDAY 20th *[Batavia]* Those who are well enough are busy at unrigging *Endeavour*.

SUNDAY 21st *[Batavia]* Captain finally received permission to have our work done, but there is no free wharf, so we cannot begin unloading our stores.

The men in my mess, accustomed to my constant hunger, tease me good-naturedly because I have no appetite. I do not know whether it is because of this weather, which is so suffocating, or some other cause.

Tupia and Tarheto are back aboard now! Tupia requested a return to the ship. He says he can breathe freer here, away from all the houses that stop the good flow of air.

It's good to have them nearby again.

I'm certain Tarheto and Tupia shall recover now.

MONDAY 22nd *[Batavia]* We managed to find a place at the wharf and the unloading begins.

TUESDAY 23rd *[Batavia]* The people of Batavia are to do the work on *Endeavour* while we wait with no purpose but to keep ourselves well. That alone is a serious business.

WEDNESDAY 24th *[Batavia]* Captain went aboard a Dutch Ship with a packet containing his Journal, his Charts, and his communications of the past two years to be sent back to England. Would that I could deliver that packet.

I have sent along a letter to Father. At least now he shall know where I am and that I will soon return. I think, with Father, it is good to give him some time to consider what he will do with me.

THURSDAY 25th *[Batavia]* The Dutch Ship sailed today on its way round the Cape of Good Hope and on to En-gland. How long until *Endeavour* follows?

FRIDAY 26th *[Batavia]* Tents have been set up for the sick onshore at Cooper's Island, and for the rest of the Company as well. Many men suffer from a dysentery they've picked up in the foul air here. I am on my feet day and night, washing them, feeding them, trying to make them comfortable. It is beastly hot here.

SATURDAY 27th TO SUNDAY 28th *[Batavia]* Tupia is settled in the sick tent and feeling better with the sea near him and the breeze coming over. I am tired beyond reckoning. There are so many sick, and Tarheto has a dreadful cough.

How could we travel so long, so far, so distant from the

English world and maintain our health, only to return to this place of civilization and be devastated by disease?

MONDAY 29th TO WEDNESDAY 31st *[Batavia]* Tending the ill.

THURSDAY 1st NOVEMBER *[Batavia]* Mr Banks, after staying beside Tupia in the sick tent for two days, returned to his lodgings and was stricken with illness. Mr Perry says he lies senseless. And Dr Solander shows signs of coming down ill, too.

But most alarming is Surgeon Monkhouse. His fever is frighteningly high. Mr Perry and I do what we can, but we cannot bring it under control.

FRIDAY 2nd TO SATURDAY 3rd *[Batavia]* The men who are able have been aboard overhauling the Rigging, making Rope, making and repairing Sails. I help Mr Perry in all things.

SUNDAY 4th *[Batavia]* Finally *Endeavour* has found a place at the Careening wharf and the work can begin. We shall not come away from this unwholesome place soon enough.

Surgeon Monkhouse does not improve, no matter what we do for him.

MONDAY 5th *[Batavia]* Surgeon Monkhouse is dead.

Mr Perry ordered me away from the body to take a strict and careful Survey of all the Surgeon's Medicines, Instruments, and Necessities.

'You are to count each piece and remark on its condition,' Mr Perry ordered. 'Do you hear me, Nick?'

'Aye, sir,' I said.

TUESDAY 6th *[Batavia]* Some of the men went to bury Surgeon Monkhouse. I could not go. There are too many sick for me to leave.

A stream of Carpenters, Caulkers, Riggers, and Slaves boarded *Endeavour* today to heave her down.

Mr Perry reviewed my survey of the medical stores. Captain has appointed Mr Perry as Surgeon Monkhouse's successor and provided money for him to replenish our medical stocks.

Mr Perry bought enough supplies to last seven months.

Seven months!

Can it possibly be that long before we arrive home?

WEDNESDAY 7th *[Batavia]* Mr Banks asked that I might come from the Company's tents and attend him, for his servants are so ill and the Malay Slaves do not satisfy him in their attention. Mr Perry said I could not be spared. I'm glad. I do not wish to be away from Tupia and Tarheto. There is so little I can do for them, and yet they both brighten at the sight of me. I cannot leave them now.

THURSDAY 8th *[Batavia]* We were battered by weather last night, with cracking Thunder that sent poor Goat into a state of complete jelly. I wonder how Lady Grey did. There is no one at Mr Banks's lodging to comfort her. They are all too ill.

FRIDAY 9th *[Batavia]* The ship is in far worse condition than any of us imagined. Once they got a good look at her, the question came to mind, why did she not sink long before we arrived in Batavia, so eaten by worms and the reefs and the sea she is. I thought maybe we should just board and take her ourselves and work on her as we sail. But the work is too great even if we had the men to do it, which we do not. Only twenty of our eighty men and Officers have health enough to carry out their duty. Even the cats have little energy for their mousing.

But every Carpenter and Caulker in Batavia has descended upon *Endeavour*. With so many hands, the work should go fast.

SATURDAY 10th *[Batavia]* Mr Banks and Dr Solander are being removed to a house in the country where the air is cleaner than the foul air of this town. They have retained Malay Women to nurse them in the hope that their care will intercede in the progress of this disease.

SUNDAY 11th *[Batavia]* The ship is alive the way a hive is with bees. Our tents are filled with moaning and cries for water and bad smells and insufferable heat.

Tarheto looks out of eyes glassy with fever. I sit with him for a moment before I am called away. I remember when he studied the colour of my skin on OTahiti, and I studied his. We have come so far since then.

MONDAY 12th *[Batavia]* Still tending the ill.

TUESDAY 13th *[Batavia]* Mr Perry said that Dr Solander took a turn for the worse last night. Mr Banks summoned a Batavian physician, who has ordered mustard plasters applied to his feet, but it looks grim.

Mr Banks, though he is ill himself, spent the night watching over Dr Solander, expecting he should die with each gasp, but this morning found him somewhat improved.

Mr Banks should not sit up with any patient. His own condition is dangerous. He must take great care, lest he follow our Dr Monkhouse.

Mr Sporing, who has often acted as recorder for Mr Banks as well as botanist and draughtsman, has been carried away to join Mr Banks and Dr Solander at the country house. Mr Banks's house, which stands beside a clean river, should be more healthful than our tents.

John Charlton and I went along to Mr Banks's house to see to the transfer of Mr Sporing. On our way back a native rushed out into the street with his dagger and began stabbing people. We quickly got out of his way, and the man, as he was about to be taken, killed himself. It was explained to us later that this happened regularly when someone, jealous over a woman, became intoxicated by the drug opium.

Blisters! This is a rotten place.

WEDNESDAY 14th *[Batavia] Endeavour's* bottom is entirely repaired now and is being cleared of the Careening gear.

THURSDAY 15th *[Batavia]* Moved *Endeavour* from Onrust to Cooper's Island, where our stores are. Soon we shall move everyone back aboard and be on our way.

FRIDAY 16th *[Batavia]* Coal and Ballast coming aboard *Endeavour.* The bad pump came off in hope of repair.

SATURDAY 17th TO FRIDAY 23rd *[Batavia]* Rigging *Endeavour,* bringing stores and water aboard. It is slow going. We have only twelve hands able to perform their duties.

Still Tupia and Tarheto hang on to life, but they do not improve.

SATURDAY 24th *[Batavia]* The tents are wet, the cots are wet, the ground beneath us is mud with rushing gullies running through, the supplies are wet. I am molding in this steaming heat.

At night frogs sing in the ditches so loud sometimes I mistake them for the sick calling.

The mosquitoes are worse here than any place we have ever been. Particularly are they hungry when the moon shines.

SUNDAY 25th TO FRIDAY 30th *[Batavia]* Still I tend the sick while *Endeavour* fills with Stores. The men who are able work on the Rigging.

SATURDAY 1st TO FRIDAY 7th DECEMBER *[Batavia]* Brought the last of the stores on board and brought the sick when all was ready for them in anticipation of getting quit of this place.

SATURDAY 8th *[Batavia]* Weighed anchor this morning and moved a little ways up the Batavia Road.

SUNDAY 9th *[Batavia]* Dirty weather this day. Tonight Captain sent Empty Casks in a boat to shore and brought on board the New Pump, along with some other necessaries.

MONDAY 10th *[Batavia]* Captain is ill. Yet he does not take to his bed.

TUESDAY 11th TO SUNDAY 16th *[Batavia]* Tarheto cannot breathe. His fingers and toes are cold. I know these signs. Of all the things I have learned in my time aboard *Endeavour*, this is the worst.

MONDAY 17th *[Batavia]* Tarheto is dead.

TUESDAY 18th *[Batavia]* Tupia grieves over Tarheto. I remember all the times he snapped at my friend and found fault with him. Tupia has found fault with nearly everyone aboard *Endeavour*, and nearly everyone of our Company has found fault with Tupia at one time or another. But above all, Tupia has been a good teacher and a good guide. I cannot watch him mourn himself to death over Tarheto without doing the same myself. My heart is a rock. I can barely move.

WEDNESDAY 19th *[Batavia]* The *Earl of Elgin* Indiaman has taken anchor in the Batavia Road, for she has lost the wind. She must now wait for the next season before she can reach China. I wish her luck that she may not lose her crew in this evil place. John Reynolds, servant to Mr Green, is dead.

THURSDAY 20th *[Batavia]* Tupia has followed Tarheto.

FRIDAY 21st *[Batavia]* Tarheto and Tupia were buried together on the island of Eadam this morning. They shall never see their home again. I could not be spared to see them to their grave.

SATURDAY 22nd TO MONDAY 24th *[Batavia]* John Woodworth and Timothy Rearden, both able-bodied seamen, died today. Captain oversees the provisioning and watering and preparations for sea, but his heart seems broken. He kept us safe and healthy for so long, and now he watches the men slipping away.

TUESDAY 25th *[Batavia]* There are Batavians who are surprised that we have lost only six men. They wagered we would lose more. 'You're lucky', they say.

I don't feel lucky. I feel tired.

Mr Banks and Dr Solander returned last night. They are thin and pale and unsteady, but it is good to see them. Somehow I can almost pretend that all will go better now that we have the Gentlemen aboard again.

'Tis Christmas.

PART XIX

Skeleton Crew

DECEMBER 1770

WEDNESDAY 26th *[Leaving Batavia]* We sailed during morning watch. The *Elgin* Indiaman saluted us with three Cheers and thirteen guns. The *Garrison* saluted us not long after with fourteen guns. We returned both of their salutes, as pleased to be under way as they were to see us on our journey. We could not get far, though, on the wind and anchored just beyond the other ships in the Road. We have forty ill and everyone weak. The only member of the crew who has not shown one sign of illness is Mr Ravenhill, the old sail maker. Mr Perry says he's too pickled for any disease to take hold of him.

Though many of the men are too ill to perform their duty, still they rose from their sickbeds to join the nineteen new men we've taken on to get *Endeavour* on her way.

THURSDAY 27th TO FRIDAY 28th *[Leaving Batavia]* Weighed anchor and stood out to Sea, though the wind does not carry us far.

SATURDAY 29th TO SUNDAY 30th *[Leaving Batavia]* The wind is somewhat better. Anchored off the Sumatra Coast tonight, where we saw a few fires.

MONDAY 31st *[Leaving Batavia]* Sailed against the wind all day. Dropped off to sleep for a moment and dreamed of climbing bread-fruit trees with Tarheto. I did not want to wake.

TUESDAY 1st JANUARY *[Leaving Batavia]* Again we fight the wind. Set anchor beside a high island the men call Krakatau. The Mosquitoes had been getting worse though we'd put a good distance between *Endeavour* and Batavia. Then Dr Solander discovered they were breeding on the Batavian water we'd brought aboard. Mr Perry fears there is a connection between the Mosquitoes and the sickness.

'Well, we're rid of the Mosquitoes now, sir,' I said. 'The men should recover, then, don't you think?'

Mr Perry shook his head. He remains remarkably unsoiled and trim, though his eyes are bloodshot and rimmed with shadows. 'If what I fear is so, Nick,' Mr Perry said, 'we've only just begun to see the trouble.'

'Then I hope your fears are wrong, sir,' I said. 'With all respect.'

'With all respect, Nick,' Mr Perry answered, 'I hope I'm wrong, too.'

WEDNESDAY 2nd *[Leaving Batavia]* Getting nowhere on this wind. We fought all day and still ended up in last night's berth.

Why don't the people of Krakatau come out in their boats to sell refreshments to us? I want the taste of fresh fruit in my teeth. I would gladly trade an entire week of roast pork for a single bite of melon.

THURSDAY 3rd TO FRIDAY 4th *[Leaving Batavia]* Squalls.

SATURDAY 5th *[Leaving Batavia]* Sailed on a weak SE wind through the night. Anchored under Prince's Island this afternoon. Mr Banks and Captain went ashore for fresh provisions. Mr Banks tried trading for turtle, but the King of this place asked too high a price, and so Mr Banks walked away. But before his boat returned to *Endeavour,* a canoe approached and sold Mr Banks three turtles with the understanding that he not tell the King.

SUNDAY 6th *[Leaving Batavia]* Mr Banks negotiated with the natives for more turtle. These natives want nothing to do with beads and iron. They want money.

MONDAY 7th *[Leaving Batavia]* The Company of ill are worse now than they were in Batavia. Mr Perry is nearly dead with exhaustion. I am no better.

TUESDAY 8th *[Leaving Batavia]* Driven too near the shore during the night. Fortunately the Officers hove us into deeper water before any damage was done. Mr Bootie refuses to admit illness and carries on.

WEDNESDAY 9th TO SATURDAY 12th *[Leaving Batavia]* Mr Banks has suffered another attack of his Batavian Fever. Mr Perry says he has been too much in the merciless sun and must rest.

SUNDAY 13th *[Leaving Batavia]* Mr Banks had more fever this afternoon. He promises Mr Perry he shall be well once we're racing over the Ocean again. Blisters! We shall all be improved by that.

MONDAY 14th *[Leaving Batavia]* Our best intentions were thwarted by a heartless wind, which, when it finally blew, had so little strength we made but small advance. The good we had of it was more fish and turtle from the natives brought out in trade.

TUESDAY 15th *[Leaving Batavia]* Still in sight of land tonight.

I spend what little time off I have on deck with Goat and Lady Grey. For old times' sake I crept inside the Pinnace and closed my eyes. John Charlton found me and woke me and helped me back out again. I had no will to do so on my own.

WEDNESDAY 16th TO THURSDAY 17th *[Towards the Cape of Good Hope – Lat. 7°32′ S, Long. 255°35′ W]* The men grow more ill by the day, some with fevers, some with purgings. There have been times when I wished to give up. But not any more. For we are sailing.

FRIDAY 18th TO SATURDAY 19th *[Towards the Cape of Good Hope]* Little wind, but still we make progress. Saw a ship in the distance as I emptied the buckets but could not make out her colours.

SUNDAY 20th *[Towards the Cape of Good Hope]* Captain gave us a portion of the day free from our duties. I spent much of the time sitting with Goat, remembering my Sundays with Tarheto.

We have left his body behind in that unhappy place. I remember the way of the natives with their dead in OTahiti. How shall Tarheto's and Tupia's souls manage in a foreign grave?

Samuel Evans found me. I asked if we might skip reading this week. But his disappointment was clear. 'I hoped to come home a learned man,' he said. So we had our lesson. He was slow as ever. But I praised what he did well, and that cheered us both.

The ships seen yesterday came closer and then passed us. There were two, and they flew Dutch colours. It hurt our pride that they should leave *Endeavour* in their wake. But we can do little more than limp through these seas.

Mr Banks, who is very good about taking his medicine, had no fever today. But many of the men are suffering still with the bloody flux.

MONDAY 21st *[Towards the Cape of Good Hope]* One of the Dutch ships has gone so far beyond us we cannot catch sight of her. The other is still within view. Some of the men said we could catch her if we tried. I think we'd have more luck catching the birds and porpoises and harnessing them to tow us home.

TUESDAY 22nd *[Towards the Cape of Good Hope]* The wind has nearly failed us and we make little way. The second Dutchman has outrun us utterly. I don't think there is a single man on board who is without physical complaint. The worst is the fluxing and the purging.

Mr Banks is ill, Mr Sporing is worse, and Mr Parkinson, who has devoted nearly every waking moment to his illustrations of plants and fish and birds, suffers with a deadly fever.

WEDNESDAY 23rd *[Towards the Cape of Good Hope]* Endeavour now rides a swell from Southward. It is all we ride, for there is no wind to carry us. I've come to know full well the feel of those deep swells and their meaning. We are in a place so far from land that the ocean rules supreme. We have lost John Truslove, corporal of the Marines, to the flux. He was a good man.

Mr Bootie cannot rise from his hammock.

THURSDAY 24th *[Towards the Cape of Good Hope]* Calm still. We've put lime in the casks of water in the hopes that the fevers and fluxes suffered by everyone will be tempered by this action. The men clutch at their bowels and are in twisting pain. Mr Sporing surrendered tonight.

FRIDAY 25th *[Towards the Cape of Good Hope]* Why can we not stop the dying? Why can we not have wind? How shall we ever get home?

Thomas Dunster is gone.

Mr Perry ordered Mr Banks into a hot bath four times. Some of his pain has been relieved, at least for the moment.

SATURDAY 26th *[Towards the Cape of Good Hope]* Smothering heat. Cleaned *Endeavour* between decks and washed her down with vinegar. Mr Banks is in agony. Mr Parkinson is dead.

SUNDAY 27th *[Towards the Cape of Good Hope]* John Ravenhill, the ever drunken sail maker, who never fell ill when all around him suffered, gave up his life last night.

MONDAY 28th *[Towards the Cape of Good Hope]* The wind has come and we have made a little progress through rain and squalls.

Mr Green, the astronomer, sent on this expedition by the Royal Society to help Captain Observe the Transit of Venus, is gone.

Mr Banks looks more frightened than ever he has been. To lose Mr Green. He would not believe such a thing possible. And yet Mr Green is dead.

Now Francis Haite is near death. In his fever he talks to me. 'I'm sorry, boy,' he said tonight. 'What have I let you in to?'

I told him not to fret over it. I told him I let myself in.

Francis Haite lay in his hammock burning with fever. I did my best to cool his skin. I did my best to comfort his soul.

I came here of my own free will. To escape my apprenticeship to the Butcher. To escape my fears and my failings. It was my choice to come. It is now my choice to return.

TUESDAY 29th *[Towards the Cape of Good Hope]* Francis Haite is dead. I was with him at the last.

I have not always felt well over these months of illness, but this morning I'd pains in my stomach, horrible pains, and I knew then that I had come down with the flux.

I raced to the deck and I think I lost my mind, for I knew I would die like all the others. But Mr Perry brought me down to my hammock, and I awoke there later in the day and I was not ill.

I don't know why I've been spared.

WEDNESDAY 30th *[Towards the Cape of Good Hope – Lat. 12°48' S, Long. 258°59' W]* Mr Banks managed to sleep for the first time since the flux came on him. We have been giving him strong opiates for his pain. He seems somewhat improved.

Mr Clerke has taken over Mr Green's computations and observations. He was the best of Mr Green's students.

Sam Moody is dead. There are only eight men out of eighty, Officers included, who are fit to stand watch, and so they stand four at a time. I am glad there are no shoals now. With so few hands, any obstacle would be too great to manage. John Ramsay says we must take on more men at the Cape. I wonder if we shall ever make it that far.

THURSDAY 31st *[Towards the Cape of Good Hope]* Four more dead: Benjamin Jordan, James Nicholson, and Archibald Wolfe, seamen; and John Thompson, our one-handed cook, who never punished me harshly, though more than once I did him mischief, and often showed me kindness for no other reason than that he liked the way I plucked a goose.

I wish I could lie down and join him. I am so tired.

Mr Banks left his bed today. He is weak, but he has the look of a man who intends to live, something I don't see much of these days. I wish we understood why he would recover and the others not. The few men left to man the sails say we have caught the trades. I went about the ill and told them, and many brightened at the news.

FRIDAY 1st FEBRUARY *[Towards the Cape of Good Hope – Lat. 14°44' S, Long. 261°40' W]* Rain off and on today, but a fresh wind from the SE and good speed.

SATURDAY 2nd *[Towards the Cape of Good Hope]* Tending the ill. Ever tending the ill.

Mr Bootie is near death. I was reluctant to come near at first, each time I came to tend him. But I am not afraid of him any more.

'I'm sorry for what I wrote in your journal,' I told him as I washed him clean this evening.

'Bastard,' he muttered. But he managed a grin.

SUNDAY 3rd *[Towards the Cape of Good Hope]* John Thurman, gone. And Daniel Roberts. But even I see improvement in some of the others.

Except Mr Bootie.

I tried at least five times today to give him water, to make him comfortable, to wipe his burning forehead.

The last time, he opened his eyes and looked at me.

'There's a good lad,' he said.

I'm not certain he meant me. But I was grateful all the same.

MONDAY 4th *[Towards the Cape of Good Hope]* Mr John Gathrey, Bosun, and Mr John Bootie, Midshipman, died today as we flew on a fine wind towards the Cape.

TUESDAY 5th *[Towards the Cape of Good Hope]* Samuel Evans is appointed Bosun in Mr Gathrey's place. Some of the men are improving. They are well enough, they went down to take a counting of the stores.

WEDNESDAY 6th *[Towards the Cape of Good Hope]* Still the trades are with us, but still men dying in the night. This time it was Jonathan Monkhouse, Midshipman, brother to Dr Monkhouse. It was Jonathan Monkhouse who, along with his brother, the good doctor, protected me when first I was discovered aboard

Endeavour. And now I am here and they are both gone.

THURSDAY 7th *[Towards the Cape of Good Hope]* Many of the men are greatly improved, but those who began this month poorly still hang between life and death. There is no medicine we can give to improve the chances of their survival. For many the Trade winds were enough to rouse them and bring them back among the living. For the rest, the illness will take its course. We can only watch and wait.

FRIDAY 8th *[Towards the Cape of Good Hope]* Captain takes his Observations daily. While he is at that business, he seems less burdened by the losses we have endured. Otherwise he looks as if he carries all our sorrow on his own shoulders.

Another Dutchman sailed into sight and out of it again, leaving us behind.

SATURDAY 9th *[Towards the Cape of Good Hope]* No one dead for three full days, though some are still quite bad.

SUNDAY 10th *[Towards the Cape of Good Hope – Lat. 20°28' S, Long. 283°22' W]* Thomas Hardman has taken Mr Ravenhill's place as sail maker.

MONDAY 11th *[Towards the Cape of Good Hope]* Mr Satterley, our Carpenter and good friend to all, died this day of the bloody flux. I wish we could have saved him. George Nowell and Edward Terrell are all we have left of our Carpenters. George Nowell will take Mr Satterley's place.

TUESDAY 12th *[Towards the Cape of Good Hope]* I don't know how we keep going with so much loss. But we do.

WEDNESDAY 13th *[Towards the Cape of Good Hope]* Alexander Lindsey, seaman, departed this life. He came aboard in Batavia. We never even knew him.

THURSDAY 14th *[Towards the Cape of Good Hope]* Dead, Daniel Preston, Marine.

FRIDAY 15th *[Towards the Cape of Good Hope]* No one died today.

Of all who came down with the worst degree of flux, only one man survived to the best of my knowledge, Mr Banks.

SATURDAY 16th TO TUESDAY 19th *[Towards the Cape of Good Hope]* Some rain. Fine wind. No deaths.

WEDNESDAY 20th TO THURSDAY 21st *[Towards the Cape of Good Hope]* Alexander Simpson is dead. He was a good man and a good sailor.

Thomas Rossiter, who is the drummer of the marines, not half the man Mr Simpson was, received twelve lashes for drinking to excess and in his drunkenness beating some of the sick. I had my eye blackened holding him back.

FRIDAY 22nd *[Towards the Cape of Good Hope – Lat. 26°5′ S, Long. 308°54′ W]* Fair wind, fair weather.

SATURDAY 23rd *[Towards the Cape of Good Hope]* Captain is about more often making observations. I don't know for certain, but I suspect he has been more ill than he let on.

It is good to see him about.

SUNDAY 24th *[Towards the Cape of Good Hope]* An Albatross. The first we have seen in these waters. As good a sign as any we've come far enough south to begin looking for the Cape.

MONDAY 25th *[Towards the Cape of Good Hope]* I tell the ill about the Albatross and the fresh winds and the nearing of the Cape, but for some, it makes no difference.

TUESDAY 26th TO WEDNESDAY 27th *[Towards the Cape of Good Hope]* The Flux has claimed three more: Mr Henry Jeffs, Mr Manoel Pereira, and Peter Morgan of Batavia, all seamen.

Captain came along on sick rounds. He has hope these will be the last and the rest will recover. But I am not certain. It is so hard to keep up hope when so many I thought would come round have slipped away. I looked to Mr Perry to see if he shared Captain's hope. Mr Perry, still trim, still carefully attired, leaned against the bulkhead, asleep on his feet.

THURSDAY 28th *[Towards the Cape of Good Hope]* We had a heavy squall this morning, which caught us by surprise. The wind split the Fore Topsail in many places before the men could stand the sails down out of the blow. This would not have happened if there had been more men.

FRIDAY 1st MARCH *[Towards the Cape of Good Hope]* *Endeavour* is shaking loose in places under the force of these gales. The men do their best to tighten her down. My ear is so accustomed to her sounds. Day and night she groans. She needs the sure and steady hands upon her that have kept her smart in the water through so much. But so many of those hands are gone.

SATURDAY 2nd *[Towards the Cape of Good Hope]* Drove forward under rain showers and fair wind with an enormous sea rising at us from the SW. At nightfall a bank of clouds pretended at being land, something we all would like to see. It would mean we were upon the Tip of Africa and soon to make way into the South Atlantic, the last leg of our journey home.

SUNDAY 3rd *[Towards the Cape of Good Hope]* A cry of Land, but Captain, below deck on sick rounds with us, said, 'No, we shall see no land today.'

Nevertheless he had the men sound. They found no bottom.

MONDAY 4th *[Towards the Cape of Good Hope – Lat. 31°34′ S, Long. 327°36′ W]* During the night we had a display of lightning to the West. My friend Goat, who managed to survive Batavia with hardly a hiccup, quaked in her straw. I sat with her for as long as I could, but there are still several men who are desperately ill and I could not mind her as I would have liked.

At first light we saw that the land spotted yesterday truly was land.

The wind rose up behind us, drawing us closer and closer to shore. The sea broke upon the rocks with a great fury. One man said that he had come through dysentery only to be dashed to death on the shores of Africa. And solemnly did many on deck agree with him. But we made, at Captain's orders, to the East and gradually came away from danger.

Isaac Smith says this place is called Terra de Natal. It is good to see such a green and pleasant place.

Mr Perry said this is a place of birth, of new beginnings. Mr Perry has much aged in these last months.

I shouldn't wonder that I have, too.

PART XX

Second Wind

MARCH 1771

TUESDAY 5th *[Rounding Africa]* Cold here. I don't know how long it has been that I have not felt temperature. It is as if I am coming awake after a long, fitful sleep.

WEDNESDAY 6th *[Rounding Africa]* Clouds, heavy and grey, hang threateningly over us, and the wind is foul. I do not mind the clouds, but *Endeavour* needs a fair wind.

THURSDAY 7th TO FRIDAY 8th *[Rounding Africa]* The weather has cleared here on the water, though we can see clouds hanging over the land and rain sheeting down. The men have noticed a current these last days that takes us here and there with no reason or predictability.

SATURDAY 9th *[Rounding Africa]* The soundings today indicate we are upon the Cape Bank. Looking into the water is like looking into thick mud. We've lost sight of land, but birds are everywhere, crying, beating, swooping, and soaring over top and beside us.

Once, whilst I was on deck watching the birds, I felt Tarheto there, at my shoulder. It made a chill climb over my skin.

SUNDAY 10th *[Rounding Africa]* The face of the water has changed from mud to clear blue. We thought to make it round the southernmost tip of Africa this very night, but the wind turned against us, coming straight at our teeth and blowing fiercely.

MONDAY 11th *[Rounding Africa]* Though the wind was no help last night, the current took us right.

Today the wind carried us where the air went thick with birds. They were everywhere around us, filling our ears with their calls.

John Charlton came to my side. 'Call back to them,' he said. 'The Company would like that.'

So I did.

Tonight the water shimmers with shining insects. Wish Tarheto were here.

TUESDAY 12th *[Rounding Africa – Lat. 34°58′ S, Long. 329°17′ W]* Cape Falso and the Cape of Good Hope stand before us with a rock between the two, upon which the sea breaks with fury.

We anchored off Table Bay, joining several other ships – eight Dutch, four French, three Danes, and one English, the *Admiral Pocock.* So many sails. What a welcome sight.

WEDNESDAY 13th *[Rounding Africa]* Wind too fresh to take a boat ashore. None in the harbour put off from their ships today.

But tonight the wind fell enough for the English Company to send over a basket of fruit.

I think we may get home after all.

THURSDAY 14th *[Rounding Africa]* Captain took *Endeavour* into the harbour to a proper berth. A Dutch Surgeon came aboard and examined our sick. Mr Perry requested of Captain that we might take the sick ashore to hasten their recovery. The Dutch Surgeon granted Captain permission.

FRIDAY 15th *[At the Cape]* Mr Perry went ashore to locate a place for the sick, while I remained aboard and tended their needs.

SATURDAY 16th *[At the Cape]* We have moved all the remaining sick (twenty-eight) to shore. Mr Banks has found rooms in a house nearby. Captain is taking fresh meat and greens on board. We, too, have fresh food to feed our ill.

Admiral Pocock has sailed for England. I watched until I could see her no more.

SUNDAY 17th *[At the Cape]* Dr Solander, returning to Mr Banks's house from the *Pocock* before she sailed, came down with all the indications of the flux. The surgeon from this land examined Dr Solander and said that he would suffer with his ailment, which comes still from Batavia, but that he will recover.

MONDAY 18th *[At the Cape]* The men began bringing fresh water aboard, while I stayed with Mr Perry and the sick onshore.

Another English Indiaman, the *Houghton*, came into the Sea Road. How good it is to see the English colours.

TUESDAY 19th TO WEDNESDAY 20th *[At the Cape]* We learn that this has been a year of great sickness and that ships from England at sea for less than a year have lost more of their Company than we have lost in nearly three years. So we must not feel disgraced.

Judging by the reaction to us from the British we have met here, I think when we return to England, our voyage will be much discussed. It is peculiar. These men say we are heroic, but they are thinking more of the losses we have lately suffered than of our other adventures. I thought about it while watching Goat tonight. She has joined us on land, where she can happily graze on fresh grass.

She, perhaps, is most heroic of all, for she takes everything in stride. And but for a bit of thunder, in nearly three years nothing has truly disturbed her.

THURSDAY 21st *[At the Cape]* On board the men work on the Rigging and the Sails whilst others bring on water. One of the Dutch ships sailed for Batavia today. You could not get me on that ship for any price in the world. I'd sooner spend the remainder of my life with Father and the Butcher breathing down my neck than return for even a moment to Batavia.

FRIDAY 22nd TO FRIDAY 29th *[At the Cape]* The water is now on board. Captain has given leave for the Company to spend time ashore refreshing ourselves. Mr Perry has offered time off to me, but I have no desire.

When I boarded, I wanted freedom. I wished to do everything, see everything, hear and taste everything without the burden of schooling or work or family. I have grown in these years at sea. I shall welcome the burden of family. And schooling, if Father should give me another chance at it. But first I must honour my contract with the Butcher. It is not something I want to do. But I shall do it if I must. And I shall do it well. And when I am done, when I am finished with the Butcher and he with me, I shall not run away as a frightened child, nor steal away like a common thief. I shall walk away as a man, with my head up.

SATURDAY 30th *[At the Cape]* Last night we were pounded by a hard gale both at anchor and on land. Today the English East Indiaman the *Duke of Gloucester* came into the Road.

SUNDAY 31st *[At the Cape]* The men brought an entire ox aboard to be cut and salted. Joseph Childs has taken over John Thompson's duties. I'm certain he's doing his best, but we all miss our one-handed cook. Mr Banks came by the tent to deliver the good news that Dr Solander, who has been deathly ill over these past days, is much weakened and lightened but has stood up from his bed today for the first time.

MONDAY 1st APRIL *[At the Cape]* Violent weather.

TUESDAY 2nd *[At the Cape]* The *Duke of Gloucester* Indiaman left for England. Will it be our turn soon?

A Dutch ship came in from Batavia and asked for immediate assistance with her sick.

WEDNESDAY 3rd *[At the Cape]* Some of the men came ashore for their refreshment. The remainder worked on the Sails and the Rigging. And still we struggle to keep our sick men alive. Mr Molyneux, in his fever, refuses my care. He thinks I am a haunt come to take him to his grave.

THURSDAY 4th TO FRIDAY 5th *[At the Cape]* Provisions going on board.

SATURDAY 6th *[At the Cape]* A little rain last night, but mild and clear again with daylight. Surely this weather should be enough to restore the men to health. I go to Mr Molyneux's side and tell him how beautiful it is, how sweet the wind smells, that he should take a breath of it. He only glares at me as I wipe the spit from the side of his mouth.

SUNDAY 7th *[At the Cape]* A good day for exploring inland. I went out with Isaac Manley and Thomas Jones, taking with me one of Mr Banks's collecting bags. Upon returning, I headed on board, straight to the Great Cabin, where I matched plants I had found to pictures in Mr Banks's books. I half expected to look up and see Mr Bootie scowling down at me. All I saw was admiration on the faces of Isaac Manley and Thomas Jones. Neither of them reads a word.

The next thing I remember I looked up to see Mr Banks regarding me. I showed him what I'd found and he helped me identify the last plant.

'You have talent, boy,'

'Aye, sir.'

'What are your plans when we reach England?'

My heart picked up its pace. 'I have a debt to pay, sir.'

'Well, look me up after you've paid it, lad.'

'Aye, sir,' I said. 'I shall, sir.'

MONDAY 8th *[At the Cape]* Another English ship has come into the Road. She saluted us and we returned the compliment. Ginger Bigfoot waltzed around my legs as I stood at the rail. I lifted the cat in my arms and showed her the English colours.

TUESDAY 9th TO WEDNESDAY 10th *[At the Cape]* Moved eleven of our sick back on board. Captain is making ready for sea.

THURSDAY 11th *[At the Cape]* More provisions coming on, bread, fresh Beef, Mutton, Salt, Wheat. I feel a great surge of excitement at the prospect of setting sail for England.

'We're leaving soon,' I whispered to Mr Molyneux. 'Be back home soon,' I said.

His eyes, so crafty in health, looked hollow and vacant. Still, he managed to turn to me and glare.

FRIDAY 12th *[At the Cape]* The Topmast rigging is up and the sails bent.

SATURDAY 13th *[At the Cape]* Brought all the remaining sick on board this afternoon. Some are still in a very bad way. Three have died since we've been here at the Cape, but Captain has hired on more men to complete our full Complement.

We shall make it home. I know it now.

Part XXI

Home

APRIL 1771

SUNDAY 14th *[At the Cape]* Unmoored and prepared to sail, receiving salutes and returning them from all we passed.

MONDAY 15th *[Leaving the Cape]* Master Molyneux died tonight. I was with him at the last. His eyes had lost their glare in the end. I was thanking him for the turtles. He looked at me, startled. And then he was looking on a world I do not hope to see for many years.

I closed Master Molyneux's lids for him. And said a prayer.

TUESDAY 16th TO THURSDAY 18th *[To England – Lat. 31°14' S, Long. 345°19' W]* Great swell rolling up and under us from the SW, but clear weather and fair wind. Birds dip and soar about the ship. I could soar with them, all the way back to London.

FRIDAY 19th TO SATURDAY 20th *[To England]* The wind fails us, coming directly into our teeth. Wicked wind.

SUNDAY 21st *[To England – Lat. 28°43' S, Long. 347°42' W]* Picked up the Trades. Growing warmer and stronger by the hour.

MONDAY 22nd *[To England]* The men exercised at small arms as we raced over the sea.

TUESDAY 23rd TO WEDNESDAY 24th *[To England – Lat. 25°6' S, Long. 351°16' W]* We are busy in the pleasant air, with the Trade wind speeding us home. While Mr Perry and I tend the remaining sick, the rest of the Company tend our boats and sails.

THURSDAY 25th *[To England – Lat. 23°28' S, Long. 351°52' W]* Crossed the Tropic today for the last time, with a fine breeze coming from the SW.

FRIDAY 26th *[To England – Lat. 21°40' S, Long. 354°12' W]* Heard a rumbling this night, like thunder or the report of a gun. But Dr Solander says the rumbling lasted too long for a gun, as there is nothing for the sound to echo off of. So it must have been thunder. Goat did not seem concerned. Perhaps she, too, thinks only of home.

SATURDAY 27th *[To England]* Repairing sails and sailing with great speed. A large shoal of whales ran with *Endeavour* today.

SUNDAY 28th *[To England – Lat. 18°41' S, Long. 358°54' W]* Isaac Smith says we have crossed the meridian at which we began this journey nearly three years ago. We have done it, we have circumnavigated the entire globe.

I told every man still ill what they had accomplished. A tear ran from the eye of Lieutenant Hicks. I wiped it before it reached his ear.

Mr Wilkinson smiled and put his hand atop my head. No more needed to be said.

MONDAY 29th TO TUESDAY 30th *[To England – Lat. 16°11' S, Long. 2°42' W]* The wind continues to carry us. Bless this fresh weather speeding us on our way.

WEDNESDAY 1st MAY *[To England]* Saint Helena came into view, her Sea Road filled with British ships. Oh, what a sight. To see so many together. Captain brought us into the Road to anchor beside them. I am torn between wanting news of home on one hand, and getting home on the other. But Captain has chosen to stop here a day or two. So it's news we shall have.

THURSDAY 2nd *[To England]* Still anchored in Saint Helena Road. From first light, as we holystoned the deck, until sunset, when I sat repairing my last shirt, my eyes have feasted on the sight of so many British ships. They surround us like enormous white birds. And just now Isaac Smith told me the fleet of His Majesty's ships shall accompany us home. I do like the sound of that! And John Charlton has promised to pass along *Endeavour*'s latitude and longitude each day until we are home!

FRIDAY 3rd *[To England]* The men worked on the sails and rigging. We prepare to embark on the last leg of our journey.

SATURDAY 4th *[To England]* Under a fair sky and a light wind the *Portland* signalled the fleet to unmoor, and by Noon we had weighed anchor and were under sail.

We make a beautiful sight. Twelve Indiamen and His Majesty's ships *Portland* and *Endeavour.*

The fleet is eager to make home quickly and relay the news of our voyage and our return. It seems most of En-gland had given up on us.

SUNDAY 5th *[To England]* We have settled in astern of the fleet under a clear sky with a good breeze.

MONDAY 6th *[To England – Lat. 13°42′ S, Long. 8°27′ W]* The fleet is still in sight, but they sail too fast.

TUESDAY 7th *[To England – Lat. 12°5′ S, Long. 10°9′ W]* We made many miles today. The men exercised the Great Guns and Small Arms. We are still in the Company of the British fleet and today pulled ahead.

Flying fish pop from the water everywhere we turn. Smoke, the cat, bounded from fish to fish, puddle to puddle, to the great amusement of the Company.

WEDNESDAY 8th TO FRIDAY 10th *[To England – Lat. 7°51′ S, Long. 14°32′ W]* As we came past the high Island of Ascension, Captain Cook signalled to the *Portland,* and Captain Elliot himself came on board *Endeavour.* Captain handed over letters and logs and journals to Captain Elliot.

John Charlton says this means we shall not stay with the fleet. They have been holding back for our sake and shall pull ahead of us now. How can they do such a thing? How can they leave us behind?

SATURDAY 11th *[To England – Lat. 6°24′ S, Long. 15°51′ W]* Steady and fair. Still the convoy is in our sights. As long as I can see their sails, I believe we shall soon be home. I refuse to acknowledge that we shall soon lose their company.

SUNDAY 12th *[To England – Lat. 4°38′ S, Long. 16°54′ W]* Light squalls with rain. It is misty and unpleasant. I can make out little of the fleet.

MONDAY 13th *[To England – Lat. 2°58′ S, Long. 17°58′ W]* They are still in sight. But they will leave us, perhaps by tomorrow. I talked it over with John Ramsay. 'Don't you worry, Nick,' he said. 'We shall find our way ourselves. We have thus far.'

He's right.

The air is steamy and very hot. Lady Grey rests her head upon my lap and listens as I stroke her ears. I practice what I shall say to Father. I practice my speech to the Butcher.

TUESDAY 14th *[To England – Lat. 1°26′ S, Long. 18°57′ W]* Eclipse of the Sun today. I miss the Gentlemen and their excitement at every blessed thing. Mr Banks has recovered from his illness, but he is a changed man.

WEDNESDAY 15th *[To England – Lat. 0°14′ S, Long. 19°43′ W]* The wind is down and the temperature up. Had to replace the Fore Topsail, it having worn out.

THURSDAY 16th *[To England – Lat. 0°47′ N, Long. 20°20′ W]* Crossed the equator. Breeze continues light. Mr Banks sits brooding in the Great Cabin.

FRIDAY 17th *[To England – Lat. 1°39′ N, Long. 20°52′ W]* We still keep company with the fleet, though the distance between us grows greater each day. From this distance their sails look like the wings of angels.

SATURDAY 18th *[To England – Lat. 3°0′ N, Long. 21°22′ W]* Thunder and rain. But the fleet still with us. Perhaps John Charlton was wrong. Perhaps they will see us home after all.

SUNDAY 19th *[To England – Lat. 4°32′ N, Long. 21°58′ W]* Captain sent a boat out to the *Houghton*'s Surgeon, who came to look at our Lieutenant Hicks. The Lieutenant has been growing worse with Consumption by the day. I fear he will not make England.

Samuel Evans comes faithfully every Sunday, and every Sunday he makes a little more progress in his reading.

MONDAY 20th *[To England – Lat. 5°38′ N, Long. 22°21′ W]* Still in with the fleet. We are subject to squalls and calms. The men say this is what comes of changing from one set of trade winds to another, and I know they are right. But it's hard to be patient.

TUESDAY 21st TO WEDNESDAY 22nd *[To England – Lat. 6°58′ N, Long. 25°28′ W]* The *Portland* shortened her sails and gave us the chance to pull ahead of the fleet again. We continue in their company.

THURSDAY 23rd *[To England – Lat. 7°49′ N, Long. 26°2′ W]* Calm mostly, with showers of rain. The fleet kept astern of us. Captain shortened Sail at Noon so they might come up closer. Then they came up fast and we needed to go full sail to keep up with them. We lost them in the haze, then caught sight of them again between the dog watches.

I have told Lieutenant Hicks about my apprenticeship with the Butcher and about taking the coins.

'I can see a job through,' I told him. 'It's just that butchering is not what I wish to do. I wouldn't mind being a botanist, or a surgeon, or a sailor. But not a butcher.'

As ill as he is, Lieutenant Hicks is not beyond caring. 'You're a fine lad,' he said. 'You'll do what's right,' he said.

'Aye, aye, sir,' I said.

FRIDAY 24th *[To England – Lat. 8°42′ N, Long. 27°18′ W]* We have lost the fleet. Not one of their sails is in sight. Not one.

SATURDAY 25th *[To England]* Lieutenant Hicks died this afternoon. This evening we committed his body to the Sea with solemn ceremony. Lieutenant Hicks suffered from Consumption even when we sailed from England so long ago. He might have survived, though, at least to see home, if it had not been for Batavia. Father apprenticed me to the Butcher to cure me of my soft heart. Surely, with all that I have seen, my heart should be nothing but stone by now. And yet I hurt.

SUNDAY 26th TO MONDAY 27th *[To England – Lat. 12°7' N, Long. 30°40' W]* Steady winds. Mr Charles Clerke has been appointed to Lieutenant Hicks's position.

TUESDAY 28th TO WEDNESDAY 29th *[To England – Lat. 15°19' N, Long. 33°2' W]* Sometimes fair, sometimes haze, but always a good sailing wind. We are certainly through the Damp Calms and on our way.

THURSDAY 30th *[To England – Lat. 17°5' N, Long. 34°9' W]* The men work daily to keep *Endeavour* patched together. She is feeling her age and the hard usage she has had carrying us round the world.

Today the sea is uneasy, and we pitch and tumble. Perhaps there was a time when such a sea did not bother us. It is hardly a whimper compared to rounding Cape Horn, or searching in the fearful southern seas for Dalrymple's Continent, or weathering a hurricane off the coast of New Zeland, but at this point even a whimper is more than we can stand.

FRIDAY 31st TO SATURDAY 1st JUNE *[To England – Lat. 20°12' N, Long. 36°41' W]* It is too much to hope, but what if I could see England on my fourteenth birthday? It is but a week from now. I shall watch for Land's End, though the men would laugh if they knew. It is still too far even to dream. But it is only dreams now that keep us going. Dreams of home.

We all return to things left behind. Nothing may have changed in our absence. Still we are changed. And so we dream of home.

SUNDAY 2nd *[To England – Lat. 21°20' N, Long. 38°5' W]* Caught sight of some Gulfweed and pointed it out to Mr Banks. With Mr Parkinson gone, he has little enthusiasm to bring anything aboard. He does not push Captain any more to stop at every opportunity. He only wills Captain to bring him safely home. We all entrust our Captain to do this one last thing.

MONDAY 3rd TO TUESDAY 4th *[To England – Lat. 23°40' N, Long. 40°4' W]* Passed over the Tropic of Cancer through more of Mr Banks's Gulfweed. Isaac Smith stood beside me at the rail this evening. He said Captain was pleased with the care I have given the sick. He said Lieutenant Gore had requested before his death that I be paid for all three years of my service and that Captain had agreed. Isaac's words were an unexpected balm.

WEDNESDAY 5th *[To England – Lat. 24°31' N, Long. 41°11' W]* 'Less Gulfweed today,' I told Mr Banks. 'The men say we'll soon be out of it entirely.'

This made something happen inside our Gentleman. He put out a pole and caught some weed, and I saw a glimpse of the old enthusiasm as he opened his books and began to identify what he had hooked from the sea.

THURSDAY 6th *[To England – Lat. 26°1' N, Long. 43°18' W]* Mr Banks gathered more Gulfweed today and came up with a shrimp in the weed never described before.

I gave him what assistance I could with leave from Mr Perry. There are not so many sick now.

But I do not have a hand for drawing as Mr Parkinson had.

Mr Banks said, 'Never fear, Nick. Soon we'll be home. We can preserve this until then, don't you think?'

'Aye, sir,' I said. 'I do.'

FRIDAY 7th [*To England – Lat. 27°22′ N, Long. 43°42′ W*] The Gulfweed spreads across the sea in long, narrow lines, stretching far beyond sight. More birds overhead, all heading East.

SATURDAY 8th [*To England – Lat. 28°50′ N, Long. 43°42′ W*] Captain takes his observations every day, faithfully, and faithfully John Charlton delivers them every day to me.

I believe Captain is as eager to return to England as the rest of us.

My birthday. I had hoped to be home. But we are nearly there.

SUNDAY 9th [*To England – Lat. 30°11′ N, Long. 44°9′ W*] We continue to have birds overhead, clear weather, and a smooth sea. Mr Banks can find little or no weed any more. I do whatever I can for him. Lady Grey seems restless. Maybe she can smell home.

MONDAY 10th [*To England – Lat. 31°12′ N, Long. 44°50′ W*] The men exercised at small Arms. We are grateful for work, for our yearning to be home would consume us if we were idle.

TUESDAY 11th [*To England – Lat. 32°16′ N, Long. 45°14′ W*] The sea continues smooth with hardly a wind. Mr Banks and I went out in the boat and brought back many specimens, but nothing new.

WEDNESDAY 12th TO THURSDAY 13th [*To England – Lat. 34°14′ N, Long. 44°25′ W*] Still the wind fails us. I would beat my fists against *Endeavour* in frustration. But I don't think she could bear it.

FRIDAY 14th *[To England – Lat. 35°48' N, Long. 43°48' W]* A light gale has come up and we have made good use of it. Passed two turtles asleep on the water.

SATURDAY 15th *[To England – Lat. 37°2' N, Long. 41°54' W]* Caught sight of a small sloop this morning. Passed by it and lost its sails by Noon. I wonder about the *Portland* convoy.

They are probably safely back by now. Soon we shall be, too.

SUNDAY 16th TO MONDAY 17th *[To England – Lat. 38°56' N, Long. 38°36' W]* Steady wind, fine weather. Sighted two ships in the distance.

TUESDAY 18th *[To England – Lat. 39°32' N, Long. 36°59' W]* Caught sight of three New England Schooners hunting for whales. Captain sent a boat over to one, and we got news that peace reigned in Europe.

As for the Americans, King George had behaved badly, these men said. But the American men had brought him to terms and all was well on that front, too.

I wonder if we shall hear the story told the same way in England.

WEDNESDAY 19th TO THURSDAY 20th *[To England – Lat. 40°29' N, Long. 33°10' W]* Saw a sail ahead, but she was a large ship and soon left us.

FRIDAY 21st *[To England – Lat. 40°53' N, Long. 30°20' W]* Travelled with good speed today. At noon we saw a small fleet. I think we have caught up with our Convoy!

SATURDAY 22nd *[To England – Lat. 41°11' N, Long. 27°52' W]* We had two sails split on us during the night. The Rigging and Sails are in such deteriorating condition, every day something else must be urgently attended to. Kept the Fleet in sight today but only just, even with Mr Banks's spyglass.

SUNDAY 23rd TO MONDAY 24th *[To England – Lat. 40°34' N, Long. 24°49' W]* We've lost the fleet again. Tacking against a foul wind.

TUESDAY 25th TO THURSDAY 27th *[To England – Lat. 41°14' N, Long. 20°59' W]* Moderate breeze but not much distance.

FRIDAY 28th TO SATURDAY 29th *[To England – Lat. 43°49' N, Long. 17°36' W]* We are thoroughly wet. But as long as there is a good wind, none complain. The rain feels familiar almost. Lady Grey frisked on deck in it, barking at Goat and Ginger Bigfoot.

SUNDAY 30th *[To England – Lat. 44°34' N, Long. 16°2' W]* Light breeze, fair sky filled with Shearwaters. Tonight they cried in the sky above our ship and I cried back at them.

John Charlton swears they stopped to listen.

MONDAY 1st JULY *[To England – Lat. 44°54' N, Long. 13°59' W]* Passed two sails standing to the SW during the night. Isaac Smith showed me our location on his chart. We're nearly home.

TUESDAY 2nd TO WEDNESDAY 3rd *[To England – Lat. 45°24′ N, Long. 10°45′ W]* Light wind, but the weather is fine, and at least we can dry out and warm up. Six sails in sight. It is hard to believe now, that we spent so long alone in seas with not a sail to be seen for month after month. We have truly led the way, charting the path for all who come after. I don't know that I shall ever feel so again as I feel now. That any of us shall.

THURSDAY 4th *[To England – Lat. 45°29′ N, Long. 9°27′ W]* Lady Grey is dead. Mr Banks found her in his cabin, lying where she generally sleeps. I threw a piece of wood for her yesterday, and she ran all round the deck with it. Mr Banks said he heard one shriek while he slept and no more. I don't think I could have heard it from my hammock. But I, too, came awake last night and looked around feeling unsettled. I broke the news to Goat. She took it the way she takes all things.

I shall miss Lady Grey. So shall Mr Banks.

FRIDAY 5th *[To England – Lat. 45°34′ N, Long 9°18′ W]* Passed through a shoal of mackerels last night. This morning there are Crabs and seaweed and many birds.

Lady Grey loved barking at the birds. She loved barking at me when I called like the birds. It is quiet without her. I asked Mr Perry, 'Did she suffer?'

'No,' he said. 'I don't think so, Nick.'

I trust him.

I sat out with Goat tonight. 'Don't you die,' I said.

Goat lifted a gold, slitted eye to me. I don't think she will.

SATURDAY 6th *[To England – Lat. 45°45′ N, Long. 8°28′ W]* Every day we spot other ships. I am glad of them. I would be happier still to see Land.

SUNDAY 7th *[To England – Lat. 46°16' N, Long. 9°29' W]* Came up with a Brig from Liverpool this morning. Then another from London. The ship from London told us no word had been received yet about us and that wagers against our survival were high. We shall be quite a surprise when we land. And no doubt put some coin in the pockets of the faithful.

MONDAY 8th TO TUESDAY 9th *[To England – Lat. 48°19' N, Long. 8°7' W]* At last we caught a fresh breeze and made good sailing of it.

WEDNESDAY 10th *[To England – Lat. 49°29' N, Long. 6°18' W]* This morning we sounded and struck ground at sixty fathoms.

I was first to spot land from the Masthead!

'Land Ho!' I cried.

Home!

THURSDAY 11th *[Home]* Sailed a fresh gale up the channel past Peverell Point.

FRIDAY 12th *[Home]* Passed Beachy Head this morning, then Dungeness, and at noon we were abreast of Dover. Before the first dog watch we landed in the Downs. John Hudson, pilot, came aboard to bring Endeavour home, while Mr Banks, Captain, and Dr Solander went ashore to great cheering.

SATURDAY 13th TO TUESDAY 16th *[Home]* Came into Galleons Reach.

Let go the small bower anchor.

Said my good-byes to the men still remaining and to Smoke and Ginger Bigfoot and my dear friend Goat.

Mr Perry handed over my discharge orders and my pay, nearly enough to satisfy my contract with the Butcher. 'I should be happy to have you sail with me again, Nick,' Mr Perry said.

'Aye, aye, sir,' I answered. 'Thank you, sir.'

Samuel Evans called after me and ran to catch me as I came down the plank. 'I can read them!' he said. 'I can read my discharge papers!'

I offered my hand in congratulations. When I brought it away again, it held three coins.

'It's what you paid us for getting you aboard,' Samuel said. 'John, Francis, and I, we talked it over a while ago, before Francis died. We thought we ought to give your money back. We shouldn't have taken it in the first place. You were a handy little lad to have aboard,' he said. And he clapped me in his great arms. 'Though not so little now,' he said.

Turning for one last look at *Endeavour*, I saw John Ramsay and John Charlton watching me from aloft in the rigging. For one moment I considered running back up the plank to join them.

But I stood tall and waved farewell instead.

I have things to settle first with Father and the Butcher.

After that, I can only endeavour to imagine.

AFTERWORD

In the late 18th century, European powers were busily expanding their empires across Africa, the Pacific and Australasia. Wealth at this time was not just measured in riches, but also in natural resources, and plants, in particular rubber, tea and cotton, were very valuable. Although botanists like Joseph Banks and Dr Solander were on board ships like *Endeavour*, to record and draw the exotic plants they discovered, transporting samples back to England was often very difficult. Like the crew, plants suffered from the storms, harsh conditions, scorching sun and lack of fresh water on board. There was not yet a protective way of transporting them and   the long journeys killed many plants. Sailors resented giving up space and rations to house the plants and so there were many arguments! Despite these poor conditions, many thousands of plants were safely brought to England in the 18th century.

Captain James Cook made three voyages of discovery between 1768 and 1779. *Young Nick's Head* documents the first of those voyages. Originally named *Earl of Pembroke,* the converted coal ship was renamed *Endeavour* in the hope of bringing the expedition good luck in its secret goals of discovering new land for the King of England, charting the coast of New Zealand and observing the passage of the planet Venus in the Pacific skies.

Nicholas Young's name first appeared in *Endeavour's* muster book on April 18 1769, eight months after the ship left England. Scholars have speculated as to how Nicholas might have boarded *Endeavour* in the first place. Some argue he was smuggled aboard by Joseph Banks. Others speculate Nick stowed away unaided. A third hypothesis suggests Nicholas was brought aboard and kept hidden by certain members of the ship's company. This last scenario seems the most likely. *Endeavour* was a small vessel. It would have been nearly impossible for Nick to remain undetected until the ship sailed unless he had help. Sailors often enlisted a young boy on such a journey for running errands, cleaning sties, washing shirts, repairing clothing, and so on. Nicholas Young would have been an excellent recruit for such duties.

Here is what is known about the real Nicholas Young. He was approximately eleven years of age at the time *Endeavour* left England. He became an official member of the crew in Tahiti and was promoted to surgeon's assistant at Batavia. He was the first to sight New Zealand: Young Nick's Head is named for him, the honor bestowed on Nick by Captain Cook himself. Nick was also the first to sight Land's End. These facts are documented in journals kept aboard *Endeavour* by Captain Cook and the famous botanist Joseph Banks, among others. Nicholas must have been well educated. He truly did write in Mr Bootie's journal, 'Evil communications corrupt good', boldly signing his name beneath his entry. Mr Bootie, on discovering Nick's comment, wrote a comment of his own. Beneath the signature 'Nicholas Young', Mr Bootie inserted the words 'is a son of a bitch.'

The remainder of Nicholas Young's story is undocumented. His hair colour, his fondness for birds, his family situation, are all author invention. Nicholas Young's character grew out of the few facts available about him.

The journal itself, though fictional, reflects faithfully the voyage led by Captain Cook around the globe. Naval officers kept journals (with inconsistent spelling, punctuation, and capitalization) as a matter of course, recording the details of their journey. Those manuscripts technically belonged to the king, and at the end of the journey they should have come into the Crown's possession. Other participants in this voyage also kept journals. That of the artist Sydney Parkinson was rushed to print, getting the scoop on this remarkable expedition. Cook's and Banks's journals, edited by J. C. Beaglehole, along with the *Endeavour* CD-ROM, produced by the National Library of Australia and the National Maritime Museum of Australia, form the backbone of this book.

There is only one other fact about Nicholas Young existing in the public domain. Though he never traveled again with Captain Cook, he did make one more voyage with Joseph Banks, a journey to Iceland in 1772.

◉ SHIP'S COMPANY ◉

JAMES COOK (40) – *Captain (First Lieutenant)*
WILLIAM HOWSON (16) – *Captain's servant*
JOHN CHARLTON (15) – *Captain's servant*
ZACHARY HICKS (29) – *Second Lieutenant*
WILLIAM HARVEY (17) – *Second Lieutenant's servant*
JOHN GORE (38) – *Third Lieutenant*
NATHANIEL MOREY – *Third Lieutenant's servant*
DR WILLIAM MONKHOUSE – *Surgeon*
THOMAS JONES – *Surgeon's servant*
WILLIAM PERRY (21) – *Surgeon's Mate*
JOHN THOMPSON – *Ship's Cook*
THOMAS MATTHEWS – *Ship's Cook's servant*
JOHN RAVENHILL (49) – *Sail Maker*
JOHN SATTERLEY – *Carpenter*
EDWARD TERRELL (19) – *Carpenter's servant*
ROBERT MOLYNEUX (22) – *Master*
ISAAC MANLEY (12) – *Master's servant*
RICHARD PICKERSGILL (19) – *Master's Mate*
CHARLES CLERKE (25) – *Master's Mate*
ALEXANDER WEIR (35) – *Master's Mate*
JOHN BOOTIE – *Midshipman*
JONATHAN MONKHOUSE – *Midshipman*
PATRICK SAUNDERS – *Midshipman*
RICHARD ORTON – *Clerk*
SAMUEL EVANS – *Quartermaster/Coxswain of the Pinnace*
JOHN GATHREY – *Boatswain*
THOMAS JORDAN – *Boatswain's servant*

JOHN READING (24) – *Boatswain's Mate*
STEPHEN FORWOOD – *Gunner*
DANIEL ROBERTS – *Gunner's servant*
ROBERT TAYLOR – *Armorer*

ISAAC SMITH (16) – *Able-bodied Seaman*
PETER FLOWER (18) – *Able-bodied Seaman*
TIMOTHY REARDEN (25) – *Able-bodied Seaman*
THOMAS HARDMAN (33) – *Able-bodied Seaman*
JOHN RAMSAY (21) – *Able-bodied Seaman*
WILLIAM DAWSON (19) – *Able-bodied Seaman*
FRANCIS HAITE (42) – *Able-bodied Seaman*
BENJAMIN JORDAN (30) – *Able-bodied Seaman*
SAMUEL JONES (22) – *Able-bodied Seaman*
JAMES NICHOLSON (21) – *Able-bodied Seaman*
FORBY SUTHERLAND (29) – *Able-bodied Seaman*
ISAAC PARKER (27) – *Able-bodied Seaman*
THOMAS SIMMONDS (24) – *Able-bodied Seaman*
RICHARD HUGHES (22) – *Able-bodied Seaman*
SAMUEL MOODY (40) – *Able-bodied Seaman*
ISAAC JOHNSON (26) – *Able-bodied Seaman*
ROBERT ANDERSON (28) – *Able-bodied Seaman*
HENRY JEFFS – *Able-bodied Seaman*
ROBERT STAINSBY (27) – *Able-bodied Seaman*
JAMES GRAY (24) – *Able-bodied Seaman*
WILLIAM COLLETT (20) – *Able-bodied Seaman*
ARCHIBALD WOLFE (39) – *Able-bodied Seaman*
MATTHEW COX (22) – *Able-bodied Seaman*
RICHARD HUTCHINS (27) – *Able-bodied Seaman*
CHARLES WILLIAMS (38) – *Able-bodied Seaman*

JOSEPH CHILDS (29) – *Able-bodied Seaman*
ALEXANDER SIMPSON – *Able-bodied Seaman*
THOMAS KNIGHT – *Able-bodied Seaman*
HENRY STEPHENS (28) – *Able-bodied Seaman*
THOMAS JONES (27) – *Able-bodied Seaman*
FRANCIS WILKINSON – *Able-bodied Seaman*
ANTONIO PONTO (24) – *Able-bodied Seaman*
JOHN DOZEN (20) – *Able-bodied Seaman*
JAMES TUNLEY (24) – *Able-bodied Seaman*
MICHAEL LITTLEBOY (20) – *Able-bodied Seaman*
GEORGE NOWELL – *Able-bodied Seaman*
JOHN GOODJOHN – *Able-bodied Seaman*
JOHN WOODWORTH – *Able-bodied Seaman*
WILLIAM PECKOVER (21) – *Able-bodied Seaman*
JAMES MAGRA – *Able-bodied Seaman*
RICHARD LITTLEBOY (25) – *Able-bodied Seaman*
JOHN THURMAN (20) – *Able-bodied Seaman*
MANOEL PEREIRA – *Able-bodied Seaman*
NATHANIEL COOK – *Able-bodied Seaman*
NICHOLAS YOUNG (11) – *Boy*

MARINES
JOHN EDGCUMBE – *Sergeant*
JOHN TRUSLOVE – *Corporal*
THOMAS ROSSITER – *Drummer*
WILLIAM JUDGE – *Private*
HENRY PAUL – *Private*
DANIEL PRESTON – *Private*
WILLIAM WILSHIRE – *Private*
WILLIAM GREENSLADE – *Private*

SAMUEL GIBSON – *Private*

THOMAS DUNSTER – *Private*

CLEMENT WEBB – *Private*

JOHN BOWLES – *Private*

SUPERNUMERARIES

JOSEPH BANKS (24) – *Naturalist*

JAMES ROBERTS – *Banks's servant*

PETER BRISCOE – *Banks's servant*

THOMAS RICHMOND – *Banks's servant*

GEORGE DORLTON – *Banks's servant*

DR DANIEL SOLANDER (35) – *Naturalist*

HERMAN SPORING – *Assistant Naturalist*

CHARLES GREEN (33) – *Astronomer*

JOHN REYNOLDS – *Astronomer's servant*

SYDNEY PARKINSON (23) – *Artist*

ALEXANDER BUCHAN – *Artist*

TUPIA – *Native of Polynesia*

TARHETO – *Tupia's servant*

◎ SHIP'S ITINERARY ◎

1 7 6 8 :

AUGUST 14–25 – *Preparations for sea*

AUGUST 26 – *Departed Plymouth*

OCTOBER 25 – *Crossed the Equator*

NOVEMBER 13 – *Arrived in Rio de Janeiro*

DECEMBER 7 – *Departed Rio*

1 7 6 9 :

JANUARY 14 – *Anchored in the Bay of Success, Tierra del Fuego*

JANUARY 21 – *Departed Tierra del Fuego*

JANUARY 25 – *Rounded Cape Horn*

APRIL 13 – *Arrived in Tahiti*

APRIL 18 – *Construction of Fort Venus*

JUNE 3 – *Observation of Venus's transit across the Sun*

JULY 13 – *Departed Tahiti*

JULY 17 – AUGUST 9 – *Surveyed Society Islands*

SEPTEMBER 2 – *Wind and cold forced* Endeavour *to turn back from 40°south latitude*

OCTOBER 6 – *New Zealand sighted*

OCTOBER 8 – *Landing at Poverty Bay*

DECEMBER 9–31 – *Rounded North Cape, New Zealand*

DECEMBER 28 – *Struck by hurricane*

1 7 7 0 :

JANUARY 15 – *Entered Queen Charlotte's Sound*

FEBRUARY 9 – *Completed circumnavigation of North Island, New Zealand*

MARCH 27 – *Completed circumnavigation of South Island, New Zealand*

MARCH 30 – *Decision to return home along the east coast of New Holland (Australia)*

APRIL 19 – *Australia sighted*

APRIL 28 – *Landed at Botany Bay*

MAY 6 – *Departed Botany Bay*

JUNE 11 – *Struck the Great Reef*

AUGUST 5 – *Departed Endeavour River*

AUGUST 16 – *Narrowly escaped barrier breakers through Providential Channel*

AUGUST 29 – *Reached the coast of New Guinea*

OCTOBER 9 – *Anchored in Batavia Road*

NOVEMBER 9–14 – Endeavour *careened*

DECEMBER 26 – *Departed Batavia*

1 7 7 1 :

JANUARY 16 – *Sailed for Cape of Good Hope*

MARCH 3 – *Land sighted, South Africa*

MARCH 13 – *Rounded Cape of Good Hope*

MARCH 14 – *Anchored off Cape Town*

APRIL 14 – *Departed Cape Town*

APRIL 28 – *Completed circumnavigation of the globe by crossing the Greenwich meridian*

MAY 4–24 – *Accompanied by Indiaman fleet*

JUNE 22 – *Spotted Indiaman fleet again*

JULY 10 – *Land's End sighted*

JULY 16 – Endeavour *brought to Galleons Reach*

◉ SOUTH PACIFIC DISCOVERY ◉

1520 – *A Spanish expedition rounds Cape Horn and enters the Pacific from the east*

1542 – *The Portuguese reach Japan where they establish a trading station at Nagasaki*

1577-80 – *Sir Francis Drake makes a voyage round the world via Cape Horn and collects spices in the Moluccan Islands of south-east Asia*

1591 – *James Lancaster leads an English trading expedition to India, losing two of three ships, but returns with a cargo of peppers*

1601 – *The English East India Company sends out its first ships to India, later extending their voyages to China*

1605-06 – *From Bantam, at the centre of the Spice Islands of south-east Asia, a Dutch pinnace sights New Guinea and lands on Cape York, North Australia*

1606 – *The Spaniard, Luis Vaez de Torres, sails along the south coast of New Guinea*

1614 – *From this time, the west coast of Australia becomes a regular landfall for Dutch ships sailing a new route directly east from the Cape of Good Hope to the islands of south-east Asia*

1642 – *Abel Tasman, a Dutchman, sights Van Diemen's Land (modern Tasmania) and lands on South Island, New Zealand*

1698-1700 – *William Dampier leads British Royal Navy ships touching Australia, Timor and New Guinea*

1702-13 – *Many French ships enter the Pacific to trade*

1714 – *The British Board of Longitude is established to find a reliable means of establishing longitude at sea and offers a prize for the best method offered*

1728 – *James Cook is born in north Yorkshire*

1729 – *John Harrison starts building his first experimental chronometer to try and win the prize offered by the Board of Longitude*

1747 – *After 1300 men died from disease on a recent Pacific voyage, naval surgeon James Lind begins research into the causes of scurvy*

1757 – *James Lind publishes* An Essay on the most Effectual Means of Preserving the Health of Seamen

1764 – *John Harrison completes his fourth time-keeper, in the shape of a pocket watch, a copy of which is used by Cook to find his longitude in 1772-75*

1764-66 – *Captain John Byron RN is sent to discover the western end of a north-west passage from the Atlantic into the Pacific and circumnavigates the world*

1765 – *Byron is certain a Great Southern Continent exists. Captains Samuel Wallis and Philip Carteret are sent to search for it.*

1766-69 – *Louis Antoine de Bougainville from France explores the Pacific and circumnavigates the world*

1767 – *The first* Nautical Almanac *is published by the Astronomer Royal to help calculate longitude at sea from observation of the sun and stars*

1768 – *James Cook is chosen to command a ship that will carry astronomers to the Pacific to observe the Transit of Venus in order to improve estimates of the distance of the earth from the sun*

1768 *April – A Whitby collier is purchased to take Captain Cook and crew to the Pacific and is named* Endeavour

1768 *May – Captain Wallis returns from the Pacific to England with information about Tahiti which is chosen as the site for observations of the Transit of Venus*

1768 *August – The* Endeavour *sails for Tahiti, which Cook finds the aid of the* Nautical Almanac, *and the Transit of Venus is observed*

1769 JULY – *According to instructions, the Endeavour begins searching for the Great Southern Continent which Wallis suspected to be south of Tahiti*

1769 OCTOBER – *Nicholas Young sights New Zealand which Cook begins to chart*

1770 APRIL – *Aiming to return to England, Cook sails up the east coast of Australia and lands in Botany Bay*

1771 JUNE – *The* Endeavour *reaches England and Cook is chosen to command another voyage to the Pacific*

1772 – *With Cook in overall command, the naval ships Resolution and Adventure sail for the Pacific to search for the Great Southern Continent*

1773 – *Using a copy of Harrison's fourth timekeeper to find his way, Cook in Resolution circles the South Pacific without finding a southern continent but discovers the Tongan Islands*

1773 JUNE – *John Harrison, aged 80, is rewarded at the request of King George III for the contribution his timekeeper has made to navigation at sea*

1774 – *Sailing on a wider Pacific circle, Cook discovers Easter Island and the island groups named the Marquesas and New Hebrides*

1775 – *Cook returns to England from his second Pacific voyage*

1776 – *Cook agrees to a third Pacific voyage to look for the western end of a north-west passage leading from the Atlantic and sets sail with the* Resolution *and* Discovery

1777 – *Cook returns to New Zealand, the Tongan Islands and Tahiti, and discovers Christmas Island*

1779 – *Cook is killed while attempting to recover a stolen boat in Hawaii*

1787 – *William Bligh, who had been with Cook, sails for Tahiti in the Bounty to carry breadfruit plants to the West Indies but his crew mutinies*

1788 – *The first fleet of convict and store ships establish a colony at Botany Bay in Australia*

1795-96 – *Mathew Flinders, who had been with Bligh, explores the coast of New South Wales, Australia, in the eight-foot boat* Tom Thumb

◉ GLOSSARY ◉

A.B. – *able-bodied (seaman)*

ARTICLES OF WAR – *a code of laws governing the crews of ships in His Majesty's navy (e.g. sailors on night duty must keep awake on pain of death)*

BALLAST – *weight carried for stabilizing the ship (stone and iron)*

BANYAN DAYS – *days without meat (Monday, Wednesday, and Friday). Boiled peas, oil, onions, and pepper were often served in place of meat.*

BARK – *a sailing vessel*

BATHING – *Men on ships were used to fleas and lice, but Captain Cook insisted on cleanliness in the hope of preserving the life of his crew and his ship. The men bathed with buckets of water and sponges. There was no soap for them in 1768.*

BOAT – *a small, open vessel propelled by oars or sail*

BOWER ANCHOR – *the heaviest anchor of a ship*

BRASIL – *earlier spelling of Brazil, taken from the Spanish and Portuguese*

BULKHEAD – *a wall separating a ship's cabins*

BURIAL – *A dead sailor was sewn into his hammock with two cannonballs at his feet and the last stitch through his nose so he would sink and not follow the ship. Burial was swift; corpses were* considered bad luck. The ship's bell would toll several times, alerting the company to the service, a prayer would be said and the body would be tipped overboard. Tupia and Tarheto were left between a rope factory and a prison on Batavia.

BUTT – *a large barrel or cask for wine, beer or water.*

CABLE – *a thick, heavy rope; the anchor chain (rope) of a ship*

CAREEN – *to cause a ship to lean or lie on one side for calking, cleaning or repairing*

CASK – *a barrel*

CAT-O'-NINE-TAILS – *nine pieces of cord fixed to a thick rope with knots at the striking ends, kept in a red woollen bag (led to the expressions 'let the cat out of the bag' and 'room enough to swing a cat')*

CHAIN – *part of the rigging holding the mast in place*

COMPANY – *the whole crew of a ship, including officers*

COXSWAIN – *the person who steers a boat*

CUTTLEBONE – *the internal shell of a cuttlefish*

CUTTLEFISH – *a squidlike sea mollusc with ten sucker-bearing arms and a hard internal shell*

DUFF – *a pudding made of flour, suet and raisins*

DYSENTERY – *a disease characterized by inflamed intestines, bleeding, diarrhoea, and abdominal pain*

FEARNAUGHT JACKET – *a coat made from thick canvas*

FLUX – *any excessive discharge of fluid matter from bowels. The water in Batavia came from disease-ridden canals; the causes of death for the majority of* Endeavour's *company were most likely dysentery, typhoid fever and malaria.*

FOTHER – *to seal a leak with a canvas patch and other materials, including oakum and sheep's dung*

GLASSHOUSES – *a greenhouse, hothouse*

GRAMPUS – *a small, black, fierce variety of toothed whale, related to the dolphin*

GREAT BARRIER REEF – *extensive ridges of rock and coral at or near the surface of the sea off the north-east coast of Australia*

GROG – *rum mixed with water, served between 11 a.m. and noon and 4 p.m. and 5 p.m. It was mixed in a tub on deck and distributed by the mess cook.*

HAWSER – *a large rope by which a ship is anchored or towed*

HEAVE – *to raise, haul or move by pulling with a rope; to cause a ship to move in a specified manner or direction*

HEAVE TO – *to stop forward movement by hauling in or shortening sail and heading into the wind*

HOLD – *where a ship's cargo and stores are kept*

HOLYSTONE – *a type of sandstone used for scouring a ship's wooden decks. Morning watch rolled up their trousers at 6 a.m. Water was pumped on to the deck, and sailors, on hands and knees, used pillow-size blocks of stone to scrub the deck. One side of the stone was flat, the other was rounded, with two iron rings* attached to it and a rope that ran through the rings. Sand was sprinkled on the wet deck, and the holystone was pulled back and forth by the rope. The dirty sand was then washed overboard, and the deck was swabbed with a mop to dry it.

HOVE – *past tense of* heave

HULL – *the body of a ship that rests in the water, excluding the spars, sails and rigging*

JUNK – *old cable or rope used for making oakum and mats; hard, salted meat*

LOG – *a device for measuring the speed of a ship*

LOG LINE – *a rope with a board (the log) tied to the end and knots tied at intervals. The speed of the vessel was measured by the number of knots run out in a set time after the log was thrown overboard, hence measurement of the ship's speed by knots.*

LONGITUDE RECORDING WEST OF 180° – *Captain Cook recorded longitude to the full 360 degrees of a circle, rather than the more modern recording of 180 degrees east or west of the prime meridian.*

MAGELLAN JACKET – *a jacket made of thick woollen fabric*

MAGGOTS – *small worms often found in ship's biscuit. A dead fish was put over a bag of biscuit, and when the fish became covered with maggots it was thrown overboard. Sailors would not eat biscuit without some maggots; they felt that if a maggot wouldn't eat it, they'd better not eat it either.*

MALARIA – *a disease with symptoms of chills, fever and sweating*

MALT – *barley or other grain softened by soaking in water until it sprouts, used to brew liquor such as beer or ale*

MAST – *a stout vertical wooden spar for setting sails (*fore: *at the front of the ship;* main: *the largest, towards the middle of the ship;* mizzen: *the shortest mast, farthest back)*

MATS – *used to stop the sails from chafing against the masts or ropes*

MESS – *a group of people who regularly have their meals together; the meal eaten*

MIDSHIPMAN – *a class of sailors assigned to British naval vessels to be trained as officers. Midshipmen were sent below to make certain no candles were burning, they accompanied the captain on Sunday inspection, and they rectified anything that displeased the captain.*

MUSTER – *weekly roll call*

MUSTER BOOK – *a document recording all on board a vessel*

NEW HOLLAND – *early name for Australia*

NEW ZELAND – *early spelling of New Zealand*

OAKUM – *untwisted old rope forced between the seams of planks to waterproof them*

PANADA – *a pudding made of biscuit and dried fruit boiled to a pulp and flavoured*

PEASE – *peas*

PICK OAKUM – *to pull apart the loose, stringy hemp fibre of old ropes*

PINNACE – *an eight-oared boat that could be rigged with masts or sails. No doubt the only regular non-human company Nick kept while he hid inside the pinnace were rats, cockroaches and the ship's cats.*

PORTABLE SOUP – *meat products boiled down (or dried) to a thick gum and reconstituted on ship with water*

PURGE – *to empty the bowels*

QUARTERMASTER – *the person who ensured the ship was being steered on the proper course and sailing effectively*

RATIONS – *the allowance of food for each sailor: one pound of biscuit and one gallon of beer per day; salt beef on Tuesdays and Saturdays; salt pork on Sundays and Thursdays; pease on Mondays, Wednesdays, Thursdays and Fridays; oatmeal and wheat on Mondays, Wednesdays and Fridays. Cheese too hard to eat was carved into buttons. Rancid butter was used to oil the rigging. If a sailor would not or could not eat his full rations, he could trade with another sailor, using the food as currency.*

REEFER NUT – *the hard, stamped middle of a ship's biscuit*

ROAD – *a protected place near shore, not so enclosed as a harbour, where ships can ride at anchor*

ROB – *a syrup made from the juice of lemons and oranges as a treatment for scurvy*

SALOOP – *a hot drink made from orchid roots*

SCURVY – *a disease resulting from a deficiency of vitamin C in the* body, characterized by weakness, anaemia, spongy gums, bleeding from the mucous membranes, etc. The first symptoms included listlessness, irritability and shortness of breath. The symptoms then progressed to swollen gums (which became infected and bled), teeth falling out, bad breath, weight loss, swollen, aching legs, and tiny haemorrhages on the stomach, backside, arms, and legs. The small haemorrhages gave way to widespread bruising, old scars opening again, severe pain in the joints and muscles, bloat, and a grey or yellow complexion. At the time of the Endeavour voyage the British Admiralty was still experimenting with ways to prevent scurvy. Ships sailed during those days with ample sailors; the Admiralty expected the loss of a fair number of the ship's company to scurvy.

SCURVY GRASS – a plant of the mustard family, with heart-shaped leaves, small white flowers, and a tarlike flavour, used in salads and medicine

SCUTTLEBUTT – a butt or cask on shipboard with fresh drinking water

SEA ROAD – see road

SHIP – any vessel of considerable size navigating deep water and not propelled by oars or paddles

SHIP'S BISCUIT – a kind of hard biscuit that will not spoil easily; hardtack. Sailors often ate their biscuit at night so they couldn't see the maggots in it.

SKIFF – *a rowing boat (may have a small sail)*

SLOPS – *clothes, bedding and other equipment issued to a ship's crew*

SOUNDING – *the act of measuring the depth of water beneath the hull of a ship, or examining the bottom of a body of water with a weighted line*

SPAR – *a long, rounded piece of timber (mast)*

SPUN YARN – *a line made of several rope yarns twisted together*

STARTING – *beating with a stiff knotted rope or rattan stick*

SUPERNUMERARIES – *persons engaged for work other than the running of the ship*

TACK – *one of a series of zigzag movements in a course against the wind*

TOILET – *Officers and supernumeraries used chamber pots or lavatory buckets; the rest used the head (seat of ease), a wooden plank with a hole in it installed over the bow of the ship.*

TOOTHACHE – *A sailor with a toothache had a choice: he could either let the surgeon deaden the nerve with arsenic and extract it, or wait for the tooth to fall out (which it often did when scurvy took over).*

TOT – *a ration of grog. 'Due north' meant straight rum. 'Due west' meant only water. Directions between north and west determined the amount of rum-to-water ratio.*

TYPHOID FEVER – *a disease characterized by headache, delirium, cough, watery diarrhoea, rash and high fever*

VICEROY – *a ruler exercising authority on behalf of a sovereign in a colony or province*

WARP – *a rope or line run from a ship to a pile, buoy or anchor and used to move or haul the ship into position*

WATCH – *Normally, sailors were on watch for four hours, then off watch for four hours (watch below). Captain Cook put in a third watch rotation in easier seas so the men would be more rested. First watch began at 8 p.m. and ran until midnight. Middle watch commenced at midnight and ran until 4 a.m. Morning watch fell between the hours of 4 a.m. and 8 a.m. The forenoon watch was from 8 A.M. until noon. Afternoon watch lasted from noon until 4 p.m., and the dog watches ran from 4 p.m. to 6 p.m. and 6 p.m. to 8 p.m. The ship had two hourglasses: one measured time by four-hour intervals, one measured time by half-hour intervals. The ship's bell struck every half hour (four bells rang in the middle of a watch, eight bells at the end of a watch).*

WATER – *Fresh water was collected from shore. Also, rainwater was collected in sails, but it tasted like tar.*

WEIGH – *to hoist anchor; to begin to sail*

WORT – *a liquid prepared with malt, which after fermenting becomes beer or ale*

YARDS – *a spar to which a sail is attached. Yards usually cross the mast horizontally.*

YAWL – *a ship's boat, with one or two masts*

THE VOYAGE OF

NORTH
AMERICA

EUROPE

Great Britain
London

Madeira

Spain

ATLANTIC
OCEAN

AFRICA

October 1768

Equator

SOUTH
AMERICA

Ascension

Brazil

St. Helena

Rio de
Janeiro

South
Africa

Cape of Good Hope
March 1771

Falkland Islands

ANTARCTIC OCEAN

Cape Horn
January 1769

ENDEAVOUR, 1768-1771

ASIA

PACIFC
OCEAN

Sumatra

Batavia

Java

January 1771

New
Guinea

August 1770

AUSTRALIA

Tasmania

April
1770

Society Islands

Tahiti
(King George's Land)

April 1769

Equator

North Island

October
1769

NEW ZELAND

South
Island

Map illustration copyright © 2001 by Jim Hoover

More classic fiction to enjoy

"Can a book be funny, perceptive, moving and
utterly absorbing at one and the same time?
This one can. Brilliant.
A 'Swallows and Amazons' for the 21st century."

Michael Morpurgo

ISBN: 0 689 82796 2

The Raging Quiet is a haunting and compelling story about
the power and determination to overcome prejudice and
injustice in a world of witchcraft, feudalism and intolerance.

ISBN 0 689 82706 7